The Phantom of Valletta

The Phantom of Valletta

Vicki Hopkins

Dedication

To everyone who shares the cry of Erik's heart.

"All I wanted was to be loved for myself."

Acknowledgements

THE PHANTOM OF THE OPERA
By Gaston Leroux
2002 Modern Library Paperback Edition
Copyright© 2002 by Random House, Inc.

HOLY BIBLE, NEW INTERNATIONAL VERSION®
NIV® Copyright© 1973, 1978, 1984 by
International Bible Society.
Used by permission of Zondervan. All rights reserved.

Foreword

"Yes, he existed in flesh and blood, although he assumed the complete appearance of a real phantom; that is to say, of a spectral shade."

Le Fantôme de l'Opéra by Gaston Leroux

My creator, Gaston Leroux, seems intent on convincing you that I really existed. Of course, that is something you'll have to decide for yourself. However, if you're not familiar with my story, let me enlighten you before you turn the page to read of my adventures on the isle of Malta.

You'll find that I have many names: Angel of Music, Opera Ghost, Phantom, and most importantly, poor unhappy Erik. My talents are many: composer, architect, magician, violinist, and ventriloquist. My skills include proficiency in using a Punjab lasso, and I have been known to develop a few ingenious methods of torture.

Like everyone else, I have a past. My humble roots began when I was born in Rouen, France. Mother expected a beautiful baby boy. Instead, she birthed a freak, whose deformity was so hideous that she immediately covered my face with a mask. My father was a stone mason; he taught me his trade but gave me no love.

As you can surmise, my childhood was not pleasant. I ran away from home and joined a gypsy fair, where I was put on display as a living corpse. Afterward, I traveled to a foreign land serving a Sultan. While in Persia, I built a palace, executed poor souls, and ended up fleeing for my life. My Persian friend did save me from an untimely death, but he believes I'm a monster.

Eventually, I returned to my homeland and helped with the construction of the Paris Opera House. I cleverly built a world of secret passageways and a home in the cellars underneath.

Life was a bit dull, until a certain young woman by the name of Christine Daaé captured my heart. I played upon her weakness and fooled her into thinking I was the Angel of Music, sent from her dead father to teach her to sing. She became my student and I her Angel, until one day, I revealed the truth to her that I was nothing more than a mere man.

She was beautiful. I have a weakness, you see, and its name is *beauty*. I long for beauty. It's the obsession of my life; and naturally, Christine became my obsession because she was the epitome of beauty in my eyes.

I wanted her to love me as a man and be my wife. Instead, she pitied me as a monster and pledged her heart to another. Oh, perhaps she did have a morsel of affection for her Angel of Music, but it was not enough to satisfy the cravings of my soul. I did the only thing I could do. She was not willing to consent to be my wife, so I took her by force. In a moment of madness, I brought down the chandelier during a performance and abducted Christine, keeping her captive in my underground world.

Well, I do not wish to bore you with further details. The entire fiasco did not turn out well. Nothing went as planned. I eventually released her to the man she loved, and died a thousand deaths in my soul when she departed.

I told everyone that I was dying of love. It was the most logical course of action; to die and disappear. A man can die of love, you know.

As I bemoaned my fate in hiding, an opportunity presented itself on the isle of Malta. The Royal Opera House in Valletta had suffered a premature end and beckoned me to resurrect it from the ashes. I purchased the burned-out shell, took a close friend and assistant with me, and moved to Malta to rebuild my life.

You'll soon discover, I could not hide from the past. It has a clever way of following you like a dark shadow until vengeance and justice is served. Such is my life, and this is my story.

I am the Phantom of Valletta.

Chapter 1

Southern Italy – Spring 1874

"I loathe my very life; therefore I will give free rein to my complaint and speak out in the bitterness of my soul."
Job 10:1

The carriage bounced hard and wrenched Erik's neck, sending a sharp pain down his shoulder. One more time and he would scream at the ignorant driver who insisted on finding every pothole in the road. He had been inside a cage on wheels for over a week now, and Erik teetered on the edge of insanity. His nerves pricked him like thorns.

He glanced across the seat and peered at his travel companions with an irritated glare. Encased in a jostling box, he was uncomfortably sharing a small space with two humans. Even though he invited them to accompany him on his journey, it did not mean that their close proximity brought him any joy.

Darius sat slumped against the side of the carriage like a limp rag doll. His incessant snoring filled the cabin, and his flapping vocal cords strung in unison with the beating of the horses' hooves. The Persian's servant had agreed to take the trip acting as his personal assistant, but Erik doubted the dimwit possessed the sense to assist a flea.

After days of traversing back roads together, he began to question the wisdom of bringing excess baggage. Nevertheless, Darius' timidity made him easy to handle. Erik thought anyone could train a dog to obey—even a ghost.

He shifted his narrowed eyes to his other companion and watched with amusement her head bob up and down like an apple in a barrel of water. Her black taffeta dress, wrinkled from days of confined sitting, bunched up at her waist. She wore a tattered hat that fell crooked to one side, hiding her disarrayed hair underneath.

Andrea Giry had celebrated her fifty-first birthday last month, but in spite of her age, Erik still thought she was an attractive woman in her own right. She insisted, however, on dressing in frumpy clothes, which made her look like an old maid. Her attire and lack of hygiene puzzled Erik. She no longer seemed to care about her appearance. He made a mental note to have a discussion with her regarding her neglect after their arrival.

Regardless of her choice in clothing, he had grown close to Andrea throughout the years. She constantly came to his aid when he needed it the most. The fact that she held her tongue from complaints over the long arduous journey only confirmed her faithfulness. Andrea tended to smother him like a mother hen, while nagging like a wife. It irritated him, but he chose to tolerate her actions because of their friendship.

He admired the ability of his old friend to sleep anywhere, which was a skill he sorely lacked. Rather than fighting the rocking, she let it lull her into a deep slumber. His fatigue, on the other hand, bothered him very little. Erik rarely slept and ignored his need for rest. He only succumbed to its demands when he felt inclined. After wandering the Garnier while others peacefully snoozed, his body had grown accustomed to a different lifestyle.

Like a nocturnal animal, he gained the ability to roam in the dim cellars and through blackened corridors using his cat-like eyes to see in the shadows. Others groped about as blind men under similar conditions.

He glanced out the carriage window and looked up at the gathering clouds tinted with dusty rose from the rising morning sun. His fingers snatched his watch out of his vest pocket and flipped open the gold lid to note the time—5:40 a.m. They were making excellent progress toward their next destination.

Erik's relax state was cruelly breached a few minutes later when the sun rose over the horizon. A burst of light sped across the country fields and flooded the carriage interior with gold streaks. The rays caught Erik off guard and pierced his dark eyes. He lost all composure.

"Damn sun!" he snarled.

After he cursed the annoying light, he roughly pulled down the window shade. Immediately, the loud snoring ceased, and the nagging hen stirred. He felt the unwanted eyes of the carriage occupants upon him. Thanks to his uncontrolled outburst, both of his travel companions were now awake and staring wide-eyed in his direction.

"Damn it, stop gawking at me!" He barked his irritation to make a point, and then settled back for a moment of stolen peace. Hastily, he closed his eyelids to escape their stares. Silence filled the cabin until the soft voice of reason met his ears.

"A bit grumpy, are we?"

He lazily opened one droopy lid and peered at Andrea's disgruntled face. A brow arched over her sleepy eyes, and an unpleasant curl of her lips challenged his behavior like a scolding mother. He remained silent and allowed her to play her usual role of calming the savage beast.

"How much longer until we arrive at port, Erik?"

He grumbled an incoherent curse underneath his breath, expressing his displeasure. The tone of her voice insisted upon an answer, so he let out a long drawn-out sigh and replied to her inquiry.

"Soon, if all goes as planned. We should arrive in Reggio di Calabria this afternoon. We'll board a ship to Malta in the morning."

"Well, I am glad. It's been a very long trip indeed."

Thankful the conversation ended, he closed his eyelid and reflected upon his last announcement. Malta—his self-imposed exile would soon begin.

The past year, filled with sorrow, loss, and regret, grew farther away with each passing mile for Erik. He was tired of running and looking over his shoulder. Convinced that the authorities were hell-bent upon making him pay for his crimes, he had fled their reaches. He entertained no desire to make any restitution for his actions and was not about to let anyone inflict imprisonment on him. He had already spent the majority of his life hiding like a rat in a hole. Society had sentenced him to an existence of solitude and rejection, and he had had his fill.

After fleeing the unfortunate outcome of his ill-conceived abduction of Christine Daaé, he had hidden in the countryside for months with Andrea. She had thankfully come to his aid during the rampant speculation on his whereabouts. Reports and rumors swirled about the Opera Ghost, who some believed had died. Other outrageous stories circulated, saying he was alive in the catacombs waiting to kill the next intruder who dared approach.

The Vicomte had spirited Christine away to Sweden, and Erik often wondered if he still feared further attempts to take Christine by force. Andrea later received a letter from Christine saying she had married Raoul and was happy. Erik gave up all desires, but was saddened to hear of her departure and elopement. He had not only ruined his own existence that night in a moment of madness, but he had also changed the course of many other lives.

As he sensed the dogs in Paris nipping closer at his heels, he knew it was time to leave if he were ever to find an ounce of peace. He feared Comte de Chagny's untimely death would be pinned upon him out of spite. Many wished to see him dead, swinging from the end of a rope. What an ironic outcome, he thought, should his own neck feel the grip of strangulation he had so skillfully used on his enemies. Though he often despised spending years in depression, he had decided long ago that no other human would take his miserable existence. He would leave that privilege to the Devil himself; and if not, then his demise would come from his own hand and none other.

Months had passed as Erik pondered his next move, until a unique opportunity caught his attention. The Paris news ran a story of a devastating fire. On Sunday, May 25, 1873, flames destroyed the famed Royal Opera House in Valletta on the isle of Malta. It was reported that during rehearsals of *La Vergine del Castello*, a naked gas jet ignited the stage scenery. The flames swiftly spread. Two hundred people, mostly singers and musicians, fled for their lives, breaking windows and jumping to the street while the fire consumed the interior. A few received injuries, but no one died.

Erik had read conflicting reports as to the cause of the devastation, and the police considered arson a possibility. One investigation focused on a disgruntled tenor not awarded a part; he later fled Valletta after the devastation. While in the meantime, blame turned upon two careless employees—a lamplighter and stage mechanic. The police arrested both men and charged them with negligence.

An interesting prospect tempted Erik, as his life had fallen into mundane boredom. He wanted to leave France, filled with painful memories, and he began to toy with the idea of purchasing the vacant Royal Opera House as a new playground of creativity. The opportunity seemed perfectly wrought at the right time, providing him with the means to start fresh elsewhere. What better way to pay for his past than to resurrect another from its ashes? By moving to a foreign land, he could begin a new chapter in his already pitiful life. It was perfect.

After making the necessary inquiries through correspondence with the owners of the Royal Opera House, he offered a rather large sum of money for the now bankrupt theater that lay dark and in ruin. Funds were no object, for he had saved and invested his years of extortion demanding 20,000 francs per month as his salary at the Garnier.

Erik had learned through further inquiries that the fire had extensively damaged the interior, requiring major repairs. The foolish owners had failed to renew their insurance before the catastrophe occurred and now stood on the brink of financial bankruptcy. Since they possessed no money to restore the famed landmark, a quick sale to recoup losses was required. When Erik's offer arrived, the gentlemen had gladly accepted his wealth to pay their mounting debts.

Tedious months of slow correspondence between the buyer and sellers had continued, with Erik insisting on anonymity and strict confidentiality regarding the pending purchase. His name on paper was Erik Dante. The close of the business transaction was set to occur within a week of his arrival. Soon, the burned- out empty shell of an opera house would belong to Erik to do with as he willed. The very thought of the possibilities that lay ahead wiped the memories of Paris far from his mind.

Andrea Giry, after Erik's persistent requests, had agreed to accompany him to Malta. At first, she had balked and hesitated over the idea to flee with him to a strange land. Erik persisted due to their close friendship and because he trusted her implicitly to protect his secrets. He planned to use her skills to manage the household matters and residents living in the dormitories and private quarters. After reconstruction, she would act as the mistress of his domain to make sure everything was in order and running smoothly.

Andrea was far more intelligent than being a mere box-keeper, but she kept her true character a secret from everyone. Upon the arrival of the two new bumbling managers at the Garnier last year, Erik had requested that she play the role of an elderly buffoon in their midst. It was an outrageous plot for Andrea to be his ears and eyes, while he continued to wreak havoc using his tricks.

Madame Giry's daughter, Meg, married as he had prophesied, and was now the wife of Baron de Castelot-Barbezac, living in Belgium and saddled with children. Of course, he hadn't an ounce of prophetic ability, but that made no difference. What he did possess was influence, and he had played a rather charming game of matchmaking behind the scenes with little Meg and the baron.

It had all worked out as planned. Andrea freely left with him on a new adventure, because Meg was happy and settled. Erik enjoyed playing a game of chess with the lives of others around him. He did so to his own advantage, smugly proud of how well he could manipulate the paths of unsuspecting people to achieve an end.

Darius, on the other hand, had been a challenge right from the beginning. He proved useful to Erik in small tasks but required grooming. The Persian, fed up with Erik's antics and his near-death experience with the Vicomte trying to rescue Christine, had strained their relationship to a breaking point. He watched Erik flee and returned to his homeland afterward. Darius, his servant, was a parting gift, one Erik couldn't refuse after all the years they had spent together.

Darius obediently agreed to the arrangement accepting employment. Erik made sure to convey early on in their relationship that he preferred to be addressed as Master. As of yet, the man had failed to prove his worthiness. Erik had no doubt the Persian had warned Darius of his insidious temper when crossed and the consequences of betrayal. If need be, Erik was determined to deal harshly with Darius should an ounce of disrespect fall from his thin lips. He resolved to mold him into a useful piece of luggage or discard him like trash at the nearest port.

Andrea had apparently noticed his dark musings and interrupted his thoughts.

"Mulling over your regrets?"

"Regrets for what?" he responded, shifting his weight as he dreaded the ensuing conversation.

"For leaving Paris, Erik. What else? You've lived there for many years."

"I have no regrets for leaving," he replied, with a shade of bitterness. "Why should I? I have no fond memories to carry with me to Valletta."

"Except perhaps one," she quipped.

"Don't start, Andrea. I'm in a foul mood." To make a point, he leaned forward in his seat with a menacing glare. "You'd think by now you would know I wish to forget who you are referring to by your remark. Do you not understand the purpose for this journey? I wish to forget and move on!"

Andrea jolted from his spewed words, and Erik saw the fear in her eyes due to his irritable behavior. He did not blame her. The poor woman had sat trapped in a cage for days dealing with his volatile temper. By now, she must feel as if she had been locked in a lion's den and clawed to death for a week. He did not wish to cause her pain; it was just his repulsive nature. He purposely softened his tone as he continued, getting the last word on the subject.

"It's done. It's over. Let it go. I have."

He was lying. It would never be over. His heart would always cry for Christine. Yes, Christine. He could say her name as often as he wished. *Christine . . . Christine . . . Christine.* He would not allow others to speak her name in his presence or even bring up her memory; that right belonged only to Erik.

At last, the carriage slowed entering a small village. "It must be time to replace the horses," he moaned. He stretched his arms above his head and yawned. The wheels halted and the driver jumped down, opening door.

"We've arrived at Rosarno. Time to change teams." Erik was thankful they were on schedule. The trip was nearing its end.

Andrea and Darius exited first, and he followed. Erik pulled his hooded cloak over his head, shielding his masked face to hide his identity. Due to his fears of pursuit by the authorities, he had decided not to sail from France to Malta. The dangers were far too great. As an alternative, he had hired a private driver and carriage to take him across Europe to Italy. The trip would have taken half the time by train, but he feared showing his half-face anywhere in public. Their mode of transportation had been tedious to say the least, but most effective in concealing his whereabouts.

"Darius, take Madame Giry to get something to eat and drink."

"Aren't you coming with us, Erik?" Andrea pleaded in concern.

"I need nothing. Go . . . leave me to myself."

He walked away from the carriage to seek a place of solitude. The days of travel had taken its toll upon his psyche. Erik strode heavily toward a nearby wooded grove. After entering the thicket, he glanced over his shoulder to make sure he was out of sight.

The dense woods provided ample shade from the morning sun. He wandered to the trunk of a large oak tree where he stopped. Erik pulled back his hood and let it drape around his broad shoulders. His gloved hands reached up and removed the mask to allow the cool morning air to soothe his putrid flesh. The pain of removal caused Erik to wince when small pieces of moist skin pulled away from his bony cheek. The interior of his mask lay tinged with blood from weeping sores, and the foul smell of rotting flesh filled his nostrils.

Weeks of travel had wreaked havoc upon his deformed face. The hot air inside the carriage rose to unbearable heat, causing his skin underneath to sweat profusely. The mask exacerbated the problem and new lesions developed daily.

Taking his handkerchief from his pocket, he took the folded white linen and pressed it against his right cheek to absorb the blood. He looked at the residue and was surprised at the amount that stained the cloth. The cool forest breeze caressed his flesh. He stood motionless with his face turned toward the wind, hoping the fresh air would help dry the festering tissue.

Erik closed his eyes. His ears tuned to the music of the surrounding woods. Treetops swayed in the breeze rustling leaves in an orchestration of nature. Amidst the calming chords, birds sang their arias. Erik lost all senses enjoying the shadows of the woods and its enchanting operatic movements, which brought a minute of peace to his weary soul.

"Master! Monsieur Dante!"

Darius' voice pierced the beautiful strains, interrupting his idyllic surroundings. The fresh horses stood ready, and the driver was anxious to push onward.

He opened his eyes and wiped the bloody remains from inside the mask. He placed it upon his face, secured it again, and ground his teeth at the discomfort. Quickly, he pulled the hooded cape back over his head before returning.

Slowly, he walked back to the carriage and pondered the physical and emotional pain that had followed his life like a curse. He concluded that forty years of physical suffering paled in comparison to the agony of losing Christine. An empty ache tormented Erik's soul. He had spent his entire life wandering the earth, seeking acceptance, longing for love, dreaming of the pleasures of the flesh, but had experienced nothing in return. Life was meaningless.

"Are you sure you don't need anything to eat, Erik?" Andrea asked, approaching him as he returned to the carriage. He kept his head bowed and his pensive gaze away from her prying eyes.

"No, I'm fine," he muttered.

"Well, I brought you some bread and a piece of fruit if you get hungry later."

Unable to thank her, he merely nodded, as he struggled with the heavy emotion crushing his heart.

"Come, let's get on with it," he announced coldly.

He assisted her step into the carriage and climbed in after Darius. The door closed, the whip cracked, and the horses galloped off down the bumpy road, jostling them to their next destination. By tomorrow afternoon, the ship would dock in Valletta and their feet would stand on Maltese soil. Erik had no idea what awaited him on the strange isle in the middle of the Mediterranean Sea. He only knew that he felt driven by a powerful desire to rebuild what he had lost. His new life would be filled with his love of music, far away from Paris and its memories. Perhaps in time, Christine's face would fade and another would take her place.

Erik glanced out of the window and longingly wondered if there was still a chance to find love. Was it too much to ask from life or from an unknown God who had cursed his existence? If not love, then he would pursue peace as consolation for the remainder of his days. He dared not hope for anything more.

Chapter 2

The trip progressed uneventfully, and the hired carriage arrived safely in Reggio di Calabria in the early afternoon. Tired from the day's travel, Darius arranged for rooms in a local inn for the evening. Footmen delivered the travelers' trunks to their quarters, which carried every possession the threesome had decided to bring on the journey to the new world.

Erik spent the remainder of the day in seclusion, leaving his travel companions to fend for themselves. He was thankful that Andrea understood his need for solitude and reflection. Erik struggled to acclimate himself again to the presence of humans, after years of hiding in the bowels of the earth. He found it difficult to force his way back into the mix of humanity that held no compassion. All his life, he had been a social outcast. It was going to take time.

Music was the only constant that remained in his life, and the most precious of personal belongings that accompanied him to Malta was his Stradivarius violin. Through music, Erik found comfort for his tortured soul. Even though he was not a religious man by any means, he knew of the mystical story of David and Saul in the scriptures. David would play his harp for Saul, and the evil tormenting spirits would leave the king for a while.

Mysteriously enough, Erik felt calm by practicing the same method to soothe his own irritation and depression. Whenever he felt overwhelmed or on the brink of madness, he would embrace his violin and release healing music.

When Erik played, he closed his eyes, lifted his violin beneath his chin, and proceeded to caress the instrument like a lover. With each stroke of the bow, music mollified the raging anger and hurt in his heart. The intoxicating melodies penned by his own hand transported him to a place of rest, where he could stand for brief moments untouched by the past, undisturbed by the present, and hopeful for the future.

He sat in his room and played for hours until weariness overtook his body, and the desire for sleep consumed him. Erik removed his mask, laying his naked face on a soft pillow, which would surely show stains of blood by morning. He waited for sleep, and if it did not come, he could induce it by indulging in his favorite flask of cognac. Tomorrow would be a full day.

When daylight arrived, they boarded a steam ship headed for the port of Valletta. Erik insisted on hiding below deck in private quarters, having already endured the stares of passengers over his appearance upon boarding. His black hood and masked face was difficult to hide. He ignored the curious whispers and made his way to the cabin, while Andrea and Darius remained above in the glaring light of day.

After he closed and secured the door, he went to the porthole and flung open the round glass window encased in grey cold steel to behold the scenery. Even he, a monster, could appreciate the beauty of nature that he rarely had the opportunity to enjoy. He had forgotten the grandeur of the sea from his years of hiding beneath the crust of the earth. The deep sun-kissed waters shimmered like sparkling diamonds, as they rose and fell in swells.

Enthralled with the emerald color of the Mediterranean, Erik spent the entire trip below deck, enjoying the beautiful views and a time of reflection. He stripped off his confining mask and allowed the sea breeze to flow through the window and gently kiss his face. The moist damaged skin dried from the salty sea air, bringing welcome relief to weeks of pain.

Poseidon granted fair sailing. As they neared the port of the aged city, Erik struggled with a mixture of remorse and excitement. They had arrived at the isle of Malta and its capital, Valletta. Steeped in history, Erik found his new home fascinating. The Greeks, Romans, Spaniards, and French had all occupied the land at one time, but it was now under English rule and part of the British Empire. Napoleon had captured Malta by storm in 1798, and Erik planned to capture the city of Valletta through the tempest of music. Of course, he was well aware the Maltese were not too fond of the French, but he hoped to win their hearts through the operatic arts and his sheer genius.

After pulling into port, Darius quickly made the necessary arrangements, procuring a carriage and having their luggage removed from the ship. Erik finally appeared from below deck and walked the plank to shore when he was assured the majority of the passengers had already disembarked. He stepped heartily upon the dock with the heels of his boots resounding with a declaration of his arrival before climbing into the carriage alongside Andrea and Darius.

Valletta claimed Erik's heart as soon as he saw the landscape. A spark of new life flowed through his veins for the first time in months. As an admirer of architecture, he found the city immensely captivating. His eyes examined the various buildings with interest, while the horses trotted down Strada Reale. A moment later, Erik caught sight of the pillared façade that would soon be his new home. Before he could say a word, Andrea blurted out her exclamation of praise.

"My God, Erik, it's gorgeous!"

Darius chimed in, "Master, look! A great building."

Erik winced at the weak female expression that Andrea used, describing the magnificent facade as gorgeous.

"I'm very pleased," he muttered. Awkwardly tongue-tied and overwhelmed at what his eyes beheld, he tried to focus on his purchase. The closer the carriage came to the building, the more thrilled Erik became over the architectural design.

The columnar structure appeared larger than the photographs in the Parisian news that had showed its condition after the fire. Four large marble columns held each corner, and four marble columns guarded the main entrance. Multiple stairs led upward from the street level to the entrance from each side. He couldn't help but wonder how the women in their pointed shoes and billowing gowns made it up the steps.

Erik quickly surmised the height of the building neared 200 feet. As he peered upward, he was greatly relieved to see the stonework exterior had suffered no visible damage. He did note the fire damage had blackened the upper portion of the building from smoke. There were numerous broken windows along the sides.

He strained his neck as they passed, enthralled by the master architect, Edward Middleton Barry's creation. It was a superb building and very much to his liking. Erik had read reports saying early in construction there were foundation problems that were later rectified. The structure appeared formidable and strong, though much smaller than the Garnier in Paris. The front portico and colonnade sides gave it the appearance of a Greek temple. Erik's heart pounded in his chest with excitement.

Anxious to forgo formalities, he wanted to see the interior as soon as possible. When they arrived at the British Hotel, Erik instructed Darius to contact the owners so they could immediately arrange a tour. If they were not available, Erik was determined to breach the entrance even if he had to break down the doors with his bare hands to gain access.

Check in was quick and smooth, and their trunks were delivered to their rooms. Erik announced to his traveling companions that he did not intend to spend an indefinite amount of time in a stuffy hotel. Darius and Andrea were welcome to do so until other housing arrangements within the walls of the opera house became available. In the meantime, Erik would take up residence quickly, regardless of its condition. In his mind, the Royal Opera House of Valletta was already home.

❊ ❊ ❊

As requested, Darius sent word to the owners of their arrival and desire to see the interior, but heard no immediate response.

"Then we'll go on our own," Erik announced. "Andrea, you may come or stay."

"Do you mean to trespass and break in without permission?"

"Yes, I damn well do!" he replied, making his way out the door.

It was late afternoon as they walked from their hotel. Erik was confident they would find a door somewhere among the many that surrounded the building. As he surmised, upon their arrival, they found the stage door ajar, but blocked by debris.

The two men pushed hard against the barrier, and shoved the debris out of the way, until the entry opened wide enough for the three of them to slip inside. It took a while for their eyes to adjust from the bright daylight to the dim darkness of their surroundings. When their vision finally adjusted, their mouths dropped open in shock.

Erik stood gazing at the ruined interior. If he possessed the capacity to cry over what his eyes beheld, he would have wept unashamedly. Overwhelmed at the devastation, he staggered down a dark hallway, which he would later learn led to the stalls, groping along the blackened walls until he reached the rectangular foyer. Light from the windows filtered through the front entranceway creating eerie streaks of dusty ash spiraling upward from the residue kicked up by their feet.

He stopped and leaned against a black wall to regain his footing and let out a long sigh of disappointment. He could not speak.

"Erik, it is worse than I imagined." Andrea's voice cracked on the verge of tears, and Darius stared wide-eyed like an imbecile, apparently unable to process a coherent thought.

At that moment, Erik wondered if he had taken on too much by his prideful desire to resurrect an opera house from the ashes. The horrible conditions his eyes beheld explained why it had lain dormant and in disrepair for six months.

After he took a deep breath, he confessed his fears. "It is far worse than the owners portrayed in their correspondence, though I should have surmised as such from the pictures."

Erik surveyed the layout. A staircase on both sides of the center foyer led upward to another tier. In front of them were a series of doors leading into the main auditorium, all of them were hanging precariously from their hinges. Erik approached cautiously to gain entrance. He reached out his gloved hand and pushed against the wood, while Andrea and Darius followed closely behind him as he entered the interior.

Erik expected total darkness within the large auditorium, but instead, glaring sunlight hit his face causing him to cover his eyes to shield himself. He squinted, focused his gaze, and then raised his eyes upward to the sky.

"My God," he howled, scaring roosting pigeons inside the auditorium causing a flutter of wings and feathers. "There is no roof!"

The fire had destroyed the very heart of the auditorium, apparently burning so hot that the roof had collapsed in the inferno. The interior contained mounds of timbers, tiles, and roofing that had fallen on the seats, crushing everything into one huge pile of rubbish. Nothing remained. The stage was non-existent. All the curtains, riggings, sets, and scene drops were a pile of ashes. The only residents were birds, who circled the area dropping their waste on the destruction below.

Erik heard weeping and slowly turned to look at Andrea, whose tears were spilling down her rosy cheeks. His own heart sank into an abyss of disillusionment. Four stories of opera boxes lined the walls as burned-out shells, all empty and black. The only thing left was the stone masonry, calcified from the heat of the fire.

"I didn't anticipate such devastation," he admitted, choking over his own distress. Oddly enough, he felt a slight release from the guilt he harbored over bringing down the chandelier during his tirade in Paris. Whatever damage he had caused was minuscule in comparison to the hell fire that consumed the Royal Opera House of Valletta.

"What will you do, Erik?"

Andrea approached and stood by his side, offering a slight touch on his forearm. He felt her trembling and took her arm to wrap around his own when he realized the poor woman needed support.

"It's far too much damage," he admitted. "I'm not sure what I'll do at this point."

The three stood as pillars of silence observing the devastation and pondering the future. Erik bent down and grabbed a handful of ash, letting the substance filter through his fingers back to the floor.

"I have no idea what I can do." He sighed heavily. "Even if I continue with the purchase, Andrea, I don't have the funds to make such extensive repairs."

He kicked the debris with his foot to express his anger over the sad state of affairs that greeted his arrival. "Damn it!" Erik paced around the small area where they stood, thinking of a plan to overcome the overwhelming problem he faced.

"Investors," he muttered. "We will need investors to rebuild." He knew even with his own funds it would take years to resurrect the opera house—two or perhaps three years would pass before the first performance.

At the end of his patience, he needed space alone to think. "Would you mind leaving me for a moment?" he asked. He looked at Andrea, his eyes pleading for privacy to mourn among the ashes. "Please."

Andrea nodded her head, turned, and grabbed Darius' sleeve, tugging him out the exit. Darius remained silent, and Erik saw the worry in his eyes.

"We'll wait for you in the foyer, Erik," Andrea told him, pulling Darius along like a puppy dog.

He watched until they retreated out of sight, and then turned to face the challenge that lay before him. He wanted to make his way to the stage area, but piles of debris blocked every step. He grabbed pieces of wood and angrily flung them to the side to vent his frustration. The sun filtered through the ashes rising from the dust path created by Erik's footsteps, and birds overhead fluttered in fear, leaving their nests built in crevasses in the empty boxes.

Finally reaching his destination, Erik stood looking down into the remains of the orchestra pit. Everything was gone. The stage was a hole to Hades. It burned completely through, giving a glimpse of the under stage area, which was dark and reminiscent of the cellars he once knew.

Erik stood motionless among the ruins for some time, wondering if he had made the wrong decision. After thousands of miles and weeks of travel, he had finally arrived at what he thought would be a glorious experience. Instead, it was the most devastating shock of his life.

It was no wonder the opera house lay in ruins not purchased by another investor. The task of restoration was monumental. The money needed to restore the building to its former glory was a staggering amount. He had saved enough to purchase the shell and do minor restorations, but did not possess the wealth needed to complete the extensive repairs necessary, from top to bottom.

Unsure what to do, he continued wandering among the remains, kicking debris out of his way. Finding a side door off the pit, he pushed his way through into another corridor and began traversing his way back stage.

Intent on examining the entire remains, he forged his way in and out of doors. The area behind the stage led to the dressing rooms and staff quarters, which were virtually untouched by flames, but had suffered extensive smoke damage. He sighed in relief over one decent discovery in the hell house he was traversing. However, as he checked the rooms, it was obvious thieves had already ransacked the majority of furnishings and nothing of real value remained.

He continued to wander and found a door with a set of stairs leading upward to the floor above. The stairs were still intact as he climbed carefully to the second, third, and fourth levels, finally reaching a door that opened to the lower roof, a level below the highest tier. As he walked to the edge, the fleeting thought of leaping to his death entered his mind. At least all his problems would be solved within a few seconds. Instead, he explored the outer rim of the roof.

He returned indoors, shut the door, and continued his wandering about the facility. The upper levels contained large storage areas. There was much to discover in the building, and even though a vast portion lay in ashes, there were still livable quarters inside. Erik decided to choose one in the meantime and take up residence to formulate his plans for the days ahead. He would live amongst the ashes and the ghosts of the opera house to consider his penance and punishment. No doubt, he was being made to pay for his sins of the past one way or the other, and it looked as if it was about to come through the sweat of his brow.

Erik returned one last time to the ruins of the auditorium to contemplate. He closed his eyes and shut out the world around him. The apparitions of performances past began to sing their arias, and the applause of the audience rang in his mind. He imagined her presence upon stage—his Christine, singing for him as she once did at his bidding. He glanced up to the area where Box 5 would have been in the Paris house, and heard an angelic voice speak to his heart.

"Masquerade, Erik. Masquerade."

Startled at the words, a smile curled his lips. It was a perfect idea to raise funds—a masquerade.

Chapter 3

Erik chaffed at the bit for an entire day, anxious to meet with the owners to give them both a piece of his mind. The fact that they had not told him of the gaping hole in the roof was about to return and haunt them.

In order to keep anonymity, Erik devised a way to keep himself hidden during the meeting. He had no desire to meet the scoundrels face-to-face. Besides, keeping his identity a mystery would give him the upper hand. He would wield the tool of intimidation to get his way.

Their hotel suite provided a rather large ample desk for use, but Erik needed a barrier between himself and his guests. A dressing screen proved to be the perfect solution, which he unfolded and placed in an upright position in front of the desk. Two chairs were in front; it was a perfect setup.

The meeting started at 1:00 p.m., and Darius went to the lobby to greet the men. Erik made himself comfortable sitting behind the large mahogany desk with his booted heels on top. He crossed his arms, and a smirk curled the corner of his lips in anticipation. A few minutes passed, and Erik heard the door open.

"Monsieur Dante will receive you now." He knew that Darius was pointing their way to the two empty chairs in front of the screen. Erik craved to see the look upon their faces, but settled for the fact he would listen intently to the inflections of their voices. As for his speech, they would easily hear what he had to say. He planned to use his deep gruff voice to get his point across during the meeting.

Erik's ears quickly took note of the reluctant footsteps and a voice of protest spoken to Darius when they entered the room.

"Monsieur, this is most unusual," exclaimed Signore Russo.

"Gentlemen, please take your seats, and Monsieur Dante will begin the meeting."

For once, Darius sounded rather good at speaking to them in a strict tone without a hint of nervousness. Erik felt pleased that his new dog was learning a few tricks of manipulation. His new assistant was beginning to show backbone on his behalf, but he wondered if it would last.

Erik listened intently to the footsteps that approached and the veiled whispers between the two men. He noted the movements of the chairs, hearing the cushions swoosh as the men sat down upon the padded velvet seat covers. Darius came and stood off to Erik's right side, keeping both guests and Erik in view for the meeting.

On the corner of Erik's desk lay a loaded pistol, a symbol of his distrust of the men that dared to sell him a shell of a building. They had deceitfully concealed the extensive damage from him during their initial correspondence and were now about to pay for their deceit. Darius nodded in Erik's direction, indicating his guests appeared to be ready to begin.

"Gentlemen, welcome," he announced, his voice deep and commanding. "Have you brought the papers?" His intent was to set the tone and begin sending chills down their unsuspecting spines.

"Signore Russo speaking, Monsieur. This meeting arrangement is quite, shall we say, unusual."

"Yes, indeed it is!" protested Signore Sabatino.

"We thought that we would be meeting you personally and not behind a barrier!"

"I prefer confidentiality, gentlemen. There is no need for you to see my face. Money is money. The picture of Queen Victoria on your Maltese Pounds is the only face you need to see." Silence filled the room and then a final relenting sigh came from one of his guests.

"Yes, of course. We shall proceed as you wish."

Erik noted the sheepish reply. He could already tell that his guests felt unnerved by the current situation, giving him the upper hand he hoped.

"The papers, please," he reminded them tersely. He heard the clasp of a case snap open and the rustling of documents. "Hand them to my assistant, please."

He watched Darius step forward to receive the items and then retreat back to his side, handing over the papers. He removed his feet from the desk and sat upright. Erik grasped the contract and rapidly perused the multiple pages, his dark eyes taking note of every line. After reading the terms and conditions, it was time to begin his unpleasant interrogation to enhance his negotiation in a reduction of price.

"I am quite disappointed with you two gentlemen." He sighed heavily. His tone was solemn and laced with annoyance as he shuffled through the documents.

"This is Signore Sabatino responding. Why are you annoyed?" he asked hesitantly.

Erik heard the man swallow hard, and he stifled a chuckle over his apparent nervousness.

"Ah, Signore Sabatino! During our recent correspondence regarding the sale of the Royal Opera House, you failed to mention that there was no roof. Was it because your quill ran dry while penning the description of the damage? Perhaps the trauma you suffered erased your memory of that small fact. However, my gut tells me that you were merely trying to defraud me!"

Erik's voice rose in anger. He slammed his fist down on the wooden desktop with a loud *thump* as he continued. "Why was I not informed of the entire condition, including the collapsed roof?"

Silence.

"Did you think you could dupe a Frenchman into a fraudulent sale?"

"No, Monsieur Dante," Signore Russo answered apologetically. Erik wondered if his eyes bulged or beads of sweat were forming on his forehead. His voice trembled when he responded. "That was not our intention, I assure you. We planned on telling you these matters beforehand when you arrived and giving you a proper tour of the structure."

"And did you plan that tour after I signed the bill of sale and gave you the money? We sit here now about to close the deal, so your explanation is unacceptable!"

The velvet chair creaked from movement, and a whisper ensued between the two men. Signore Russo asked a question.

"Might we inquire as to how you obtained entrance to the theater?"

"Since you did not repair and secure the doors, it was quite easy, frankly. Do you know that most of the furnishings have been ransacked and stolen as well?"

"I'm afraid, Monsieur Dante, that we have not visited the remains recently," confessed Signore Sabatino.

"What about the debris? Why have you not removed the debris?"

"Well," Signore Russo answered, "we thoroughly intended to, but . . . "

"Spare me the details," Erik interrupted abruptly. "I've already investigated the two of you and am quite aware of the vast amount of debt you owe your many creditors." Erik paused shortly before taunting them further. "I always view bill collectors like angry dogs nipping at your heels." His voice turned sarcastic. "Perhaps I should walk away from the sale and just let them bite you!" Erik growled like a dog to emphasize the point.

Darius glanced at Erik conveying their discomfort, and he nodded with satisfaction.

"I'm afraid then that the terms of our sale will need to change drastically," he announced, after a few moments of silence. "Surely you cannot believe the building is worth the price you are asking for without a roof!"

Picking up a quill pen, Erik dipped it in the ink soaking the tip. With a quick stroke over the contract, he crossed out the price and penned in another a third less than the original offering. As he handed the documents to Darius to pass to the men, he explained his decision.

"Here is my new offer. Take it or leave it. There should be more than enough to settle your accounts without making a deceitful profit at my expense." Leaning back in the chair again, Erik continued speaking of his new conditions. "Oh, and before I take occupancy, I expect all debris to be removed and hauled away."

"Monsieur," Signore Sabatino protested. "It will cost us thousands of additional pounds to have the debris removed. You cannot be serious?"

"Oh, indeed I am," Erik answered emphatically. "Must I tell you how to do everything? I'm sure the local jailer would be happy to loan you a few lowly criminals for a month's worth of hard labor to haul the filth and debris away as a service to the fine city of Valletta. I get the impression the general public desperately wishes to have their opera house repaired."

Their voices lowered, and Erik could barely hear the whispered conversation ensuing between the two would-be swindlers. He glanced at Darius and shot out a question for amusement.

"Darius, does Valletta have a debtor's prison?"

He smiled in return and before he could answer, the voice of Signore Russo answered. "We will accept your offer, Monsieur."

Erik smiled. "Good!" Pleased they had agreed to the wisdom of his persuasion, he initialed the new figure on the documents and passed them to Darius. "Have the gentlemen sign first, and initial where I have indicated the new price." Handing him the paper and pen, Darius helped with the signature process and then returned the documents to Erik, who countersigned and retained one duplicate for his records. After penning a check for the exact amount payable to both, he handed it along with the documents back to Darius.

"Return the sale documents and check to the former owners."

Erik pushed his chair back and stood behind the desk, his voice carrying further orders across the divide. "You have one month to clear the debris from the building. Take no longer, or you shall be sorry, I assure you." One last portion of business remained. "Have you brought the architectural plans as I requested?"

Sabatino answered, "Yes, Monsieur." Hearing Darius grasp the rolled sketches, a smile curled Erik's lips at the thought of touching and examining the drawings. Darius handed him the plans. Erik grasped them eagerly, exhilarated over the simple act of clutching the design. In the palm of his hand lay his future domain.

"Show them out."

He listened as the chairs released their occupants and their feet strode to the door. "Thank you, gentlemen," he called after them, concluding the meeting.

Darius closed the door and returned to reassure his master of their departure. "They've gone."

"Good!" Erik came out from behind the screen. "Well done." All had transpired as planned and a victory was won. Satisfied that he had taken care of two obstacles in one day, plans for future work flooded his mind.

"We need to make sure they do not renege on their promise to clear the debris. I want you to make sure that it is accomplished. I don't care if you have to hound and threaten them daily. Make sure it gets done."

"Yes, of course, Master."

His next course of action was to take up residence in the opera house and oversee matters as they progressed. He could not do so locked up in a hotel surrounded by human bodies. The building called to his soul, and he wanted to become one in spirit before he resurrected it from the ashes.

"You and Andrea stay here for a month, and then you can move to your rooms at the opera house. Our first order of business during restoration will be to repair the living quarters."

There was much to do. His restless heart wanted to leave and find solace in the dark hallways of his new residence. Evening could not arrive soon enough. His ghostly presence would claim its territory. He would learn every inch of the opera house, with architectural plans in hand, as he formulated his revised design.

Erik carefully unrolled the plans on his desk. His eyes grew wide when his fingers traced the outline and structure as conceived by its former architect. It would take time to read each detail and reconstruct to his preference. When he was through, he would resurrect a destroyed house from the ashes. In the years ahead, the Royal Opera House of Valletta would be revered and glorified in its restored state, and perfect music would fill every inch. It would be his and unlike any other in the world.

❋ ❋ ❋

Within a week's time, Erik found his place within the charred walls. He knew that his living quarters would have to change; this was not the Garnier. There were no catacombs to hide in the darkness underneath.

Even though he had moved thousands of miles away, the importance of his concealment was paramount in his mind. He would still be an Opera Ghost of sorts, a Phantom, a spectral shade moving about in the shadows known only to his close confidants. This time, no foolish patrons or managers would stand in the way of his creativity. The masses would pay his salary to see spectacular productions, excellent casts, and a well-run theater. The glory would belong to him alone.

The opera house contained various dressing rooms, storage rooms, an office, and basic living quarters. Its accommodations were very different from the 700 individuals the Garnier could house, but at least 75 staff could comfortably live within the walls of the Royal Opera House, if needed. With the architectural drawings in hand, Erik studied his new home in depth, considering the space available to him.

After careful examination of the conditions of the rooms, Erik found a perfect location that contained a row of comfortable quarters for living and dining. He would initially house Darius and Andrea, and perhaps a new principal staff member to be hired. A newly constructed door would barricade off their rooms, so other employees or patrons would not be able to gain entrance without a key.

His intention was to prepare quarters for his own use. They would be hidden and unnoticeable down the same corridor of the main living quarters, but no door would exist. Only a panel in the wall, unnoticeable to the naked eyes, would give way to an entrance when trigged by a secret mechanism. This would allow him to live secluded, but free to wander in the shadows of his newly constructed secret corridors.

The security measures seemed reasonable. Anyone who intended to breach his domain would first need to know where his quarters were located. Secondly, they would require a key to enter the first doorway. Thirdly, they would have to locate and then engage the secret mechanism to slide open the panel leading into his suite. It was no lair, but Erik felt it was relatively safe.

Within a week, Darius and Erik began the tedious task of retrofitting the hallway to add another doorway to secure the row of quarters from the remainder of the opera house. When they finished that task, Erik removed the obvious door to his suite and replaced it with a new panel-like feature that blended perfectly with the hallway walls.

It took weeks of work. He wished to have it completed before general construction began and the opera house became filled with strangers. This way, the only knowledge of its existence would rest with Darius and Andrea. He decided, however, after much reflection, that he would show both his companions how to trip the mechanism. It only made sense to have a backup plan should he need to be reached in case of emergency.

Construction on the door and paneling was slow and difficult. Erik's temper often flared over Darius' inability to understand his simple instructions. His workmanship as a carpenter was shabby, and with the perfection that Erik demanded, he would often tell his assistant to rip it apart and start again until it was right.

Andrea visited during the process bringing food and drinks for both, as well as scolding Erik for his lack of patience while she was there. She insisted on helping in the process too, so Erik directed her to start cleaning the rooms for personal quarters. Andrea soon discovered the displeasure of her duties. Smoke damage clung to everything, and she found the smell putrid. All the rooms needed cleaning and repainting, as well as the carpeting torn out and replaced.

When Erik's two companions returned to the hotel at night, he continued to examine the architectural prints, redesigning the dressing rooms and living quarters for the staff. Some rooms would remain secure, while others would provide various egresses and ingresses that would be unknown to its occupants. His need to spy on the unsuspecting never waned an ounce, and he cleverly ensured that one room could be entered from his own quarters. Of course, he had no idea what he would use it for, except that it was reminiscent of his entrance into Christine's dressing room.

Within a week, a crew of men arrived with horse-drawn wagons to haul away tons of debris. The former owners had used his idea and procured able-bodied men from the local jailer, sentenced to hard labor as restitution for their crimes. They began the laborious task of hauling out beams, glass, wires, masonry, seats, floorboards, and everything else imaginable. Erik thought it would be a good time to tackle the numerous bird nests inside the opera boxes in the upper tiers. It looked more like an aviary than an auditorium.

Finally, the weeks progressed and the debris that had riddled the interior was gone. The opera house was now an empty shell ready for his handiwork. As he planned the redesign, Erik envisioned perfection. He wanted the opera house to consume its inhabitants and bring them into a world of music they had never experienced. His insatiable desire to succeed in this endeavor became his new obsession. The Royal Opera House of Valletta was now the driving force waking him each day, causing his lungs to inhale and exhale, and his heart to beat with purpose.

Only one obstacle to his success remained, and that was the lack of funds. He planned to rectify that problem with his next course of action.

Chapter 4

After a few more days of final touches and the delivery of furnishings, their quarters were complete. Darius and Andrea took up permanent residence behind its walls, and everyone settled into a routine as they planned their future together.

Erik took particular pride in his own private residence, decorating it to his peculiar delights and taste. He purposely wanted to deviate from his past morbid idea of sleeping in a coffin, while maintaining a certain aura of darkness so he could sleep. To that end, Erik purchased a rather ostentatious Tudor-style mahogany canopy bed, with heavy brocade curtains that could be closed for privacy. He adorned it with deep blood-red silken covers and pillows. Since everything in Erik's life required perfect order, the remainder of the room held a dark mahogany dresser, nightstand, and armoire aesthetically placed to his liking.

Erik's parlor contained a piano, divan, two armchairs, and bookcases that he fully intended to fill to the brim. He placed a side table, with a crystal decanter of cognac that sat upon a polished silver tray, near a small desk.

One obsession he continued to feed was his love of flowers. He strategically placed multiple bouquets of various colored roses throughout the room for the sole purpose of filling his nostrils with his favorite aroma.

He chose an eclectic mixture of abstract and fine art. Andrea was not too keen on his preferred subject matter, which she expressed to him on more than one occasion as being rather dark and morbid. He merely smiled at the comment, finding the scenes of hell and ghouls being dragged to their ultimate torment rather entertaining.

In contrast, Erik thought her taste in art boring. Andrea preferred still life pictures of flowers and fruit, which lacked emotion and depth, in his opinion. He sneered at her choices of dull subject matter.

As they settled into a daily schedule, Andrea and Erik created a morning ritual of eating breakfast together. Darius, a devout Muslim, retreated up the stairs to the lower roof of the opera house to face Mecca and pray each morning. Erik allowed his private beliefs to continue, but shared no interest in seeking anything divine.

Valletta appeared to have its share of domed Catholic churches, which he could see from the rooftop. He enjoyed surveying the city landscape from that vantage point as he eyed the various architecture of the city. The roof also became his favorite place for reflection, as he retreated at night to view the harbor in the distance and overlook Valletta.

Even though the upper part of the roof had collapsed from the fire, the outer lower ridge was still intact. The architectural structure provided for various roof levels. The entire length and breadth of the opera house on the first roof level was actually a walkway easily accessed by a staircase and doorway. Once on the outer level, the roof raised to a second tier smaller in circumference. The flat roof at the very top of the structure had collapsed into the auditorium during the fire.

Finally, after everyone moved into their housing, it was time to discuss the future. Erik asked Andrea to join him in the auditorium, which was finally clear of debris. The bowels of the opera house were clean and empty, waiting and ready for Erik to fill them once again. However, there remained that one small problem—money.

As they strolled about the stone floor inspecting the final work, Erik shared his plan with her.

"I think now that we finally have room in the auditorium, we should have a masquerade to celebrate."

"A masquerade?"

Andrea's eyes grew wide with excitement and curiosity over his suggestion. Women always enjoyed parties. Erik, however, kept a solemn face while he walked through the vacant auditorium. He lifted his head upward and peered at the clouds threatening rain.

"Yes, a masquerade. What better way than to procure funds from the rich of Malta to rebuild this shell of a building filled with bird waste?" Erik walked toward the stage area, longing to see it completed. "It's either that or steal the money from a bank. Would you prefer I try that ploy, Andrea?"

"Oh, Erik, of course not!" she protested.

"I thought not," he smugly replied. Erik pondered his course of action. It probably would have been easier to steal than to beg from society, but desperate times called for desperate measures and only one choice remained. Certainly, with a little persuasion, he could raise the necessary funds through donations from obliging patrons. He toyed with the idea of offering shares of ownership, but decided that would be unacceptable. He wanted total control.

There remained one looming problem. He needed a front man of sorts to do his bidding at the masquerade. He envisioned someone acting on his behalf, a representative who could persuade people to donate. Darius lacked the qualities needed for the job, but Erik had another person in mind.

"Andrea, I only have enough funding to finish half the structure. There is no other way. We must raise money."

Erik continued to stroll along side Andrea, his hands clasped behind his back. "We'll invite the social elite, the governor, government officials, titled aristocrats, and military officers to open their wallets and purses. I'll play upon their desire for the arts and the social necessity that the Royal Opera House rises to its former glory. It will cost funds to have the masquerade, of course. I'll spare no expense on alcoholic refreshments, food, and decorations. After our guests eat, drink, dance, and are merry, I'll have someone convince them that the new owner's desire to rebuild is worth sharing their Maltese pounds."

"Who will convince your guests? Do you think the public will wish to invest in your opera house without even knowing who the owner is behind the endeavor?"

Erik braced himself for the usual lecture about to spew from Andrea's lips, and tried to keep his growing irritation in check as she continued to badger him.

"They will need surety that the owner exists and possesses the ability to resurrect this house from the ashes. People do not like to risk their investments. You should make yourself known, Erik. This is the perfect time."

As he suspected, her insistent drive to push him into facing society met his ears. His nostrils flared in anger, and he quickly strode from her side, his heels clicking across the stone floor. They were about to repeat the familiar, yet never-ending, argument.

"Are you suggesting I show my face, Andrea, what I have of one?" He flung the comment over his shoulder, as his feet took him farther away from her peskiness.

"No, of course not, not your full face, but you cannot hide for the remainder of your life, Erik! You must find your way back into society."

He heard Andrea's footsteps approach from behind, but continued to walk in the other direction to put distance between them.

"Erik, stop, and listen to me, will you!" she cried.

Relenting, his feet came to a halt, and Erik spun around, resting his dark gaze upon her face. Andrea, he noted of late, was flashing a bolder presence when they were together, and he wondered how far she would attempt to push his limits this time. He shoved out his chest and asserted his superiority to put her back in her place.

"I will do what I damn well please," he hissed. "I will live my life as it pleases me, not you!"

Andrea stood her ground before him.

"Well, I for one think you're a fool, Erik!"

Erik's brow rose when she stood tall and puffed out her own chest, releasing a huff of air from her lungs. Aghast over her brashness, he took a step in her direction, closing the gap between their bodies. He clenched his angry jaw and lowered his head to hover above her 5'5" frame. His eyes, turbulent and dark, examined her closely. Andrea did not flinch.

"I plan on finding someone to represent me, Andrea, if that is all right with you. Perhaps some day, I shall reveal myself, but I have no desire to do so now. The discussion is over."

Erik turned and walked away, his fists clenched with anger.

"And who will you find to represent you, Erik?" she nagged, following again. "You refused to even meet the owners in person. You'll have to show yourself eventually, you must."

"I don't need to be told what to do," he snarled. "Especially by some hen-pecking damn woman!"

He strode a few more steps and then stopped in the middle of the auditorium and turned his head up toward the gray skies that threatened rain. A tinge of weariness washed over his soul. A drop released from the clouds and hit his uncovered cheek, followed by another and another until one by one they left their wet marks on the dusty stone floor.

"I hope to hell it doesn't rain on the eve of the masquerade." He turned around and grabbed Andrea's arm softly as he passed. "Come, you'll be soaked in no time. Let's go inside, and we'll have a cup of tea to calm your righteous nerves and soothe my foul mood."

She was always pushing him, challenging him, trying to change him. The only problem with her plan was that Erik had no intention of changing. He was too accustomed to his personal misery.

Erik escorted Andrea to their dining room where they sat and chatted for some time.

"You know, I'll need your help and expertise to plan the event." He looked at her, hoping she would find pleasure in his request. "I'm sure Darius can be of some assistance with the logistics."

"Yes, it would be good to use Darius," she replied. "Though I'm not sure how much help he'll be." Andrea chuckled.

Erik was not surprised that Andrea had finally acknowledged Darius' shortcomings, though this was the first time she had voiced her opinion candidly.

"We'll have to erect some type of canopy or tent structure indoors since we have no roof. If I know my luck, it will rain the evening of the masquerade," he noted, convinced of his bad fortune. "I wish for it to be a merry occasion, if there is one to be had in Valletta, and we'll spare no expense. There must be music as well. We will feed them and get them drunk then ask for their money."

"I think it's a fine plan, Erik, now that I hear what you envision."

Erik rarely smiled in response to anything Andrea said, but he allowed a small opening to part his lips, causing the corner of his mouth to rise.

"Andrea, I cannot wait to restore this building. You have no idea how it burns in my soul. I plan to secure only the best performers and musicians to fill this house with music, and we'll hold auditions for singers from around the world." Erik paused with satisfaction. "I may even return to composing again."

He shifted his gaze to the floor as he thought. "It's my only food," he admitted soberly. "Music is all that keeps me alive now. Without it, I'd go mad." A few moments passed, and he looked up at Andrea. "Let's hope that we have fair weather, a large turnout, and the investors we need."

Andrea smiled and raised her teacup in his direction. "To your success!"

"To my success!" Erik roared in return, his deep voice filling the room. "Now, all I need is a front man."

Andrea's eyes widened in bewilderment. Erik sported a sly grin, and took another sip of tea.

Chapter 5

The plans to find a front man went well. It was not a difficult task. The gentleman had announced where he was going upon his retirement. Erik took note and found out exactly where he had relocated, after making a few inquiries. Many speculated Richard Mercier had disappeared to Australia or Germany, but Erik knew that Venice was his ultimate destination.

He had not retired either, but just upped and left Paris, tired of the Ghost. He accepted a position elsewhere. Apparently, Mercier only wished to retire from the Phantom's pranks, which amused Erik immensely.

Erik dispatched a letter dangling a carrot in front of Richard's nose. Within a week, the answer came. He was interested in the prospective offer of head manager at a new venue. Richard accepted the invitation to travel to Valletta to meet with the owner, and a week later stood on Maltese soil. A meeting was arranged a day after his arrival, with instructions to report to the newly constructed office at the Royal Opera House.

Darius waited for Richard in the defunct foyer, and upon arrival escorted him to the mysterious owner. At last, the time had arrived for the former manager of the Garnier to meet the real Opera Ghost in the flesh.

Erik had respected Richard for many years, though he never revealed his human appearance to the man. He was wise in that he consistently obeyed the Opera Ghost, unlike the fools Armon and Firmin, who later arrived on the scene.

Richard repeatedly displayed intelligence to Erik and never argued or questioned the Ghost's demands, especially when they were suggestions on how to run the theater better. Whether he obeyed out of curiosity or fear, Erik never really knew, but he surmised that Andrea had often persuaded Richard to comply.

Armon and Firmin, on the other hand, were foolish idiots who thought they could usurp the Ghost's authority over his domain. Of course, they paid; they paid dearly. Erik made sure of it, by bringing down the chandelier.

As he pondered the incident that had occurred over a year ago, he carried little remorse for the outcome of its crash. Only one died that evening, who was merely a victim of necessity in Erik's mind, and a poor soul in the wrong place at the wrong time.

When the door finally opened announcing the arrival of Mercier into his office, he watched Richard's face with great interest. As soon as Richard's eyes met Erik's masked countenance, the poor man's blood drained away, and he appeared ashen. He looked like a ghost meeting the Ghost. Erik knew he had always wondered about him, and now the time to wonder had abruptly come to a surprising end.

Erik approached Richard and stretched out his arm. "Go ahead," he told his guest, offering a gentleman's handshake. "Touch me. I'm not a ghost, Richard. My name is Erik. In Valletta, I've taken the name of Erik Dante." No use mentioning any other last names he had used in his lifetime. Today he was Dante; the Devil.

Mercier glanced at Darius quickly. Erik noticed his servant give the man a reassuring nod and smile. After a few moments of hesitation, he reached out, took the Erik's hand, and clasped it tightly.

"It's good to finally meet the apparition who haunted the Garnier for so many years," he declared, nearly choking on his words.

Erik watched in curiosity as Richard eyed him from top to bottom. He seemed to take note of his finely made wig of human hair, and his clean white mask that covered his deformity. His inquisitive eyes traveled over his tailored suit.

"Take a good look. Make sure I'm real." Erik encouraged Richard with a smile before turning away and walking over to a side table. He poured two glasses of cognac, returned to his guest, and handed one to him. "You look like you could use a drink. Have a seat, please." Erik gestured toward a nearby chair and sat down as well.

Darius stood in the doorway, with a hopeful look upon his face, as if he wished to stay. However, Erik denied his request, as he wanted privacy. "That will be all, Darius. We'll speak later."

Darius' countenance fell in disappointment, but he nodded obediently, turned, and closed the door behind him. When the latch clicked, Erik focused his attention back on his guest.

"So, tell me, Richard, what have you been up to? How's retirement?" He grinned at him with a snide smirk. "You really didn't think I thought you'd retire, did you?" Taking a sip of his cognac, his eyes flashed with amusement. "You were just tired of the Ghost. Confess it, my friend!"

Richard took a large gulp of alcohol. Erik noticed his hand shake, surprised that he was so nervous in his presence. He felt a bit pained the man feared him so much, but he probably thought he had killed the derelict stagehand. There was no using arguing his innocence. Richard would never believe him anyway.

"Yes, you are quite right. I was tired of the Ghost and have settled in Venice. I'm the assistant manager of La Fenice."

"And your salary, Richard, do you find it adequate?"

Mercier raised his brow at the odd question. Erik could tell he was confused, so he decided to move things along. He rose to his feet and walked over to his desk, dipped the quill in the inkwell, and wrote a figure on a piece of paper. Folding it in half, he approached Mercier and handed him the note.

"Open it." Erik appeared smugly confident, fully anticipating Richard's favorable response. "This is what I will pay you if you come to work for me."

Mercier's fingers fiddled tensely with the edge of the paper. He flipped it open, read the figure, and his jaw dropped open. "You . . . you cannot be serious!"

Richard's wide-eyed astonishment amused Erik. "Quite serious. I need you. Frankly, I respect you. I know that sounds odd coming from someone who gave you so much hell. However, I believe we could have a rather good working relationship together now that you have met me in person. As you can see, I'm no apparition. I'm not a lunatic, as some suspect. I'm a musician and architect with a passion for excellence in the theater."

Erik took a sip and then sat back down in the chair. "I've purchased the Valletta opera house. This building you are now visiting belongs to me, but as you can see, it lays mostly in ruin and needs to be rebuilt." Erik sipped his cognac and then continued speaking with frankness.

"As you are already aware, I don't necessarily prefer to have a public life. I prefer one of solitude. Nevertheless, to run an opera house on such a grand scale as this, I will need a good manager. I'm looking for an assistant, one whom I intend to pay handsomely to do my bidding. I believe, Richard, you are that man." Erik nodded toward the note still in Mercier's shaking hand. "As you can see, I'll pay you well for your services, if you agree to come and work for me to raise this house from ashes to glory."

Erik took another sip and let his words sink into his guest's obvious spinning head. Mercier appeared interested, but the poor man looked as if he were too terrified to answer.

"If I promise not to strangle anyone, will you agree?"

Mercier lifted his head and laughed nervously. "For some reason, I don't think you'll keep your promise." He paused. "However, at the price you're offering, I'm more than willing to turn a blind eye."

A sly grin curled the corner of Erik's lips. "You are a wise man indeed, Richard. Welcome to *my* opera house."

The two men spent the next hour behind closed doors coming to an understanding on many levels. Mercier asked questions about Erik's past life that he wanted answered. Erik responded to those he felt comfortable revealing, while keeping silent on others that he did not wish to discuss.

It was decided that Richard would relocate as soon as possible from Venice to Valletta. His position would be that of general manager and the main publicity figure and contact for the Royal Opera House. Erik Dante would stay in the shadows, anonymously directing all that was to occur, including the reconstruction, hiring of staff, auditions, and productions. Erik decided to forgo a ballet corps, which seemed more important to Parisian patrons than the Maltese.

Erik felt pleased with Richard Mercier. He hoped the man would eventually become a close friend and was confident he could trust him implicitly. He was a good choice in character and stature, and able to hold his own in the public eyes.

Above all, Erik hoped Richard was still in love with Andrea. Overall, his plan was a good mix of manipulation and control. Erik was proud to have thought of it in his devious way. He knew for the sake of Andrea, he would keep his loyalties intact. In the process, he might be the merry matchmaker once again and bring them back together.

When they finished their discussions, Erik stood to his feet and offered his hand once again. In a gesture of confidence, he reached out his other hand and placed it on Richard's shoulder.

"I trust you, Mercier, to run the show with my guidance, and I know that you are no fool to cross me." Erik's eyes spoke of the consequences.

"Then I shall earn your trust," Richard replied, convincing his employer.

Erik smiled and then began his game of chess. "Oh, and by the way, Richard, an old friend accompanied me from Paris to Valletta," he added nonchalantly. "I believe you two are acquainted."

"Who is that?"

"Andrea."

Richard's eyes sparkled, though he withheld a smile, which answered Erik's curiosity.

"I'm glad to hear of it," he replied awkwardly. "It will be good to see her again."

Their handshake ended, and Richard Mercier left to return to Venice with the understanding that he would be back in two weeks. Erik's next order of business was to break the news to Andrea.

❋ ❋ ❋

"You'll never guess who I saw this morning," Erik announced with a sneaky grin on his face.

Andrea lifted a cup of tea to her lips and peered over the rim of her cup, clearly wondering what he was up to this time. "And who would that be?"

"Richard Mercier."

Her face went blank, and Erik had to look closely at Andrea's chest to make sure she was still breathing. Her cup began to shake in her hand. Slowly, she lowered it to the saucer. Erik enjoyed her reaction, amused over how many times the china cup clanked until it finally rested in the small rim circle.

"Erik, how did you find him?"

"Oh, come on, Andrea." He was surprised at her question. "It's me; the mastermind. Did you didn't think I'd let him wander off to retirement without keeping tabs on him?" He felt offended over Andrea's question. She knew he could do anything. Why did she doubt his abilities? "You wound my ego," he moaned. He fiddled with morning newspaper in his hand and shook it once to flip it open.

"Oh, look, an article about the Royal Opera House." Erik ignored her sniveling in the background and cleared his throat before reading the notice aloud.

"It had been rumored that the Royal Opera House was recently purchased by a mysterious unknown investor—"

"Put the damn newspaper down and talk to me!" she interrupted.

Erik lifted his eyes in her direction and looked at her red nose. "I think you need a handkerchief." He pulled one out from his inside vest pocket and passed it across the table. "Wipe your nose, and then we'll talk."

Andrea grabbed it, and flipped it open, looking quite happy to soil his white linen with her tears. She blew her nose loudly. When she was finished, she demanded answers.

"What are you doing, Erik? Tell me what you're up to!"

"No good. I'm up to no good."

He was about to continue reading, enjoying the torment he was giving his old friend, when she grabbed the newspaper from his hand and flung it across the room, sending the sheets flying. Erik moaned.

"All right. It's obvious you want answers," he relented. Her tears stopped, and her eyes glared at him.

"I've hired Richard to be my front man, Andrea. He's currently an assistant manager at Le Fenice in Venice making a pittance of a salary. I offered him a large sum, which he probably thinks I owe him after all I extorted out of his pocket throughout the years."

"What do you mean a front man?"

Erik's face turned serious. "I don't wish to be known. With him in the public eye, I can hide and direct things anonymously. This is my preference, despite your insipid nagging." Erik picked up his cup of tea, took a sip, and pensively thought of all the ways he could use Richard.

"He will do everything. He'll host the masquerade, oversee the reconstruction, hire the staff, and take my directions throughout each step without complaint."

"You could have chosen someone else," Andrea told him in a low tone tinged with emotion.

"I could have. However, whatever drove you two apart is not my concern. Resolve your issues with him or be miserable. Frankly, I don't care one way or the other when it comes to matters of love. It's all a pain in the ass." Erik knew he sounded cold, but it was times like these that women and their emotional states irritated the hell out of him. He never understood the creatures and probably never would.

"You drove us apart!"

She flung her words at him like sharp knives. It wasn't often Andrea dared to shout, but apparently this was one time he would take note.

"We constantly argued over my loyalty to you. He only paid you and did your bidding because I begged him to do so. Do you know how hard it was for the two of us during those days, do you? You were so obsessed . . . "

"Enough!" Now she had hit a nerve. His eyes narrowed, and his amused expression faded into one of darkness. Erik stood to his feet, picked the paper up from the floor, and replaced each sheet in its place perfectly, as if it just came off the newsstand. He set it upon a nearby table.

"Now if you'll excuse me, I have architectural plans to look over."

Her boldness grew by the hour. Once afraid of his very shadow, she would do as she was told, deliver his messages, and never talk back. She knew better. Now, however, since he had taken her to Malta and they had formed a deeper relationship, she was beginning to test their boundaries. Those boundaries were not to be crossed. At times, it was all Erik could do to suppress the rage within that he wished to display in response to her words. He would never hurt her physically, but his anger needed release. He found that storming off out of her presence became his only response to cope with her female emotions.

He left the room and slammed the door to make a point. Upon arriving at his private quarters, he went inside, locked the paneled door, and headed straight toward his desk. He unrolled the architectural sketches with great care. For a fleeting second, a sense of madness flowed through his veins. It seemed as if an eternity had passed since an opportunity to construct had presented itself. The Royal Opera House was his new playground of creativity.

The exterior structure stood strong, but the interior auditorium and outlining hallways were a mess. The intense heat of the fire had calcified the stonework, and only the finest of masons would do for restoration. He decided to hire the original sculptor who had worked on the initial construction.

Erik began to draw to scale new corridors and secret hallways, carefully laying out a labyrinth behind the walls. Unfortunately, this was work he and Darius would need to perform alone to keep their existence a secret. Months of construction stretched out before him, but in the end, his domain would be secure.

It was a new era in his life. He smiled as he planned his own Box 5, which would grant him secret entrance and exit to come and go at will. With Richard in place to play the social persona, he could remain the Opera Ghost as long as it damn well pleased him; a part he played well.

Of course, the Ghost wouldn't need to use his former methods of menacing control over its owners and idiotic managers. This was his opera house, and he was going to enjoy every second of overseeing its daily operations. The crew, cast, and employees would be hand-picked and approved by him. The productions would come as he ordered and staged. He would return to composing and pen another opera.

As he thought of finding a soprano whose voice would fill his ears, Erik fell into a brooding mood of dark memories. He wondered if Christine was now performing in Sweden and hoped she continued to pursue her career in his absence. There was no doubt in his heart that he missed her angelic voice, which he had toned to perfection. Would she always be thankful that he had taught her how to sing? The thought shrouded Erik like a cloak of sadness, and he poured himself a large glass of cognac to take the edge off the pain.

Chapter 6

Erik smoothed the sleeves of his black velvet tuxedo. A long red opera scarf draped around his neck and hung down the front of his pristine white ruffled shirt. Tonight he would wear a black mask that would cover both sides of his face, both the good and the bad. There was no need to cause speculation as to what lay underneath. He would just blend in like the rest of the crowd, with a masked face.

He shoved his hand into a black glove and then adjusted the fingers one by one until they were tight, doing the same with the other hand. One last gulp of a glass of cognac for fortitude, and Erik exited his quarters, walking down the long hall. Darius stood at the end waiting for him.

"Everything is ready, I trust?" he asked in anticipation.

"Yes, Master, everything is ready. Carriages are arriving now. Monsieur Mercier is at the entrance greeting the attendees."

"Very well, then. Make one quick walk through of the auditorium. Make sure the servers have their trays filled with champagne flutes, tell the orchestra to start, and check with the caterer to make sure the buffet tables are stocked and ready."

Darius bowed in acknowledgement and left his side. Andrea exited her quarters and strode down the hall to catch up with her escort. She was dressed outrageously in a bright green gown with peacock feathers bobbing in unison as she walked. She looked more like a bird than his right-hand confidant, but it brought pleasure to Erik to see her well dressed for once.

"You look wonderful, Andrea. In fact, I might dare to add, very pretty. Shall we mingle and eavesdrop?"

"Well, a flattering remark from the Phantom himself! I'm speechless," she teased, with a broad smile on her face.

"I want you to go shopping," he told her, offering her arm in escort. "You need to buy yourself some fancy dresses. I'll give you the money."

"That's very nice of you. Are you trying to prep me for Richard's eyes," she accused him teasingly.

"I have no response," he replied in an uncommitted tone. "I'm merely a ghost, wandering the halls, minding my own business."

After Richard Mercier had arrived, he was shown his living quarters next to Andrea. She scolded Erik for an hour behind closed doors over his motives. He merely listened with delight.

Erik had been privy to their secret affair in Paris. Andrea and Richard were once a couple, carefully hiding their secret romance from the cast and crew. Erik, however, saw and heard everything. Nothing escaped his notice as he wandered through his secret corridors. He would eavesdrop on their times together, which brought him an odd sense of enjoyment. He intended to do the same when the Royal Opera House filled with new live-in cast and crewmembers. They would all be under his scrutiny. It was Erik's way of keeping informed and in control.

Tonight, his attention would rest upon Richard's performance. Afterward, Erik would wander through the crowd unnoticed, picking up tidbits of conversations here and there to ascertain the attendees' willingness to contribute.

Of course, Andrea wished he would reveal himself and be a normal man. She was disappointed in his decision to remain a spectral shade and remained heaven-bent on his redemption. He, on the other hand, remained hell-bent on his solitude. Nothing would persuade him otherwise, as he did not wish to take the risk of being discovered.

They arrived inside the rectangular foyer filled with glowing candelabras that cast a golden hue on the bare stone walls. Bouquets of roses decorated the entranceway, greeting the guests with a stifling floral aroma that Erik found soothing. He grabbed two flutes of champagne passing by on a tray held by one of the servers and handed one to Andrea.

Erik stood tall and confident with nothing to hide in his appearance, though he struggled at the thought of throngs of humans surrounding his body the entire evening. However, to secure his future, he would grin and bear it. Alcohol would help.

He stood by Andrea, sipping champagne, while he watched Richard greet the guests. The man was tall, with broad shoulders. His salt and pepper hair gave him an air of maturity. Richard's long sideburns met his upturned mustache that Erik thought he should have shaved long ago. It made him look older than his years. Erik leaned into Andrea, feeling teasingly wicked, when he whispered in her ear.

"Tell me. Does his mustache tickle when you kiss him?"

Andrea shot him an evil look and elbowed him in his side. "Erik, how can you ask such a thing?"

He chuckled, intent on teasing her often. "Fine, I'll drop the subject." His eyes twinkled from the candles in the room.

Erik felt good. Things were going as planned. One by one, aristocrats and government officials entered. When Darius, who was dressed in a dashing uniform, introduced the most important arrival at the door, Erik took note.

"The Honorable Governor of Malta, Sir Henry Roberts, and his wife Lady Roberts."

"Welcome, your esteemed Excellency," Richard greeted, as he bowed at the waist to honor the dignitary and his wife.

"Signore, it's a pleasure to meet you," the Governor replied.

Erik examined the official, dressed in his finery, wearing a sash across his breast with medals dangling everywhere to declare his importance. Apparently, he appeared too proud to partake in the festivities of wearing a masquerade costume. His arrogance caused Erik's eyes to narrow, and he shifted them to his wife, glaring at her outrageous gown and tall wig reminiscent of Marie Antoinette. Erik smirked, wondering how far her head would roll if she lost it in a guillotine.

"The pleasure is all mine," Richard replied, giving another short bow. "Thank you for attending our masquerade this evening. I hope you enjoy it."

Well done, Richard, you're playing the part splendidly, Erik thought to himself with amusement, while sipping his flute of champagne.

He leaned into Andrea's ear and whispered, "So what do you think of your Richard now, Andrea? Quite the man of the hour, I would say."

Andrea shot him an annoying glare, causing a sly smile to curl his lips in delight. He was about to retort back with another smart remark to edge her on, but stopped as the cackling voice of the Governor's wife caught his ear.

"Mercier," she mused, sticking her nose in the air. "You're French then, Monsieur?"

"Indeed," he replied with pride.

"Well," she huffed, "I told my husband a thousand times the Royal Opera House needs to be restored for the sake of society and the arts of Valletta. Music is the mainstay of society. Don't you think so, *Monsieur*?" She paused and then continued, "I'm sorry, what is your name again?"

Richard smiled. "Mercier."

Erik raised his brow over the woman's confession and glanced at her husband, who rolled his eyes, no doubt bemoaning the Frenchman who stood before them.

"I do hope," she added, shaking her closed fan in Richard's face, "that the new owner plans to restore the Governor's box to its original design. Is the box still there? Do the grand statues still support the overhang?"

"You will see upon entrance, Madame, that the majority of the interior was destroyed. The demolition, I'm afraid, did remove the box and supporting statutes, but I'm sure its restoration, as designed by the owner, will be pleasing. We will do our utmost to restore the opera house to its former glory, if not better."

Very good, Richard. You are doing quite well. Erik was pleased to say the least. He would probably give the Governor's wife her box back, along with its outrageous overhang, if they contributed enough money to make it worth his while.

Richard extended his hand toward the theater doors, inviting them to join the celebration. "Please, enjoy the evening."

Everything was under control, so Erik escorted Andrea into the main auditorium to mingle. As the crowds thickened, so did his anxiety. Living in a lair was far more appealing than rubbing elbows with high society. He would have gladly retreated for the evening had it not been for his lust for the pocketbooks of aristocrats.

He wandered among the crowd, champagne flute in hand, listening to conversations of potential investors. They discussed beforehand that Andrea would mix with the crowd too and report any overheard conversations that might give him a feel for how the evening was progressing.

The interior of the auditorium appeared clean and cleared of all debris, though the ninety-seven burned out opera boxes were an ugly eyesore. To compensate, Erik had commissioned banners to hang from the boxes draping downward to cover most of the destruction. They depicted in bright colors the various productions planned after the gala reopening. In addition, one large sign hung over the stage area declaring the words, *the Royal Opera House – Ashes to Glory.*

At the foot of the missing stage, a thousand fragrant roses surrounded the orchestra pit, which contained dozens of musicians playing waltzes by several well-known composers. Tables lined the outer walls, overflowing with food, and servers in black footmen uniforms walked among the attendees, passing out copious amounts of alcoholic beverages. The ambiance played upon the gaiety of the crowd. Erik was pleased.

Richard arrived to make his rounds and answer questions. An architectural scale created by Erik sat upon a table, showing the potential investors the changes planned during restoration. Of course, Erik did not reveal his numerous new hidden corridors weaving throughout the building. The mockup attracted a large gathering of men, who stood examining it closely.

He glanced above at the missing roof feeling extremely thankful fate had given him a star-filled night. Erik had purchased canopies for the occasion, but once assured the weather would be clear, he decided against erecting them. The stars played upon the atmosphere, which was much better.

"It seems to be going well," Andrea observed, approaching his side. "I've been milling about. Comments are very positive."

"I'm pleased, I must admit," Erik replied, his eyes skipping about the crowd.

"However," Andrea's voice lowered with a tone of concern, "there is a woman who wishes to speak with you privately. She's standing to the left of the orchestra pit dressed in an outrageous scarlet gown, red mask, and raven-colored hair."

Erik turned his eyes toward the area and discovered the stranger staring at him intently. "What does she want to speak to me about?" he asked, curious about her appearance.

"She wouldn't say." Andrea clutched his forearm and looked into Erik's eyes. "Whatever it is, I have an ill feeling regarding her presence here, and I'm not one to have such premonitions," she emphasized.

Erik shrugged off her words. *If anyone should have an ill feeling about someone's presence, it should be her*, he thought to himself. His dark eyes roved over the stranger's frame, wondering what she could possibly want with him. No one knew who he was, or so he thought.

"I'll go talk to her." He turned and assured Andrea first. "Stop worrying. I'll handle it."

As he walked closer to her waiting figure, he examined her closely. Her eyes remained fixed on his movements. He returned the gaze unbroken. He stopped and allowed his tall frame to hover over her scarlet-clad body and peered down into her dark eyes.

"You wished to speak with me?"

"Why, yes, Monsieur Dante," she responded in French. "My name is Sybelle Renard." She stretched out her hand waiting for his lips to touch. Erik was unaccustomed to obliging women in this manner and looked at her gloved hand with reservation. He thought it best not to spurn her should she wish to invest, so he swiftly lifted her hand to his lips and left a perfunctory kiss that merely grazed the fabric of her glove. He felt like spitting afterward.

"How do you know my name?" Erik responded in French, hoping to keep their conversation private from eavesdroppers. "I don't believe anyone has properly introduced us."

The woman took a step closer toward Erik and peered into his eyes from the darkness of her own. She studied his masked face, keeping her intense gaze.

"An evil eye, Monsieur. I see within you an evil eye."

Erik's brow rose in surprise over her odd superstitious remark. "Oh, really?" he questioned with a smirk. "And what does that evil eye tell you, Mademoiselle?"

The woman's mouth curled into a wicked grin. "You've murdered before, perhaps?"

Erik's blood ran cold. "What is it you wish to discuss with me, since you seem to know so much about my evil tendencies?" His voice was curt and menacing, studying the dark woman that stood before him with boldness.

"You may rebuild your Royal Opera House," she told him confidently. "But the ground is cursed, and it will be destroyed again. One never knows when such things will happen," she added, void of emotion. "But it will be a pile of rubble again one day. I assure you." She leaned in close to his ear and lowered her voice. "The spirits beneath are angry."

Erik's irritation grew with each word. "You presume much, Mademoiselle," he responded in a drawl of disgust. "You conclude that I am the owner of this building. You appear to have intimate knowledge that I've killed in my lifetime. Now, you stand before me like some idiotic soothsayer who can see the future of the building in which we stand." He paused and then spat out his thoughts. "Arrogance and rubbish!"

His knuckles tingled with temptation, as he looked at her scrawny neck. He hadn't felt any evil tendencies to strangle the life out of anyone in a long time. The unknown guest had succeeded in resurrecting a darkness buried in his soul, and he wondered why.

"And how do you know the future of the ground we stand upon?"

"I sensed it when I arrived from France, Monsieur. Premonition is something that once given to a human, follows them no matter where they roam upon this Earth. I read signs, and spirits speak to me. I know the future. I'm gifted in telling fortunes." She lifted her chin with smugness and spoke confidently.

In a surprise move, she stepped closer to Erik, her perfume wafting up his nostrils as she whispered in his ear. "Do you wish to hear your future, Monsieur? I find it quite interesting."

"I know you damn fortune tellers," he spat in disgust. He stepped back from her sickening sweet scent. "I had my fill as a boy living among the tricksters and liars of traveling fairs. You think I believe you?" He threw his head back and laughed, shrugging off her ludicrous statements.

"I'm surprised you are not a believer! Nevertheless, I will tell you what you so arrogantly refuse to hear." Her eyes glazed over as if she had slipped into a trance, and her voice lowered. "You think that you have purchased your freedom and a new life, but you have only dug another grave for yourself. Hell awaits you, Monsieur, and so does the destiny you fear."

Erik watched her closely when she stared boldly into his dark eyes. She reached out, trailing her index finger from the base of his neck down his chest until it stopped above his heart.

"And here, Monsieur Dante, is your fate." Her fingertip rested heavily upon his vest making her point. "You wish for beauty and love. Love you will find, but without beauty, and it shall pierce your heart like a dagger. In the end, it will be your undoing and death."

The woman let out a grotesque chuckle and then pulled out a calling card from her sleeve, shoving it into Erik's coat pocket.

"Should you wish to know more, you may find me at that address. Good evening, Monsieur." She turned, her skirt rustling with its layers of silken fabric, but then she abruptly stopped and peered over her bare shoulder to leave her last words.

"Oh, and you shall do quite well this evening. You will raise the funds needed, and you will rebuild. Whether the building stays erect for centuries to come is entirely another matter, oui?"

The woman winked at him and then walked away, leaving Erik standing alone in a crowd of people. Erik's heart thumped hard in his chest. The woman knew who he was. How? What did she really want?

"My God, Erik, what did she say?" Andrea asked, quickly coming to his side.

Erik shook his head. "Nonsense. She said nothing but nonsense." He took a sip of champagne that had grown warm in his hand from clutching the glass as she spoke her venom. It wasn't often that anything riled the Ghost, or caused him uneasiness. Frankly, this was the first time, and it irritated the hell out of him coming from a damnable woman no less.

"There are always a few lunatics among the sane." He laughed it off. "If you'll excuse me, I'm off to mingle."

He left Andrea's side and kept a wary eye on Sybelle Renard, who spoke with other guests in the crowd. He wished she would leave. Her words burned into his mind and kept repeating like a haunting musical score sung out of tune. Her presence agitated him at a most inopportune time.

After a full hour of revelry, drinking, and dancing, Richard walked to the front of the orchestra, instructed them to stop playing, and turned to greet the guests.

"Ladies and gentleman!" Richard's voice carried loudly through the auditorium aided by the acoustics of the hall. The crowd hushed, and all eyes turned on his tall commanding appearance.

"Welcome to the Royal Opera House of Valletta. It is my pleasure to be the new manager of this fine establishment without a roof." He pointed his hand and head upward, amusing the attendees. "At least we've been graced with a vision of the stars above this evening. However, I come to you with an urgent request." Richard toned his voice appropriately for the event. "It is the desire of the esteemed owner of this superior structure to return splendid divas to the stage and fill this house with musical entertainment that will leave you breathless."

Richard changed the tone to one of jest. "Of course, to do that, we must first empty your pocketbooks and wallets just a wee bit." Richard raised his thumb and index finger together, leaving an inch of space. The crowd laughed.

"I have no qualms, I assure you, in investing my own life savings into this endeavor. Tonight, if you wish to participate as well, I invite you to do so. Help us raise this wonderful structure from ashes to glory. Become a patron of the Royal Opera House reconstruction, by making a generous donation this evening. In your honor, we shall inscribe your names into the stone walls as a tribute to your generosity. Let us rebuild together and bask in the glory that awaits us!"

Erik stood tall, listening to the thunderous clap from the attendees. Richard did well. *Bravo!* The man commanded the audience. He was very pleased with his performance.

"And who is the new owner," a voice surprisingly rang out from the crowd. "Why isn't he here tonight?"

"Yes, who is the owner?" another demanded. The crowd all agreed, shaking their heads. Erik watched the unfolding scene with interest.

"Why, it's a ghost!" Richard replied. "A ghost who prefers to walk among you even now." Heads turned back and forth while people looked at other faces covered with masks. "He's here among the crowd, I assure you. He prefers a relationship of confidentiality with his patrons. I'm here as his voice."

Erik's eyes rested upon Madame Renard, who caught his eyes. She smiled, raised her flute to him, and then took a drink. In her hands at that moment, she had the power to reveal his identity, but she merely stood silent, staring at him with her dark eyes. Erik needed to take command of the situation to his own benefit, and he did so quickly.

"Every opera house needs a ghost!" he yelled over the heads of the crowd. "As long as the man raises Valletta's opera house from the ashes, I say let him hide!"

"I agree," added Sybelle Renard loudly. Erik's heart stopped. "I will be the first to invest as a patron. Who else will join me?" she asked, spurning on the attendees.

Richard pointed toward Darius, who was sitting at a table ready to receive donations with his pen in hand and an open ledger ready.

"Please, continue to enjoy the wonderful evening, ladies and gentlemen. My assistant will be more than happy to take your money and your names."

Erik watched the throng of costumed attendees line up. The confident prediction of Madame Renard proved correct. The night was a complete success and more than enough funds were donated to continue onward and rebuild.

When the last carriage departed, Erik shoved his hand into his pocket and pulled out the woman's card and read the embossed letters. "*Madame Sybelle Renard, Prophetess – Fortunes, Readings, and Séances.*" He flipped the card over and found her handwritten destiny, which caused his heart to skip a beat.

"*And here, Monsieur Dante, is your fate. You wish for beauty and love. Love you will find, but without beauty, and it shall pierce your heart like a dagger. In the end, it will be your undoing and death.*"

Chapter 7

"No, no, no!" Erik cried, exclaiming his displeasure to Richard. "This stonework is shabby! Tell the workers I will not pay them until the job is done correctly."

Richard noted in his small black notebook the next complaint spewing from Erik's lips. The man was impossible to please.

"Nothing will get finished if we keep redoing everything," he responded in exasperation. Richard thought he might as well give his opinion.

Erik answered with a brash reprimand. "Don't try and second guess me, Richard. You may know something about architecture and construction, but nothing compared to what my keen eyes see. I will not have this opera house open to the public unless it meets my standards of perfection."

Erik continued walking down the line of boxes. "Look!" He pointed up above him. "See . . . see there? There's a hairline crack in the stonework. That needs repair; otherwise the entire facade will eventually fracture and fall off."

Richard squinted trying to see where Erik's eagle eyes pointed, but it was useless. He merely noted the inconsistency in his pad to bring it to the attention of the mason.

Each day at the end of the workers' shift, Erik would emerge from his quarters and make his rounds with Richard throughout his domain. Erik had been spending his days with Darius behind the walls working on his secret labyrinth. The work was nearly finished, and Richard wondered about the torture Darius had to endure working alongside his master's ranting and raving for perfection.

Richard, however, was happy that Erik was pleased with his managerial skills. After the masquerade, Erik had given him a sizable bonus for doing such an outstanding job, as he put it, dealing with the public. He was relieved the event was a success and sufficient funds were pledged to start construction.

In all honesty, Richard had to admit that he was enjoying the task of being Erik's front man. Erik possessed the genius to succeed, but Richard possessed the gumption and persona to deal with the public and oversee the workers.

After his initial shock of finally meeting the masked man who had tormented him for years, he had comfortably slipped into a business-like relationship with Erik. In the past, their association was strained and one of total anonymity on Erik's part. Andrea had acted as the intermediary between the two, delivering the Ghost's notes and demands for payment and instructions.

He had often wondered about the man who lived underneath the Garnier that succeeded in placing such dread within his own heart. The dangerous tendencies of the reclusive Ghost had finally played out in the death of one of the workers. It was then Richard reached his wit's end. He blamed Erik for the murder, which in turn produced contention with Andrea, who came to his defense.

Their argument was so great over the matter that Richard decided it was time to leave the wretched haunting and move elsewhere. He had asked Andrea to go with him, but she refused, retaining her loyalty to Erik. It had angered Richard enough to end their relationship. He feigned his departure using retirement as an excuse, taking the position in Italy leaving and them both behind.

When he first received correspondence regarding a head manager position at the Royal Opera House, he was immediately intrigued. Of course, unbeknown to him, Erik was luring him back into his web of control.

It took time to get used to the Ghost he had once thought of as an insane monster. As the weeks passed with constant interaction between the two, he saw the man beneath the mask and recognized Erik's humanity. The Ghost was a human with a past, and much bitterness; some of which for good reason. In Richard's honest assessment, Erik was a product of his deformity, upbringing, and society's cruel response and lack of compassion.

Richard appreciated the fact that Erik was driven to succeed, driven to write music, driven to perfection to compensate for his physical imperfections. When he complained of shabby work, he knew it was because of his insatiable desire to surround himself with beauty.

In addition, he recognized Erik's need for ultimate control. His tools of human manipulation were unlike any other, and Richard often found himself analyzing Erik's every move and mood to anticipate his needs or discover his motives. It was an emotionally draining exercise each day to please the man. How Andrea ever put up with him for so many years was beyond his comprehension.

As they neared the end of their inspection of the reconstruction, Richard turned toward Erik and looked into his frustrated gaze to offer assurance.

"It will be finished." He sighed. "I shall see to these matters immediately. Perhaps within the next month or two we can start planning the grand opening ceremonies."

Erik glanced up above him at the partially reconstructed roof, which was the most daunting project. "I'll be glad when the damn roof is back and reconstruction of the stage and seating areas begin."

Richard saw his gaze fix on the stage area, which spurred a thought. "Do you mind if I ask you a question?"

"You may ask," Erik replied coldly, "but I retain the right not to answer."

Always the same response, he thought. "Do you ever miss Paris and the way it was before?" Erik's eyes grew dark. Richard wondered if he would answer truthfully.

"Some things I miss, yes, but there's no use living in the past when I have a future to build."

Richard easily surmised what Erik truly missed, and it wasn't a building; it was a woman. His obsession continued to haunt him thousands of miles away.

"True, one should look to the future," Richard agreed, not wanting to push the matter further. He closed his black notebook. "Will there be anything else?"

"Not tonight," Erik replied.

Richard noted the moody response. "Well, then until tomorrow. I think I'll visit Andrea, I have some things to discuss with her this evening."

"It's about time," Erik noted, as he wandered away with his hands shoved in his trouser pockets. "I would have thought by now you would have taken care of those matters, Richard."

"Indeed," he admitted somewhat sheepishly. "I should have."

Erik, perceptive as usual, had touched his own sore spot. He had purposely avoided Andrea since his arrival. However, Erik had made sure he placed them in close proximity of one another. When Richard moved into the opera house, he discovered his quarters were next door to hers. Obviously, the setup was a planned ploy by the architect.

Andrea, it appeared, had not totally come to terms with his return either. Their relationship since his arrival was strained and cold. Perhaps it was for the best, he mused, considering the circumstances and voluminous amount of work involved in the restoration process.

Andrea spent her days overseeing the living quarters and hiring the new general staff, such as housekeepers and cooks. Like the Garnier, when the opera house was finished, an entire community of individuals would live underneath its roof like one big family.

Richard said nothing further to Erik, and walked resolutely to Andrea's quarters, determined to make amends. When he reached her door, he stood thoughtfully looking at the handle, wondering if she would give him the time of day. Instead, he braced himself for the worst and a shooing of her hand accompanied by one of her disapproving looks. He wanted to offer her an olive branch of peace, if nothing else. After all, they were now in the uncomfortable position of living next to each other and working side-by-side.

He rapped on the door with his knuckles and waited for what seemed like an eternity. His heart pounded in his chest. A moment later, the door opened and Andrea's face shifted to a sour expression upon seeing him on the other side of her threshold.

"Yes?" she asked, one eyebrow lifted in disdain. "You wish something?"

"What I wish, Andrea, no doubt you'd refuse me," he confessed. "All I want at this time is a civil conversation between old friends."

He watched Andrea pull her mouth to one side, showing her disgruntlement over his unwelcome visit. Her eyes studied him for a few moments, as if she were trying to decide whether she cared to let him in or not. Finally, with a relenting sigh, she bid him entrance.

"You may come in."

Richard quickly stepped inside and closed the door behind him, before she could change her mind. Andrea walked over to her divan and sat down, while Richard glanced about her quarters noting the interior. Her furnishings were modest and drab. Dull lifeless paintings, dim lighting, and dark green upholstery gave the room a dreary atmosphere. The room appeared shrouded in sadness rather than joy, and Richard could not help but wonder if it was an outward reflection of her heavy heart.

She still wore the same dress he had seen for the past three days, and Andrea's dark hair coiled on top of her head in a bun. He remembered how he hated the style before, and he hated it still. He wanted to walk to her side and pull out every hairpin to release it from captivity and let her curly locks fall down her shoulders.

She was an attractive woman, who for some reason insisted on hiding her true beauty. More than one person in the Royal Opera House wore a mask of sorts. Andrea's was invisible to the naked eye, but visible to Richard's heart.

Richard studied her face, trying to ascertain her feelings, but she did well in showing no emotion except indifference. He wanted to see a glimmer of affection. If it was still there, she held it locked away.

He possessed a thousand questions about the time he had been absent in Italy. Much had transpired with the Ghost and her daughter, and Richard was anxious to fill in the gaps.

"You look well, Andrea," he noted affectionately. "Tell me first, how is Meg?"

"She's fine, Richard. Married, with children, and a baroness!"

Richard saw the pride in her eyes. "A baroness you, say? I seem to remember Erik prophesied as such. Did he arrange the marriage?"

"Their meeting," she replied. "But love took its course afterward. He foolishly prides himself as a matchmaker, you know."

Her eyes averted Richard's, and he knew why. Was Erik trying his hand at it once again between the two of them? Erik's actions were indeed a mystery. He had never experienced the love of a woman, but had no qualms in arranging the happiness of others, if it was in his power to do so.

Andrea interrupted his thoughts. "You see, Erik is not the selfish monster you thought him to be."

Richard sighed. They had returned to the point of contention that had driven them apart. He had to admit, though, that his feelings had changed somewhat.

"Perhaps I did think of him that way in the past, but I now see he is more man than monster." He hesitated, wondering if he should spill his entire thoughts, but decided honesty was best if they were to move forward. "I still question his sanity at times, Andrea, and believe if pushed far enough, he still possesses violent tendencies."

Her face turned bitter with disapproval.

"You needn't worry. He hasn't strangled anyone lately, if that's what you're thinking."

Richard quickly changed the subject, wanting to dig further into the reasons behind their relocation.

"What happened in Paris, Andrea? Why did he choose to come to Valletta?"

"Well," she huffed, as if he should know the reason behind it all. "Valletta is not Paris; it's that simple. Things happened after you left, I'm afraid. A sordid state of affairs between Christine and the Vicomte de Chagny unfolded. It was quite ugly. Erik lost his senses, brought down the chandelier, abducted Christine keeping her captive for days in his lair, and nearly killed the Vicomte and the Persian. Sadly, a horrible accident transpired too, and Comte de Chagny died; but Erik swears he was not responsible for the man's demise."

Andrea shook her head, as if she tried to erase the scenes from her memory. "It was quite bad, I will admit. After it ended, Erik disappeared and people assumed him dead. The Vicomte and Christine moved to Sweden and married."

Richard watched Andrea as she appeared to struggle with her next words. Her eyes fell to her lap, and she fiddled with her hands nervously. "If I tell you something, Richard, swear to me that you will not mention it to Erik."

"You have my word, Andrea," he assured her, while leaning forward from his seat in anxious anticipation.

"I have kept in touch with Christine by correspondence, though we only occasionally write to one another. Erik would strangle me, not literally, of course," she quickly clarified. "Though I think he would see it as my own betrayal. Christine is quite happy with Raoul, and she has a beautiful daughter now."

"And does she sing?"

"Occasionally, she pursues her career when she is able, but of course it's more difficult with a child. She sings at the Royal Swedish Opera."

"Well, that is good news," Richard concluded. "I am, however, sad to hear of the Comte's passing."

"I can only say that Erik lost control and slipped into a season of insanity. He couldn't have Christine willingly, so he took her by force. Thank God, he finally came to his senses and freed her, along with the Vicomte and the Persian. Afterward, he moved to the country, and I went with him. We settled in a small village near Rouen where he was born. He sunk into a deep depression for some time, until the news of the Royal Opera House reached his ears. It was the perfect opportunity to leave and start a new life."

"And the authorities, do they still search for him?"

"He believes they do, though we are not aware of any formal charges filed. The strangeness of the Comte's death, I believe, caused much speculation. Hence, his decision to continue to live as a Ghost within these walls, rather than show himself to the public." Andrea hesitated and then added, "You are a godsend to him, Richard."

"Yes, it is a shame," he admitted, "that he cannot live the life of a normal man. I do pity him in that regard." He paused before confessing his conclusions. "I've come to respect his genius, Andrea. He is remarkable in many ways."

"As you can see, he's still the master of manipulation having brought me here." She finally shared a smile in his direction. "He found new purpose and inspiration for his life, so coming to Valletta has been a good thing. I think it has helped him come to terms with life."

"And have you come to terms with your own?" he inquired nervously, opening up what could very well be Pandora's Box.

"I'm happy here if that's what you mean."

Her voice turned terse, and Richard recognized her sensitivity. He moved uncomfortably in his seat, fighting with the next words he wanted to express. Finally, with a slow, heart-felt confession, he spoke his feelings.

"I do hope in time we can perhaps rebuild our relationship, Andrea. I must declare that I have missed you terribly." He raised his eyes in a hopeful gaze, searching out her response. "I shall not pressure you though."

"Please don't," she responded, barely audible.

Richard's countenance fell at her words.

"I will say that I am thankful you are finally seeing the man behind the mask who I served for so many years. You never wished to look behind it before. You were too damn stubborn. Perhaps you will see he was worthy of your respect. Do you finally understand why I chose, and still choose to serve him?"

Not really, he thought to himself. Why did one woman feel obligated to such a man as he? Yes, he deserved compassion for his fate, but still, his sordid past was nothing to admire. Richard wondered, as he pondered, if Erik had her under some type of spell that clouded her wisdom. Her dedication was a mystery, but an integral part of the woman he adored.

"I am trying," he admitted with hesitation. Richard said nothing more. He had built a small bridge between Andrea and himself and was satisfied with their progress. He looked at her admiringly and realized his love remained. She was an exceptional woman, who saw the good in the ugliest the world had to offer—Erik being a perfect example. The years they had fought over her dedication to him now seemed a large waste of time. If only he had been more understanding in the past, they would be married now.

He stood and nodded. "Well, I have my latest orders and must be off."

Reluctance toned his voice, as he headed toward the door. Turning to face Andrea once more, he smiled softly, his mustache curling at its tips.

"I'll be glad when opening night arrives and things finally settle down into a normal routine."

"If it's any consolation, Richard, I will be too. I have my own struggles dealing with a grumpy owner who demands perfection." She flashed a warm smile that he took to heart. "I've been looking for housekeepers and cooks to staff our residences, and he even wishes to be involved in those decisions."

"Well, if anything," he added in jest, "we both suffer the same fate from the Master of the domain."

His hand finally found the ability to turn the doorknob. Richard wanted to raise her hand and press it to his lips. He refrained from following the impulse and swiftly exited, closing the door softly behind him.

A chill ran up his spine when he thought of what lay ahead. Much needed to happen, and he was going to have to endure Erik's ranting and raving. The man was a genius; perhaps that was how Andrea rationalized his behavior. He would try the same tactic and see if it helped any. However, he had his doubts.

Chapter 8

There were days when Erik believed he stood on the brink of insanity. The construction progressed much slower than anticipated, and he was anxious for completion. Every day he would make demands, which he fully expected to be fulfilled quickly. Instead, it would take days of ranting and raving at Richard and the irritating incompetent staff to carry out his will.

It had been two long years since the night of the masquerade. Investors were antsy like Erik to see the Royal Opera House fully restored. If he did not finish soon, he would burn the damn thing down to the ground with him inside it.

The stress and pressure often drove him to his decanter of cognac. He began to reek of alcohol in the presence of Richard and Andrea, who no doubt thought he was turning into a drunk. He did not care and ignored Andrea's frequent judgmental glares when he drank too much.

To calm himself, Erik returned to his private quarters at night and attempted to compose. The act proved futile. Eventually, he would pick up his violin and play haunting dark scores to soothe his pain. He felt empty and void inside. Sleep was difficult to achieve, and when he finally did succumb, the faces of those he had tortured or murdered returned in his dreams with a vengeance.

At the beginning of the third year, the end was finally in sight. A new roof hung over the auditorium. Erik was pleased with the interior stonework carved to perfection. The reformed sculptures added to the artistic elements of the interior. The outrageous Governor's box protruded over the dress circle, as it had before, supported by two massive pillars. The remaining five tiers of patron boxes were ready for occupants, including his own with its secret entry and exit. The red velvet seats for the audience were soon to arrive, and after installation, the final plans for the gala opening night would follow.

The completed hardwood stage stood bare; but in time, it would hold the sets for scheduled opera productions. The riggings, curtains, multiple ropes, pulleys, and catwalks above were all in place, tested, and in good working order. Erik made sure he could prowl around, as he had in the past, whenever he felt so inclined. It was like old times, oddly bringing a devious smile to his gloomy face. He enjoyed traversing the catwalks while gazing at the stage below.

The next order of business was to hire a stage crew and performers. The latter, however, would certainly try Erik's patience. The former stage crew applied for jobs, but Erik was hesitant. He wanted to make sure if any returned, they would not be like the bumbling idiots who were possibly responsible for burning the place down the first time.

After discussions with Richard over his planned performance of Gounod's *Faust* for the opening night, he placed advertisements throughout Europe at various operatic venues searching for talent. In addition, the local news announced auditions scheduled to begin in the weeks ahead. As a result, they were inundated with responses.

Erik studied the interested applicants, his eyes scouring for names that were recognizable, as he hoped beyond hope that he would see a certain soprano's application from Paris or Sweden. He soon threw such fanciful hopes to the side and faced reality that he would never see or hear from her again.

Among the responses, however, he did find an ounce of amusement that caused him to roar with laughter. He had received a letter from Carlotta, written in her usual narcissist form, praising her abilities. After a good husky laugh, Erik wadded up her penned inquiry and tossed it into the trash.

In the end, Erik reviewed his choices with Richard and Andrea, and appointments for auditions were set. They sat in the front row, while Erik sat in Box 5 unseen, listening from the shadows and making his own assessments of the various singers. Afterward, the three gathered and discussed each audition, but Erik gave the final word after considering his friends' opinions.

The most tedious of auditions was finding the right soprano, who sounded half-way decent. Erik knew there wouldn't be an *angel* among the entire lot. How could there be? Instead, he settled for the best he could find, which he felt still needed copious amounts of coaching.

In the end, he chose a young soprano by the name of Maria Lucia Cardona from Italy. She had performed in a variety of productions, but did not appear hardened or spoiled by too many years of success as a celebrated diva. Maria seemed pliable and could be molded to his whim, which he would do by giving instructions through Richard and his new maestro, Paul de Marco, to better her performances.

The chosen tenor for *Faust* was a local man by the name of Renaldo Rossini. Erik highly approved of his ability. Apparently, he had been one of the original performers before the destruction of the opera house. He was a logical choice. The remaining performers who auditioned came from the former production company, while others were from various countries abroad.

When the tedious years of rebuilding and hiring cast and crew finally concluded, the first rehearsal was scheduled. Erik chose a gala opening date of May 25, which was the anniversary of the destruction of the Royal Opera House. It seemed appropriate to revisit that date with its resurrection to glory. To celebrate the victory, he invited Richard, Darius, and Andrea to meet him inside the completed auditorium. He brought champagne and glasses to toast their success.

All three arrived together. Erik watched from on stage as they came down the center aisle. He could see their faces admire the decorated interior of brilliant red velvet cushioned seats and golden boxed alcoves papered in dark red. The completed interior easily accommodated 1,100 patrons, with the ability to hold another 200 standing. A large chandelier hung in the center, similar to the one Erik had brought down in Paris.

He watched his cohorts examine the beauty within and gloated with pride while he stood center stage. Erik waved his hand across the expanse before him and asked for their final opinions.

"Now what do you think of Valletta's Royal Opera House?" A heavy red brocade velvet curtain hung behind him, decorated in an grandiose golden design.

Andrea stood wide-eyed, clearly overwhelmed. "Erik, I have no words to describe what I feel!" His friend freely showed her enthusiasm. "You've done a magnificent job. I never thought . . . "

"Never thought what?" he asked, looking at her with amusement. "That I could rebuild something so beautiful out of ashes?"

Erik took a step forward until he reached the edge of the stage and raised both arms into the air, as if he were embracing his creation. A guttural laugh escaped his throat, echoing throughout the auditorium. He had conquered his demons and proved his enemies wrong. He had risen from the ashes to a new life. The dream of owning and operating an establishment finally arrived. This was *his* opera house.

"No longer am I destined to be at the whim of owners and mangers, eh, Richard?" Erik looked at him, clearly relieved. "At last this is mine! I own every inch! Nothing shall take it from my hand. Nothing!"

Erik's voice rose in challenge to Madame Sybelle's foolish warning over the peeved spirits that lived underneath. "This house shall stand for eternity in witness that Erik Dante, the Phantom of Valletta, reigns!"

He glanced at Richard and Andrea, whose faces looked as if they were watching a lunatic on stage. Perhaps he was, but he knew in his soul he had come to a place of dominion in his life, and it felt damn good. This was his world, his livelihood! He would succeed and continue in its glory until his dying day.

He heard Andrea clear her throat, bringing him back to lucid thoughts. "You've done well, Erik. Very well." She turned to Richard, whose face looked white as a ghost, and Erik snickered.

"You have anything to say, Richard Mercier?" Erik poked at him to get a response. "I promise not to bring the chandelier down upon the audience. Will that help?"

He watched as the man gulped, glanced over at Andrea for a quick assurance, before expressing his thoughts. "Andrea is right," he conceded. "You've done well."

"And Darius, cat got your tongue?" he asked.

"No . . . no Master," he stuttered, clearly flustered. "You have done magnificently."

Erik took in a deep breath and raised his head to the large crystal chandelier. He remembered the moment of his insanity, the screams of the audience, the victims that had been hurt by madness on his part. Silently, he swore he would never destroy what he loved again—not like before.

"A toast then," he announced, as he popped the cork off the champagne bottle and watched it fly across the stage floor. "Come up with me here, and let's hail our accomplishments."

Erik poured the glasses and handed one to each of his friends. His heart raced in his chest, as he expressed his joy and raised his glass.

"To our glorious future and success!" Each glass came together, the crystal ringing in unison.

"To our success," they all repeated. Everyone smiled and took a sip.

❆ ❆ ❆

Finally, opening night arrived. It was a full house of nobility, government officials, high society, and even army and naval officers. The Governor participated in a ribbon cutting ceremony, and by 8:30 p.m., the curtain pulled back and the performance of *Faust* began.

Erik had instructed the maestro, director, cast, and crew to push everyone to their limits until absolute perfection was displayed on stage. It paid off. When the final curtain fell, the patrons jumped to their feet in thunderous applause, while shouting accolades of, "*Bravo.*"

Erik watched from Box 5 with great pride. All the sweat, money, and time had paid off. Life had reached a point of personal perfection, and for the first time in his life, he sensed an ounce of true joy. It was surreal to experience such genuine happiness. It touched him to the core, and uncharacteristic tears welled in his eyes when he watched the cast give multiple curtain calls. After the last of the attendees left, Andrea, Richard, and Darius shared his enthusiasm.

"Wonderful, Erik!" Richard exclaimed. "It came off quite well, and already sales for future performances are booked solid. You have a hit, my friend!" He grabbed Erik's hand and gave it a hearty shake with a pat on his shoulder.

Andrea stood and cried like a baby. "Well, I can see you are, pleased. Happy you came now?"

"Oh, Erik, I'm so proud of you. Would you mind terribly if I gave you a hug?"

Erik cringed at her request, since it wasn't his favorite bodily expression. However, he couldn't deny his old friend after she had risked her life to follow him on yet another adventure.

"Of course." Erik opened his rigid arms. Andrea quickly gave him a squeeze and released him, no doubt aware of how uncomfortable he felt over the act. Nevertheless, she shared his joy.

When morning came after a sleepless night, Erik was quick to arrive for breakfast grabbing the morning newspaper before anyone else had the opportunity to read the reviews. In no time, he had turned the pages until he reached the arts section, his eyes quickly grabbing the words off the page.

"Brilliant, excellent, bravo!"

A genuine smile of relief spread across Erik's face. "Listen to this, Andrea and Richard." He read the article aloud.

Last night's gala reopening of the Royal Opera House of Valletta proved to be the highlight of the year. Restored to even more beauty and glory than the original design, the audience was enthralled over the excellent performance of Faust that resulted in multiple curtain calls. Though the current owner continues to remain shrouded in mystery, one must give the man credit for the superb job in restoring the arts in all their glory to the residents of this historic city. Whoever you are, we salute you!

"I told you!" he exclaimed, putting the paper down in his lap. "We're the talk of the island and soon to be the talk of southern Europe. Mark my words!"

"It's so exciting," squealed Andrea. "Don't you think, Richard?"

"Yes, indeed. We will soon be the talk of all of Europe."

Erik was excited, however, being the talk of all of Europe could bring attention. He wondered if Christine would hear, or if the authorities would find him. He did not know. For now, he would glory in his success and push his anxious thoughts aside. It was time to enjoy life.

Chapter 9

Erik entered the auditorium and strode down the center aisle. Things were going extremely well. The weeks passed with overwhelming success and sold-out performances.

Each night after the show, Erik celebrated his achievement by walking through the auditorium to make his private inspections and reflect on the performance. The housekeeping staff had already cleaned the floors, picked up the debris, and returned everything to pristine order both on and off stage. If Erik discovered one discarded program during his rounds, he would make sure the crew heard about it the next morning.

Everything appeared to be tidy and in its place, as he surveyed the seats and boxes. The chandelier hung dark, but a few gaslights near the stage burned, adding enough illumination in the theatre. As he strolled toward the front, he spotted a lingering light in the orchestra pit that caught his attention. Erik heard shuffling noises and movement and quickly halted his step. He listened intently, trying to ascertain if one of the musicians had perhaps lingered behind for some odd reason. Cautious and not wishing discovery, he stood motionless, waiting to hear further sounds before proceeding closer.

Suddenly, a recognizable pluck of a violin string met his ear, randomly flicked by a human's finger. The plucks continued, with no semblance of tune, accompanied by the soft giggle of a female voice.

Irate that someone was daring to toy with an instrument meant for sounds of perfection, he strode angrily forward until he peered over the edge of the pit. There before him, with her back to his burning gaze, stood a petite golden-haired young woman fingering the instrument as if it were a mere plaything.

Twang, twang. The sounds reverberated again and another giggle ensued. His unbridled displeasure over her actions caused him to fling his words at her without a second thought.

"What in the hell do you think you're doing?" he snarled, sounding like an angry bear about to claw its victim. He boldly stepped into full view, daring to show his masked face to the intruder to make a point. "The violin is not yours, Mademoiselle, and I insist you cease from handling the instrument with such disrespect this instant!"

A startled gasp escaped the woman's lips, and she quickly turned around to face her accuser. Instantly, her hand came to her mouth to hold back a scream of fear, which managed to escape her lips anyway. Her wide-eyed expression met his, and Erik's dark eyes glared in return.

Ignoring the steps down to the orchestra pit, Erik walked to the rim and jumped in front of her, landing with a loud *thud,* as his booted soles hit the floor. He straightened his back and looked down upon the young woman with disdain. She was like a quivering child about to be scolded. In reaction to his hasty arrival, she stepped backward into a stand, knocking it to the floor. Sheet music spewed about landing at Erik's feet, which pushed his irritation level to new heights.

"Have you nothing to say for yourself?" he demanded. The woman looked petrified. Her complexion paled to a white porcelain hue.

"I'm . . . I'm sorry," she stuttered, her voice trembling. "I . . . I was just looking at the violin."

"Who are you?" Erik snarled.

The woman lowered her gaze from his piercing eyes and stared at the floor as she responded. "Désirée Martin," she answered, her French accent giving away her origin. "I'm a housekeeper here, Monsieur."

Erik narrowed his dark eyes pondering her answer. He found a strange familiarity to her countenance and quickly noted her youthful beauty. "I've seen you before, have I not?" he asked, stepping a foot closer to examine her face.

"I don't know, Monsieur. I have worked here for a few months now. Perhaps you have seen me around and about doing my duties."

"Do you know who I am?" Erik towered above her tiny frame in a show of superiority.

"Oui, Monsieur, you are . . . you must be the mysterious owner everyone talks about." She hesitated and swallowed hard before asking. "Are you?"

He stood eyeing the golden-haired woman from the top of her head to the hem of her garment. *A brilliant deduction on her part*, he thought, perhaps his masked appearance led her to that conclusion. He was unsure whether he wished to confirm her suspicions or not.

She looked curiously at his face, which bothered the hell out of him. "If you wish to know what's underneath, I can only say it's nothing a lady should see, so stop staring at it."

Désirée pulled her eyes away and glanced at the violin.

"Why are you here fiddling with the instruments? If you wish to keep your job, I suggest you do not handle things you know nothing about."

He walked over behind her and bent down, lifting the fallen music stand and returning it to its rightful place. Afterward, he gathered the sheet music from the floor and reverently put each one in its proper order for the score.

"I'm curious." Her slight boldness piqued Erik's interest. "I've always wished I could learn to play the violin. That's why I was plucking the strings."

"Play?" Erik picked up the violin she had handled and brushed the wooden surface beneath the palm of his hand, as if to remove her finger stains. He caressed it like a lover underneath his square chin. "You mean like this?" he offered, as he picked up the bow and began to slide it across the strings in one melodious tune.

As he always did, he closed his eyes to commune with the violin. He caressed it as if it were a delicate woman, showing his obsessive passion as he played. His fingers pressed the strings, picking notes and making music that filled the empty auditorium with glorious sounds of rapture. For minutes, Erik lost himself in the music, oblivious to the audience that stood dumbfounded before him. Finally, he stopped and glanced at Désirée, surprised to her eyes filled with tears. Her reaction stunned him.

"It was beautiful, Monsieur." She wiped the moisture with the palm of her hands. "I only wish . . . "

"Wish what?"

"That I could learn to play."

Erik chuckled under his breath at the absurdity of her wish. *A woman play,* he thought to himself. She must have sensed his thoughts for she quickly spat her defense.

"What? Do you think a woman could have no talent?" she demanded, pressing herself a step closer.

"If you know so much, name me one famous female violinist," he challenged her in return. Erik watched as the insolent young woman assertively responded with a name.

"Regina Strinassachi, for one!"

"Huh!" He shook his head in disgust. "An anomaly, I assure you, in the world of proficient musicians." Surprised she could even name one, he turned away, frustrated over his inability to dissuade her wish.

"If one has the desire," she added, "one should at least be given the opportunity to find out if talent lies within. Would you deny every woman that quest?"

Erik turned around and latched onto her bold eyes. As he stood before her, the flash of memories regarding his former days of tutoring, and the satisfaction of sharing his knowledge of music to another human tugged at his hardened core. With the restoration finally complete and the opera house restored, he knew he would need something beyond everyday management to carry his interest between productions. Perhaps this was it—an insolent woman, who possessed the audacity to think she could learn to play a violin.

Carefully, he laid the violin down on the musician's chair, making a mental note to reprimand the man for leaving his instrument out of its case when not in use. His eyes lifted to Désirée, who remained defiant before him.

"Very well," he relented. "I need some amusement in my life. I will teach you." His lip curled at the slyness of his offer.

"Amusement? You think it will be amusing, do you?" She swung away from him with an attitude and headed toward the stairs that led directly out of the pit.

"Well," he responded, clearly irritated by her feisty behavior. "Do you wish to learn or not?"

She stopped abruptly before turning around and looking at him. She stood firm and spirited in her response. "Yes."

The word was enough to carry Erik's feet toward her body. He peered down into her eyes, which he noticed were the color of a deep blue ocean. They were oddly attractive and mesmerizing.

"I will teach you, Mademoiselle, but you will say nothing about our meeting. The majority of the staff here knows nothing about Monsieur Dante, the owner, nor have they seen me. I prefer to keep it that way." A brush against her body, a darker gaze to make a point, and Erik continued. "Do we understand each other?"

She nodded in return, her face ashen from his close proximity. "We can begin tomorrow evening after the show. Report to Monsieur Mercier's office at 10 p.m., and he will escort you to me."

Erik motioned to Désirée with his outstretched hand to climb the stairs before her, and she quickly obeyed. "I suggest you now leave these instruments alone and return to your quarters. It's late."

Her feet scurried down the aisle and out the door with nothing further being said. He wondered where she was from, surprised at meeting another French woman in Malta. In any event, he already felt amused with his newfound hobby.

❊ ❊ ❊

"Désirée Martin," Erik announced, throwing his newspaper down on the morning table and walking up behind Andrea before sitting down. "What do you know about her?"

His actions startled Andrea, and she dropped her fork on her plate with a *clang*. "Would you stop sneaking up on me like that!" she barked. "Damn it, Erik, you startled me."

Without a word, he sat down, poured himself a cup of black coffee from the carafe, and insisted on a response. "Who is she?"

Andrea grabbed hold of her napkin, dabbed her lips, and took her time answering his question, just for the sheer pleasure of making him wait. When she was ready, she laid down the napkin alongside her plate, and her eyes finally rose to meet his impatient gaze. She chuckled under her breath when she realized he was irritated to no end. It felt odd to experience a sense of control in Erik's presence.

"She's from Paris and used to work here at the Royal Opera House before it went up in flames."

"But she's French," he noted, pointing out the disparity.

"Yes, her family is French. They came here to Malta during Napoleon's occupation. From what I understand, however, they are all dead now. She came begging for work and a place to live, so I felt pity on the poor girl and gave her a job." Andrea wondered about the inquiry, after watching Erik's reaction to the information. "Why . . . why do you ask?"

"I found her last evening after the performance in the orchestra pit fiddling with one of the violins, which I found most irritating. I spoke of my displeasure and warned her to stop toying with the instruments."

"You warned her? You mean you revealed who you were?" Andrea was dumbfounded that Erik had crossed that line with anyone on the staff.

"Yes." He sighed over his rash actions. "I'm afraid my anger got the best of me, and I jumped in front of her, telling her to put the damn thing down. Before I knew it, she asked if I was the owner. I neither confirmed nor denied it at first. I swore her to secrecy if she wished to get what she wanted."

"Wanted?" Andrea was definitely interested in what she could possibly want from Erik.

"Lessons," he replied, rather indifferently. "Violin lessons."

Andrea laughed.

"And what's so damn funny?" he barked, annoyed at her response.

"You've found a new student it appears."

"She'll amuse me," he replied dryly. "You know how quickly I get bored when I have nothing to challenge me. This will no doubt be a challenge indeed."

"Yes, indeed," she replied with delight.

"Do you know anything else about her?" Erik wondered what else he could find out about his new pupil.

"I'm afraid I don't. I do find one thing a bit odd about her, but I can't quite put it into words."

"What do you mean odd?" He leaned forward, showing his curiosity.

"She works well. I have no complaint whatsoever regarding her housekeeping skills, but I always get a slight feeling from her that she's hiding something. I just cannot put my finger on it."

"Hiding what?"

"I don't know, Erik. It's just a feeling. You're the great judge of character between the two of us. Perhaps you'll discover it yourself as the lessons progress."

"Progress?" He questioned his newest endeavor soulfully as he stood to his feet. "I must be mad thinking I can teach a housekeeper how to play the violin with any proficiency. I would much rather be tutoring . . . " His voice trailed off as he stopped the thought abruptly.

"A soprano?"

Andrea's comment was barely audible, but Erik's keen ears heard the words. It was enough to raise the hair on the back of his neck and turn his relaxed countenance into an angry scowl. He roughly pushed the chair back, rose to his feet, and stomped to the door.

He said nothing, and Andrea knew that she had hit the nerve she often wished she could leave untouched. However, when she tested its sensitivity, it only proved to her that Erik was still raw and vulnerable. It made her wonder where it would lead him with his newest student. She was no fool. The golden-haired girl was fair, blue-eyed, and petite-framed, reminiscent of the Scandinavian beauty Erik had once loved. It gave her cause for concern.

"Did she inquire why you wear a mask?" she called out as he reached the door.

"She stared at it, and I promptly told her she should never wish to see what lay beneath. That should be the end of her curiosity."

Erik left the room, and Andrea picked up her dropped fork. *Oh, dear God, please. Let this not be another one,* she pleaded to heaven.

Chapter 10

Erik paced the orchestra pit like a caged animal, as he struggled with a mixture of emotions. He was angry for revealing his identity to some unknown housekeeper, but oddly excited at the prospects of teaching again.

There was no doubt in his mind the woman would be dreadful, so he braced himself for the inevitable. He planned to stuff cotton in his ears to endure the screeching sounds she would elicit from the strings. Whether he could hold his temper would certainly be a test of endurance.

He spoke privately to Richard about his new undertaking, who made no comment one way or the other. Erik was thankful he kept his opinions to himself, though he wondered if he would do so in Andrea's presence.

He had arranged for his new pupil to report to Richard's office after the performance at 10 p.m. Erik would wait in the pit for their arrival. He thought it only proper during their first lesson that she be escorted. Afterward, Richard would retreat and lock the doors. No one would see or hear the two of them. Erik held no ulterior motives and thought nothing of the arrangement being improper.

At Erik's request, Richard chastised the musician who dared to leave his violin unattended. Erik did not know whether to thank or curse him for having caused this new state of affairs through his careless act. In any case, the circumstances had produced entertainment for Erik, and he was going to take full advantage of the situation.

While waiting for their arrival, his fingers traced along the stands. His musical mind thought of each instrument, ranking them in order of perfection and personal preference in sound. He was not always pleased with the performances of the musicians, and he had recently been pressuring the maestro, Paul De Marco, to add additional rehearsals. Richard conveyed his displeasure on his behalf. Erik did not care if their fingers were raw from strings or their lips swollen from blowing horns. Performances were to be flawless.

The door opened interrupting his thoughts, and Erik stood rigid.

"Mademoiselle Martin, as requested, sir." Richard assisted her down the stairs into Erik's presence. "I'll lock up, as instructed," he added.

"Fine, return in a half hour, Richard, to retrieve the Mademoiselle. Our first lesson shall be quite short and basic."

Richard retreated and Erik looked at his pupil, whose eyes widened when Richard mentioned locking the doors.

"I won't hurt you," he assured her, glancing away and feeling like an ass for having to make her feel safe. "I just prefer privacy and do not wish others to know of my existence. Do you understand?" His eyes spoke of his insistence of anonymity.

"Of course," she replied apprehensively.

Erik examined her closely, since he was too irritated during their first encounter to notice her finer points. He allowed his gaze into her blue eyes to linger, finding them mesmerizing and calming. Her deep blue irises stunned his senses, her lashes fluttered dark and full, and her eyebrows arched to perfection.

Her face, flawless and pure, sat framed by her golden hair that flowed with long curls. They draped across her shoulders and down the front of her breasts. Erik wondered if her hair glistened in the noonday sun. It looked soft to the touch, and he quickly restrained an urge to lift his hand and feel the silk strands between his fingertips.

Erik cleared his throat in uneasiness, bringing his faculties back in line. He appreciated her beauty, but felt the familiar tinge of jealousy. She was one of the lucky humans gifted at birth with perfection. While he, on the other hand, felt cursed by God.

Désirée wore a modest dress with a high neck and long sleeves, but appeared clean and neat. An odd sense of regret that she lacked a more glamorous gown stabbed his heart, while he wondered why she wasted her beauty working as a housekeeper. Not particularly caring to pry further, he turned his focus to the lessons.

"How much do you know of a violin?" he asked, picking up the one he had brought with him. He asked Richard to purchase a violin for the occasion; he had already decided that if she excelled, he would give it to her as a gift.

"Very little, I'm afraid."

At least she's honest, he thought to himself, as he held the instrument. "Then I shall explain the various parts of the violin first." As he started to form in his mind where to start, the thought struck him cold.

"And do you know how to read music, might I ask?"

Her eyes averted his gaze, and rested upon the sheet music laying on a nearby stand. "I'm sorry, but I don't." She acted ashamed and shook her head.

"Oh, hell," Erik cursed aloud. "This is going to take longer than I thought." His fingers fiddled with the strings. "Well, we'll just have to remedy that as well. You must be able to read music before I can teach you to play anything."

"You don't mind, do you? I'm a fast learner. I've always wanted to learn," she assured him.

Her voice sounded desperate, but Erik couldn't determine if it was due to eagerness or an attempt to convince him otherwise.

"We'll see how fast a learner you are." A sly devious twinkle shined in his eyes, thinking he would break her spirit quickly. "As I said, we'll start with the basics of the violin itself."

Erik's heart rate increased, as his long fingers held the instrument before his pupil. His gaze shifted from one beauty to another like an obsessive lover. The tone of his voice became smooth and melodic, while pointing to each piece of the violin with reverence.

"Watch my fingers," he instructed, as he moved across the instrument, indicating the various parts starting from the top scroll and ending at the chin rest. After his explanation of each part, he stopped and glanced up to see if she was paying attention.

When he was through, he handed the instrument to her warily. "Now, it's your turn. Point and name to me what I have just recited."

Carefully, she reached out with her delicate small fingers to touch the instrument for the first time. Her hands shook. A pang of remorse stabbed his heart thinking she feared him. Erik softened the tone of his voice.

"Go ahead," he urged. "Don't be afraid."

Finally, in silence, she reached for the violin, stared at it for a moment, and then with a deep breath, she repeated her first lesson.

"The scroll, the tuning pegs, the neck, the fingerboard, the upper bout . . . " Her voice hesitated, and

Erik saw her swallow before continuing. "The bridge, the lower bout, the tail piece, the chin rest." She stopped and her eyes looked into his, begging for approval.

"You've forgotten one very important part," he reminded her softly, trying not to show his disappointment in her error. He reached out and pointed to the F holes.

"The F holes!" she blurted out. A slight rosy blush ran up her neck.

"Correct, Mademoiselle, the most important part where the melodious sound escapes to touch the soul of its listeners." Erik smiled at his profound, but truthful statement, that music possessed power.

"Désirée," her voice whispered, interrupting his thoughts.

"I beg your pardon?" His eyes widened in shock.

"Désirée, Monsieur. Please call me by my first name."

Erik shifted in his stance, uneasy over the familiarity she requested. He wanted to keep their teaching sessions strictly professional, and calling her Mademoiselle gave him the power to do so. Her given name spoken from his lips felt terribly uncomfortable.

"I cannot do that, I'm afraid," he spoke bluntly. "We must keep such interactions between us formal. To you, I am Monsieur Dante, and you are to me Mademoiselle Martin." His spine straightened from its lax position until he towered above her, asserting his dominance.

"As you wish," she relented, fumbling with the violin in her hand.

"Give me the instrument," he demanded, slightly aggravated. Erik positioned the violin under his chin. The bow rested on the strings, until his arm began to move it back and forth, playing a few swelling measures.

"Do you see the position of the violin underneath my chin and how my hand is positioned upon the stem?" He withdrew it from its resting place and handed the instrument back to Désirée. "Now show me how you would hold the instrument." He watched with impatience when she fiddled with the violin like a child unable to grasp a ball.

"No, no, like this," he commanded, stepping closer to her. With both hands, he positioned the violin, lowered her chin until it touched the rest, and then proceeded to reach out and adjust her hand around the stem. Her flesh felt warm to his touch. His lack of hesitancy to handle her surprised him.

"One must learn to caress the violin as if it is your lover," he instructed seriously. "You need to embrace it firmly but gently, until you become one with the instrument. Inspiration will flow from your soul, through your arm and into your hand, causing you to skillfully stroke the strings, like lovers stroke each another until ecstasy is released."

He ground his teeth over the absurdity of his statement, inwardly cursing himself. How could he teach someone to stroke a lover when he had never experienced such pleasure? Nevertheless, in his own mind, his violin embodied the perfect example of how it would feel to make love. His bow would glide over the strings of a woman's body, and touch the right notes to elicit the precise melody of bliss. The result would be perfect harmony, as flesh upon flesh produced an aria of satisfaction. They would ultimately be one with the music, their souls united in rapture.

The thought so troubled him that he stepped back and wiped his brow as it beaded with sweat. It was at that instant he realized his weakness. He returned his gaze to Désirée, who stood quietly with flushed cheeks, no doubt aghast over his gross analogy.

"I will need to purchase music books for you to learn how to read notes." He changed the tone of his voice and facial expression to emphasize the seriousness of the situation. "You have much to learn, Mademoiselle, and it will take time. Richard will deliver your study materials to you, and when we meet again, we shall go over the basics of reading music."

"Whatever you wish," she replied, lowering the violin.

Her arms held out the instrument toward Erik, and he noted her hands still shook. In haste he took it. The half-hour had flown by quickly. Erik heard the door open and saw Richard walking down the aisle. He heaved a sigh of relief.

"That's all for this evening, I'm afraid. Meet me here in two days time and we'll continue." He lowered his attention to the music stands to avert her eyes. "I have other things I must attend to tomorrow evening before we resume our lessons."

Erik lifted his gaze with a cold aloofness to make sure she understood their relationship.

"Thank you for teaching me," she responded. "I know you must think this could be a waste of time, but I am truly devoted to learning."

Erik had nothing more to say. Her assurances were dull, and he felt stifled in the close proximity of the orchestra pit.

"Until next time." He turned to leave and stopped Richard on the way up the stairs to whisper in his ear. "Make sure you escort her back to her quarters."

Erik disappeared and returned to his own private room, closing the panel securely shut. He felt irritated and ill at ease and headed straight for his side table to pour himself a hefty drink of cognac to settle his nerves. He thought he had possessed control of his male urges and desires since Christine departed. It was obvious he had not, even though he swore never to entertain such thoughts again. Rejection had torn his soul apart once, and he wished for no repeat performance.

However, as he gulped his drink, his body confirmed that he had not obliterated his thirst for love and beauty. He lowered the glass and closed his eyes. Désirée's deep blue irises flashed before him in a vision of loveliness, which he found both troubling and enticing. He heaved a sigh, feeling anxious to be in her presence once more, and wondered what it would be like to kiss another woman's lips.

Chapter 11

Richard knocked on Andrea's door, and as she opened it, a surprised look crossed her face.

"Mind if I come in?" he nervously asked.

He hoped she wouldn't say no. They were beginning to mend their strained relationship. It had taken months of working side-by-side doing Erik's bidding, but it had driven them together whether they wanted it or not. One thing they had in common was Erik's overwhelming demands for perfection, which they seemed to enjoy complaining about to one another when the master of the opera house wasn't around.

"No, of course, not. Please, come in." Andrea closed the door, and Richard walked to the divan and sat down.

"What is it, Richard? You look disturbed."

"Has he told you about his latest endeavor?"

"You mean the girl?" Andrea sighed, walked over, and sat next to him. "Yes, I know."

"Well, I don't know about you," he began, shaking his head back and forth, "but for some reason it bothers the hell out of me." He wasn't sure if Andrea understood why. However, it was obvious that Erik had a tendency to obsess over women.

"I wouldn't worry too much," she reassured him, reaching over and patting his hand. "I think this is much different. The two of us know this isn't his obsession with Christine Daaé. It's just something to keep him occupied. You know how he loves to tutor."

Richard shifted uncomfortably in the seat and sighed. "I don't know. Something doesn't sit right with me. Why would he bother trying to teach some woman how to play the violin? It's undoubtedly the most difficult instrument to learn, and you and I both know he's not about to give her a job in the orchestra when he's done with this endeavor."

"Well," Andrea answered with a huff in defense of her sex, "I think it's rather nice he is at least giving the girl an idea of what it's like. I mean, Richard, just because she's a woman doesn't mean she doesn't have any talent."

"Perhaps, but I have my concerns."

"Are you thinking about his moment of madness when . . ."

She stopped her thoughts abruptly, and he was surprised that Andrea did not have the strength to speak of the incident.

"After he brought down the chandelier in a fit of insanity and dragged Christine against her will to his lair?" Richard was more than willing to say the words that Andrea could not, to remind her of his capabilities.

"You only heard about it, Richard, so don't go judging him. It was a difficult time, but it's over now. Christine Daaé is married to the Vicomte de Chagny. The obsession is done and over. I don't believe this new interest will turn into another one or even a romantic interest, if that's what you're so worried about."

Richard mulled over his own worries regarding Erik. Andrea knew him better than any other person and tended to focus only on the positive qualities. However, Richard could not shake the fear that Erik held some mental instability deep within his psyche, waiting to be unleashed. He was convinced the man had murdered before, though Andrea would never admit to such monstrosities. When one of his crew died, he had blamed the Ghost, though he had no proof of his involvement. And what about Comte de Chagny's demise? Did Erik have any involvement in that unfortunate affair? Richard could not believe the Opera Ghost was suddenly a reformed man and free from his dark tendencies. Far from it.

There was no use arguing with Andrea, however. If he wished to keep the peace between them, he needed to keep his mouth shut. They would rehash the same argument that had broken the two of them apart years before. Richard did not wish to lose what ground he had gained in healing their relationship. In an effort to show otherwise, he grasped Andrea's hand.

"Well, I hope you are right, my dear. I won't worry," he lied.

Andrea smiled but it quickly faded. "When I look at him, Richard, I still wish he'd find happiness. The man has suffered so much in his life. He's despised his existence since the day of his birth, hid his face in shame, and only yearns for love. I believe he has the capacity to love if given the chance, but with whom? Who would love a monster?"

"Yes, who would love a man who looks like a monster," he agreed, separating the two. "Though I've never seen his true face, I can only imagine." Richard let go of Andrea's hand and stood to his feet. "I will admit the man is a genius. I'll give him that much credit. I've never met anyone so musically brilliant and skilled. If there is a God, he's given the Ghost the gift of intellect to make up for giving him half a face."

Andrea stood to her feet and walked Richard to the door. "Yes, gifted indeed, but he lacks the greatest gift of all—to love and be loved."

Richard saw a glimpse of tenderness from Andrea that touched his heart. Dare he? He dared, and bent down to kiss her on the cheek. He stood tall and looked into Andrea's eyes. "I must be off. The Master calls." He opened the door and left her alone, sulking over his own unrequited love.

❄ ❄ ❄

Désirée nervously arrived at the manager's office as instructed at 10 p.m., filled with anticipation over her next lesson. The staff had retreated to their quarters for the evening, and the opera house remained quiet.

Monsieur Mercier answered the door and invited her into his office. "Good evening." He showed her to a chair in front of his desk. "Your teacher will be meeting you here in the next few minutes. They'll be no lessons in the orchestra pit this evening. I believe he has other plans."

"Oh," she replied, swallowing hard when she watched him leave. He merely nodded his head goodbye, and she noted his furrowed brow that spoke of his displeasure. The arrangements were all quite strange, she had to admit. Perhaps he wondered what they did together.

The door closed, and she sat apprehensively thinking about being alone with her teacher again. Désirée nervously glanced around her surroundings and restlessly rearranged her skirt until she heard the doorknob turn. A thousand prickly needles ran up her spine, and she sat up straight in her chair sensing his presence enter the room. It was uncanny how she knew, just by the movement of his body, and the sound of his breathing.

"Mademoiselle." His soft deep voice gave her a chill. She glanced over her shoulder, watched him lock the door, and walk toward the desk. In his hands were books and musical sheets. She realized this would be a night of study and no passionate caressing of a violin.

He sat down at the desk and carefully laid the papers upright with his long fascinating fingers. His eyes bore into hers, and she lifted her lashes to look at him in the face; the face of flesh on one side and a mysterious mask on the other.

"I trust you are well and ready to begin your studies. We really must teach you to read music before I teach you the joys of bringing the bow across the strings to make music."

"Yes, of course." Her voice quivered in his presence. Just the nearness of his body put her nerves on edge. She studied him more closely this time. His eyes were dark and intense. The flesh side of his face was clean-shaven, smooth, and his jaw strong and square. His hair was black as midnight and coarse. She wondered if it was a wig, but couldn't tell from where she sat. Every strand was in perfect order. She felt no desire to explore what lay underneath the mask or the wig.

"Bring your chair closer," he instructed her, as he lay out a blank piece of paper with lines. "You must be able to see what I am about to show you if you are to understand."

She obeyed and scooted her chair closer to the edge of the desk. After she did so, her nose picked up the scent of his cologne. It surprised her. For some reason, she thought it an odd thing for a man like him to wear.

Her eyes scanned over his fine clothing, from the perfectly stitched black velvet jacket to the white linen ruffled shirt and ascot around his neck. He always dressed neat, each button firmly closed, everything tucked where it should be, no creases in his coat, trousers, or shirt; impeccable in his style.

Désirée looked at his dark eyes and discovered he had been watching her during her observation. She wondered if he was pleased or disturbed, but could not tell. Immediately, her eyes darted back to the paper on the desk, and she looked at his hands holding it between his fingers.

Erik returned to the lessons, and Désirée tried her very best to follow his explanations.

"You will notice here five lines and four spaces; this is the staff. In each space and on a line, notes are placed. In addition, there are indications for timing, a clef sign, key signature, and other various marking that set the overall tone of the musical score."

Désirée was confused already by the strange marks. Erik continued his monologue over clefs, trebles, notes, and her eyes glazed over.

"You're going too fast," she exclaimed. He was spouting everything as if it were second nature to him. To her, it was a blur of lines and definitions she couldn't understand. "I know I can learn," she added, "but I just need you to slow down and realize that I don't know what you're talking about!" She raised her voice, letting her frustration spill out.

Erik pulled up one corner of his mouth and raised a brow, as if he were annoyed. She heard him sigh and knew he was already frustrated with her inability to comprehend.

"What is it that you don't understand?" he asked, clearly perturbed. He glanced down at the musical language, which Désirée clearly saw he understood to perfection.

"Just start once again, only slower this time. Don't go so fast. I need time to comprehend."

Erik started from the top, taking her cue, obviously straining with every word to find patience. "All right," he began, pointing his fingers at the five lines. "These five lines are called a staff. The notes either sit on the line itself or in between the blank spaces."

Finally, she thought, he was explaining it in a more rudimentary way, but it was helpful. By the end of his long detailed account of clefs and trebles, the light finally dawned in Désirée's mind. As a result, she couldn't contain her excitement. She reached out and grabbed his hand. "I understand it now!"

As soon as she touched him, she quickly retreated. He mentioned nothing about her movement and just lifted his eyes.

"Forgive me, Monsieur Dante," she whispered. "I didn't mean to—"

"No, no," Erik interrupted her apology. "That's quite all right. I would much rather see your enthusiasm over learning than watch you yawn, because I'm putting you to sleep."

Désirée saw a pleasurable twinkle in his eyes, but no smile curled his lips. The remaining hour they spent together poring over the basic education of reading music. When they were through, Erik gathered up the papers and books and gave them to his student.

"Take these and study when you have time on your own," he instructed her. "When we meet again, we'll go over it one more time. I will bring one of my scores, a simple portion," he clarified. "And you can tell me the notes as you read the music. Does that sound reasonable?"

"Yes, very," she agreed, withholding a yawn from the late hour.

He stood to his feet. "Come with me, and I'll escort you back to your quarters. No young lady should have to make her way down a dark corridor alone."

Désirée saw his hand outstretched, and she took it as he lifted her from her seat. He let go, and then opened the door, escorting her down the hallway untouched without a word. As they arrived at the dormitory door, he merely looked at her with an expressionless face, and said his goodbye.

"Good evening, Mademoiselle."

"Thank you," she replied. She entered her room and closed the door behind her, sighing in relief.

Chapter 12

Erik retreated to his quarters heading again for the decanter of cognac, ready and waiting on his side table. This time, he poured four fingers rather than two, walked over to a chair, and flopped down.

His free hand grabbed the ascot wrapped around his neck, which he tried to loosen without success. He let out a string of curses, fumbling at the knot that was refusing to untie. After finally pulling it off, he let out a chuckle at his inability to stand his neck coiled by anything that resembled a noose. His thought triggered memories, and the ghosts of those he had executed arrived to taunt him once more. To push away the tormented faces, he drank his cognac and thought about Désirée instead.

A feeling of irritation and intrigue returned, while he pondered her interesting personality. She was eager to learn, slightly short-tempered but determined. He liked that. It was obvious by her trembling hands that her nerves were still edgy when in his presence. He felt bad that she exhibited fear when near him. There was no telling what stories she had conjured in her mind about why he was so secretive about his existence. The fact that he was tall and overbearing with a half-masked face might also have something to do with it, he mused.

Erik stifled urges of familiarity, even though he demanded their relationship be professional. He wanted to speak of personal things and inquire about her past, her likes and dislikes, but he was not quite sure why he should bother. Erik glanced down at his hand where she had touched him earlier in the night, remembering the warmth on his usually cold flesh. It was only a quick glance of her fingers, but the lingering graze had been enough to trigger a rush of desire in his body.

He brought the glass to his lips, sipped, and his eyes narrowed as they stared blankly ahead, observing nothing in particular. Erik lost himself in thought, letting his mind wander to her gold tresses, her fair complexion, her gorgeous blue eyes. She dressed plainly with a high collar and long sleeves when they were together, too modest perhaps. Nevertheless, he could see enough of her beauty to wonder what it would be like to rest his lips upon hers, feel the warmth of her kiss, and peek at her bosom in a low-cut gown. He wondered how soft her breasts would feel in the palm of his hands.

Erik closed his eyes and felt his body respond to the forbidden, as he thought of what it would be like to fondle the beautiful naked body of a woman. In anger, he stood to his feet, threw his glass against the wall, and watched it shatter and fall to the fall. He clenched his teeth over the human needs his body demanded but fate refused. Angry and needing a breath of fresh air, he grabbed his hooded cloak and headed out the side door.

As soon as he walked out onto Strada Vittoria, the cool night air met his face. He flipped the hood over his head and lowered his gaze to the ground, his footsteps pounding down the shadowed streets. It was an overcast night, and a misty wind swept in off the harbor.

After a few months living on the isle, Erik had started exploring the city late at night when sleep failed to give him rest. He discovered Valletta to be a fascinating capital steeped in history and filled with lavish architecture, which he found intriguing. Many of the streets were narrow pathways of stairs, which gave understanding to Lord Byron's penned words after his visit to Valletta: *"Adieu, ye cursed streets of stairs!"* Erik found the stoned walkways exhilarating instead. It gave him an opportunity to broaden his world beyond the walls of the opera house, which kept him concealed from the world outside.

In his spare time, Erik read books about the isle of Malta. He discovered the fascinating history and legends of the Knights of Hospitaller, and read about the various empires that had occupied the small island. To his surprise, there were miles of underground catacombs in nearby communities, which he longed to traverse but could not. There were buildings and architecture to explore, but the reality of his life made it impossible. Instead, he crawled about at night, like a rat in the gutter, feeding upon small morsels of what Valletta had to offer in the darkness of night.

As Erik walked pensively down the street, he shoved his hand into his pocket fiddling with the card he had kept since the masquerade. *Madame Sybelle Renard, Prophetess – Fortunes, Readings, and Séances.* He pulled it out, stopped under a streetlight, and read the address, realizing he was near where she lived.

Curious, he found the residence and stopped to scrutinize the building. It was unpretentious, with no visible sign of the woman's business hanging over her door. He thought it strange that she did not advertise her services publicly, but not surprised since the Maltese were known to be superstitious, yet deeply religious.

The curtains were closed, but a light lit the inside. Once again, he flipped the card and read his fortune.

"You wish for beauty and love. Love you will find but without beauty, and it shall pierce your heart like a dagger. In the end, it will be your undoing and death."

Irritated, but unable to shake her words that had somehow branded on his psyche, he strode down the street in the shadows, making his way back to his quarters. Since the strange fortuneteller had not attempted to contact him since that night, Erik reinforced his beliefs it was time to forget about her foolish omen.

He shoved his hand back into his pocket, scrunched the card up into a little ball, and tossed it down a sewer grate he passed by. Enough was enough. There was no beauty, no love, no undoing, and no death. Death would only come when Erik allowed it, and though there were days he wished the cloaked dark angel would finally take his life, he somehow knew it would not be any time soon.

❊ ❊ ❊

"So how are the lessons going?" Andrea examined the dark circles underneath Erik's eyes. "You're not sleeping again, are you?"

"She's a slow learner," he replied sarcastically. "And I don't need sleep."

"Well, you look like hell," she told him, flinging her unwanted opinion at him. "Honestly, you should stop wandering the city by yourself at night."

"Observant as usual," he retorted. "I enjoy the night. You know that I love the dark, Andrea. Let me amuse myself in the shadows as I see fit."

Andrea watched his face sneer resentment knowing the next few moments between the two of them would undoubtedly be unpleasant.

"I have no cellars to crawl about here in Valletta, though I've heard there are some rather interesting catacombs not many miles away. Perhaps I will go there and live among the skulls and bones of the dead. It would suit me more than my fine quarters here, don't you think?"

Andrea ignored his rather gruesome remark and pulled her eyes away from his glare. She poured herself another cup of tea and sipped it, wondering what had set off Erik's foul mood this time. He had been happy for months since the opera house reopened. Now, since he had started tutoring Désirée, his personality had taken a dark turn back toward depression.

She felt powerless, because she did not possess the miracle Erik needed to find an ounce of happiness in his life. He needed to be healed from the pain of his past, but Andrea had long ago accepted the fact she was not his healer or guide. The man had a mind of his own. He loved to wallow in his own misery when he grew crabby. Apparently, the new relationship of student and tutor had resurrected buried emotions of former days, which concerned Andrea even further.

"Well, I must say, the performances are going well, don't you think?" Andrea attempted to pull him out of the pit.

Erik huffed with disgust. "I need to speak with Richard about Mademoiselle Cardona's pitch. Did you hear her last night? She's beginning to sound like La Carlotta."

"She sounded fine to me, but of course I don't have your ear for music."

Andrea thought before pressing matters further, but her curiosity was nudging her to poke him. "So tell me about Désirée. You say she is a slow learner. Will you continue your lessons then?"

Erik picked up his cup of coffee, took a sip, and then put down the morning paper. "Yes, she is determined. I give her that much recognition, but I'm afraid teaching her the violin is no easy matter. She can't read music. I need to focus on that problem first. I'm hoping by the time she learns the placement of notes, she'll be able to follow along while I play."

Andrea smiled feeling somewhat relieved he joined in the conversation. She thought of Richard's concerns, wondering if he was right. Erik, however, as if he could read her thoughts spoke suddenly.

"You needn't worry," he declared, glaring at her. "I won't lose my sanity over this one, if that's what you're apprehensive about."

Andrea pulled her eyes away from his gaze. She never could stare at him for very long when he gave that narrowed-eye dark look of displeasure.

"I didn't mean anything by it, Erik," she replied defensively.

"Like hell you didn't," he flung back. "I'm no fool. I suppose you and Richard talk about me all the time and discuss my stability, as it were." A spiteful sneer curled his lip. "You know, Andrea, there's only one woman for me. Do you think another could capture my heart? I think not." Erik drove the point home like a nail into a wooden coffin. He continued to gaze angrily into her eyes.

"Tell me, Andrea, is Richard still the only one for you? Have you two lovers finally mended your ways or are you still arguing over your loyalty to me? I wouldn't wish you to be unhappy," he concluded, with a snide drawl aimed to hurt.

Andrea stood to her feet and threw her napkin down on the table. "After all I do for you, Erik, you can still be the most monstrous bastard I've ever known," she retorted, heaving her words like knives. "Frankly, I'm at the point where I don't give a damn if you ever find love!"

She exited the room, slamming the door behind her while wondering if Erik felt an ounce of remorse over his cruel behavior. She had served him for years, but there were times he crossed the boundaries of her life she never wished him to enter. No one could tell him how to love, how to feel, how to live his life, but he always stuck his nose in everyone else's business.

Angry, she huffed all the way down the hall, intent on ignoring him until his foul mood went back to hell. The man was insufferable, but she loved him like a mother and cried over his unhappiness.

Chapter 13

Désirée arrived at Monsieur Mercier's office as instructed with her notebooks tucked underneath her arm. She had spent the entire afternoon studying what looked like Greek, but made progress, hoping to please and surprise her tutor.

She knocked, expecting the manager to answer, when instead Erik opened the door, appearing gloomy. "Oh," she muttered, wide-eyed, looking into his gloomy eyes. "Monsieur Dante, you startled me. I was expecting—"

"Monsieur Mercier," he said rather sharply, cutting her short before she could finish. "Yes, I know, but I have no need of him this evening."

His voice sounded strained and curt, and his words were laced with a tinge of coldness that unsettled her nerves. Désirée sensed something different about him and wondered why. His eyes were dark and brooding, without any welcoming sparkle she had seen before.

He showed her to the seat before the desk, and then sat quickly fiddling with a few pieces of sheet music. A violin lay on the opposite corner of the desk. Désirée wondered if tonight she would learn a note or two.

"The next step in our lessons will be how to read notes." He pushed a piece of sheet music in her direction.

Désirée smiled. She reached out to the paper and then glanced in his eyes warily. "May I?"

Erik released his grasp, surprised over her movement but making no protest. Her index finger pointed to the first note on the treble clef, and she announced it confidently, "C." After a moment of hesitation, she took a deep breath and continued her recitation in perfect order as her finger pointed to each line and space. "D, E, F, G, A, B, C, D, E, F, G."

Désirée glanced up Erik's intent focus, which encouraged her to continue. She moved to the bass clef. "B, A, G, F, E, D, C, B, A, G, F." She abruptly stopped, inhaled a deep breath in relief, and smiled over her accomplishment.

Erik sat up straight in his chair with a surprised look on his face. Désirée hoped he was pleased with her progress but he said nothing. Perhaps it was just too elementary in his mind to receive any praise. Her voice broke the silence. "I studied today."

"I see," he finally replied, his tone softening. "You've done well."

Désirée let out a puff of air, and Erik grinned hearing her release of pent-up anxiety.

"Oh, Monsieur Dante, I'm so glad you approve."

"Erik," he told her, repentantly. "You may call me Erik."

Désirée's mouth dropped open wondering why he had suddenly changed the rules between the two of them. She really did not care and quickly responded with the same offering. "Désirée, you may call me Désirée."

The room grew strangely quiet. Désirée watched Erik's eyes. A part of her wished to understand who was behind the mask, but another feared his every movement.

"All right, Désirée, show me what else you've learned today." Erik pulled back the musical score from her hand

and started pointing. "What does it mean when the note is empty inside?"

"Whole note."

"And this?"

"Half-note."

"Tell me the rest," Erik insisted, his voice laced with excitement. Désirée continued to recite all she had learned that day and identified the notes correctly.

"And timing," Erik pressed further. "What did you learn of timing?"

"I . . . I'm afraid nothing," she confessed. "I had other work to do for my housekeeping duties. I'm sorry."

"Yes, your duties, of course."

"I'm confused over the beats," she confessed, daring to pull the music back from his hand to look at it again. "I think I understand that 4/4 means four beats per measure, is that correct?"

"Yes, yes." He pulled the music back his way, showing his eccentric love of his gift.

"Look at the notes here, two full notes, four half-notes. Do you see, that's four beats in the measure?" Désirée was startled as he reached across the desk and took her hand. "Make a fist."

She did, and he gently took her hand and rapped it on the desktop ever so slightly just to make the music of the beat, *tap – tap – tap-tap-tap-tap*. "Do you hear the beats in the measure?" he asked, taking her hand once more and pointing to the next measure, knocking upon the desk to make the music of the beat.

Désirée smiled as she watched the genius at work, teaching her at such a simplistic level.

"Thank you," she blurted out.

Erik abruptly stopped and lifted his eyes. She saw a twinkle of pleasure in them; an understanding as to why she felt moved to say what she did. He replied to her softly and simply, "You're welcome."

The next hour, Désirée pored over the lessons with Erik, finding pleasure in learning. When they had finished their review of measures, beats, rests, and volumes of notes, she begged him for what she craved the most when they were together.

"Please, Erik, play for me before I leave. Play something, anything. I want to hear you play."

He looked at her thoughtfully trying to decide what to do. Erik then stood from his chair, walked over to the far corner of the desk, and lifted the instrument, cradling it underneath his chin. When he held the bow over the strings and closed his eyes, Désirée did the same.

The dark foreboding that had permeated the atmosphere earlier fled from their presence, and in its place ushered in melodious strains of music that made her soul soar. Her heart thundered in her chest when she drank in the music, as if it were life-giving water.

Erik continued to play sounds that elicited the same reaction as before. Without thought or effort on her part, tears trickled freely down her cheeks. There were no sobs of pain or heartache—only tears of release. She felt as if the darkest night of her life was washed away by simply listening to Erik play the violin. Désirée wanted the moment to never end, but then it did. The music ceased, and she heard his voice speak.

"Here, take this."

She opened her eyes and saw his outstretched hand offer his handkerchief. Taking it, she inhaled his scent, and then wiped her tears gently, leaving the moisture behind.

"I don't know why I cry each time you play," she confessed. "It's so very beautiful. I've never heard such wondrous music that touches my heart."

Erik sighed and lowered the violin back to the desk, setting down the bow next to it. "Music is healing to the soul, Désirée. It's very powerful."

"Yes, healing," she repeated, wistfully wanting it for herself. Why was she finding healing from what he had to offer?

"It's time to go," he told her, reaching out his hand.

Désirée gave back his linen handkerchief wet only with her tears. Erik carefully slid it into his pocket.

"I'll escort you to the dormitory."

They exchanged no other words. Erik saw her safely back and said goodnight. Désirée did not want to leave his side. She wanted him to play again and fill her soul with peace and healing. After he departed, she walked over to her bed and fell into her pillow, releasing another flood of tears. Her heart was torn, and her path clouded.

"What am I to do?" she sobbed. "What am I to do?"

❄ ❄ ❄

Erik returned to his quarters. He felt fatigued, confused, and emotional, as he headed for bed. Once there, he sat down on the edge and slowly pulled the handkerchief out of his pocket. It was still wet.

He let his fingertips feel the moisture. He hesitated, fighting the urge, but then brought the linen to the side of his unmasked face and allowed the cloth to touch his skin. His flesh reacted unexpectedly. In a rare response, Erik's pained soul released. Before he could stifle the emotion, tears spilled over his lower eyelids and rolled down his cheeks and into the cloth that held the tears of Désirée.

The moment broke him, and for the next few minutes, he pressed the handkerchief to his flesh, catching his tears to mingle with hers. Erik struggled with raw emotions that threatened his tough exterior, but he could not fight the attraction he felt toward Désirée.

The realization he could offer anyone something of beauty was more than he could comprehend. He could unmercifully move a person to tears through cruelty, but to move someone to tears by simply playing his violin felt peculiar. Yes, his compositions at times could be terrible and all consuming—but beautiful? He wondered what Désirée felt inside when she heard the cords and strains of his violin, which triggered such emotion to rise from her soul.

Unsure of how to respond, he tried to control the passions threatening his resolve and playing upon his vulnerability. He removed the handkerchief from his face, folded it in half, and placed it inside the nightstand drawer.

Erik thought of the sheet music strewn upon his desktop. He stood up and walked over to it, sliding one hand over the papers of random unfinished scores. Ever since he lost Christine, he had felt an internal struggle to compose. The joy of composing for someone left and only empty notes played between the measures and lines, bringing no melody.

Tonight a new motivation infused Erik, as he picked up a pen and started again. He realized that he could create beauty that made someone cry, and her name was Désirée. Like a maniac on a mission, Erik sat creating music with new desire. He would write for her alone. He would teach her to play his compositions upon the violin with proficiency and then they would be one in music. No longer would his sleepless nights have no purpose; he had found again the fountain of inspiration.

Chapter 14

Darius began his usual morning inspections, while reflecting upon the years that had passed since he arrived in Malta. He tried hard to please his master, though he sensed Erik's disappointment over his lack of abilities. Whatever he did was never good enough, and it caused him despair.

He feared Erik too. The Persian had told him horror stories of Erik's previous escapades calling him a monster. It was enough to make the hair on the back of his neck stand up after hearing tales of tortures and strangulations executed by his skillful hands. Darius, however, was by nature a true servant at heart; and a servant must be faithful to his master, whether good or evil.

When he first arrived upon the isle, Erik had relied heavily upon Darius' services, until he hired Richard Mercier. The former manager was far more intelligent and perceptive in the ways of the world, so Darius understood his master's need to use him in matters of more importance. Without complaint, he continued his duties, assisted with construction, and rejoiced in Erik's ability to erase the devastation and return the structure to glory.

Erik had assigned certain tasks for Darius to perform now that the opera house was operational. Matters of maintenance and security were his responsibilities. Two roles he felt prepared to carry out, or at least he hoped, to Erik's satisfaction. He acted as the custodian, making sure that everything was in working order. In addition, he was the keeper of the keys. He locked and secured the doors at night.

As he walked the catwalk above the stage, inspecting the ropes and riggings like he normally did, he hoped that nothing new would catch his eyes. Everything appeared to be normal, until he spotted something wrong.

He bent down, examined the rigging, and discovered a partially cut rope. The cut was deep enough to start the twine unraveling but not clear through. A few more pounds, a few more sways on the catwalk, and it would snap sending its occupant to the stage below, gravely injuring the unfortunate worker.

Carefully, Darius inspected every rigging, tie, and rope in the maze above the stage. This was the second in a month, and even he with his simple mind realized it was sabotage. He had let the first occurrence slip and did not report it to Richard or Erik. He was afraid of upsetting his master. Unfortunately, he could no longer keep another incident silent. It was a matter of safety, and a mystery too.

He climbed down the riggings and headed through the long hall that led to Monsieur Mercier's office. A quick rap of his knuckles on the door, and he heard Richard's invitation to enter. Upon doing so, he found Erik in the room as well, and silently dreaded his master's reaction. He shut the door and approached, trying not to show his nerves.

"I need to speak with you, Master," he announced, his face etched with worry. He slipped his eyes toward Richard. "Monsieur Mercier, you need to hear this as well."

Darius lowered his voice, so no one could hear the conversation through the door. To hide his jumpy nerves, he shoved both hands into his pants pockets and began fiddling with coins between his fingers.

"Today I found one of the ropes on the riggings above the stage slashed, cut by a sharp knife. The slice was not all the way through the cord, but far enough to weaken its tie. It is frayed and will soon break if not replaced. If it does give way, some poor soul will fall to the stage below!"

Erik's eyes turned dark. "Cut, you say?"

Darius nodded. "Yes, Master, and I'm afraid this is the second time this month. I thought perhaps the first was an accident, and I sloughed it off and just replaced the rope. I can see now it was not. It's been slit on purpose so it will break and cause a fall."

"My God, who would do such a thing?" Richard asked, sitting down behind his desk stunned by the news.

Darius saw Richard shift his eyes toward Erik and wondered if he thought the same thing. It sounded reminiscent of the Ghost at the Garnier when he used to play tricks. Surely his master wouldn't sabotage his own domain. It was a mystery.

In a gruff voice, Erik attacked Darius' oversight. "Why in the hell did you not report this the first time?" He stepped closer, showing his irritation. Darius retreated in response.

"I . . . I just replaced the rope, Master. I wondered if it just wore through, but now I know it's something else. I'm sorry." Darius gulped. Inwardly, he prayed to Allah. *Please, don't let him ask me any more,* but his plea came too late. The prayer had no sooner left his rattled thoughts when Erik asked another question.

"Anything else?" Erik demanded, seething through his teeth. "Are you keeping anything else from me?"

Darius shifted unsteadily on his feet. Allah would know if he lied. He looked into Erik's angry eyes, then over to Richard and back again. "Yes," his voice squeaked. "But,

Master, I swear to you, I've been very careful. I don't know how it happened." His eyes bulged in fear.

"How what happened?" Erik snarled, as he reached forward and grabbed Darius' shoulders tightly with both hands. He shook him hard for the answer.

"I . . . I lost my second set of keys. I kept them in my drawer in my quarters and discovered they were missing. But," he added, shoving his hand inside his coat pocket where he retrieved the master keys and jingled in front of Erik. "You see, I still have the originals. It's only the copies that are gone." He smiled thinking that would please his master.

Erik pushed Darius back into the closed door, slamming his body hard against the barrier. "You damn fool!" he yelled.

"Erik!" Richard screamed in response. He jumped to his feet from behind the desk and flew to Darius' side for protection. "Let the man go, Erik. Let him go!"

Darius felt as if Erik's eyes were burning a hole in his soul. He had let his master down. He had not been faithful, and he lowered his head in shame. "Please, Master, don't hurt me. I'm sorry. I'll have an extra set made as soon as possible. Please, I beg your forgiveness."

He brought his hands together, looking like he was praying for his very life. He felt Erik's fingers dig into his shoulders and feared he would soon draw blood.

"Damn fool! I knew you were a damn fool I couldn't trust." Erik released his grip and flung around toward Richard, his fists clenched at his side. "Don't presume, Richard, that you have the right to tell me how to act either," he growled. Erik stepped away and paced back and forth across the room.

"I will have the rope on the catwalk replaced immediately." Darius looked warily at them both, his voice still shaking. "The keys," he asked. "What do you wish me to do about the keys? Shall I have a second set made?"

Erik flung a sarcastic answer at him. "Oh, do please, Darius, have a second set made so those can be stolen too," he said mockingly.

Richard interjected. "We should change all the locks, but I'm afraid it will take time and money." Turning toward Darius, he asked, "What keys are we talking about, Darius?"

"All entrances to the opera house from the exterior, and all the interior door locks, Monsieur Mercier." Darius was saddened to see the disappointment in Monsieur Mercier's eyes too.

"What possessed you to keep all those keys on one ring and keep them just shoved in a drawer somewhere?"

Darius shrugged his shoulders. "I . . . I don't know," he admitted, thinking nothing wrong over his actions that they thought were careless.

"Change the locks on the exterior doors first," Erik grumbled. "I'm more worried over uninvited guests wandering our halls when we're asleep at night. We should post watches in the meantime, Richard."

"Yes, yes, of course. I'll see about additional security."

Erik turned to Darius and explained the severity of the situation. "You do realize, Darius, that someone burned this opera house down once. They never discovered who was responsible for the devastation. Did it ever occur to you that perhaps the same disgruntled individual may be wandering about Valletta wishing for an encore performance?"

Darius's eyes grew wide and his jaw dropped over the thought that someone might try to destroy everything his master had resurrected. "No, I didn't."

Erik turned away, uttering just one word. "Go."

Darius took the short command and obeyed it immediately. *No more questions! No more questions!* he screamed in his mind. It was clearly wrong to lie, but it wasn't wrong to keep secrets. Relieved, he spun around, opened the door, and flew into the hallway. As soon as he closed the door behind him, he sighed in relief. His hand came to his head and ran through his scalp of thick black hair. *Praise be to Allah!* He did not have to tell the master everything; otherwise, he would be dead!

❅ ❅ ❅

As soon as Darius left, Erik turned to Richard. "This is not good."

Richard stood contemplating the situation and nodded his head in agreement.

"I must see it for myself," he declared, leaving the office and heading for the stage. Erik needed space. He was peeved at Richard for daring to tell him how to behave and enraged with Darius for being such a simpleton.

Richard did not understand him; he was sure of it. Erik needed an outlet for his frustrations that boiled beneath the surface. If he did not express his anger, it would seethe inside until it exploded into violence. His act of pushing Darius against the wall was to make a point and vent his frustrations. He did not intend to strangle the man, though the thought had crossed his mind. At any rate, he noted Richard's insolence in his mind as he strode toward the auditorium.

Erik climbed the back stairs to the catwalks above and came out on the planks, traversing back and forth like a cat with claws. He inspected all the ropes, ties, and riggings with his own eyes and found the one Darius had mentioned. It needed immediate replacement before the next show.

A sharp knife had cut half way through the rope. Erik remembered the times he brought down sets at the Garnier to make a point. However, this could injure or kill someone. It carried no indication of being a mere trick or joke to cause havoc. Who would do such a thing? He had no answers, and it gnawed at him like an irritating bug.

He climbed down and headed back toward his quarters. A door flung open before him, and he nearly ran into Darius carrying a replacement rope for the rigging. Erik grabbed him by the arm and stopped him in his tracks.

"Make sure you do a good job," he growled.

"Yes, Master, I will. I promise," he replied, scurrying off toward the stage.

Erik returned to his room. The night lay ahead with a performance of *Faust* to a sold-out crowd. Business had been good, with patrons consistently returning nightly. He basked in success and profits.

Tonight he would attend the performance from his box in the shadows and check on the soprano's progression. There were times he itched to reveal his identity and teach her to project her voice with more clarity. She was good, but not that good.

Still antsy about the total lack of excellence, he swore that one day he would have every one of the staff obeying his orders to perfection. He was beginning to toy with the idea of revealing himself to the cast and crew, but decided to wait a few more months to make sure that once he did, he would be in no danger.

As the night progressed and the performance began, Erik anxiously waited for the crowd to dissipate and the tutoring session to begin. He arrived first, bringing the violin he had purchased for Désirée. He restlessly waited for her arrival. Erik needed something to take his mind of the disturbing news of the day, and this would do the trick. Richard was to bring her to the orchestra pit, as he had done before.

When he arrived, he said nothing, but his face showed concern. Erik, still on edge, threw Richard his own look of disdain. Was he worried about him spending time alone with Désirée? Did he think he could not handle himself like a gentleman? Whatever the reason, he surmised his concern was no doubt the result of a discussion between Andrea and Richard, which he would soon put to an end.

"Thank you, Richard," he noted, dismissing him. He watched Désirée descend the stairs. She approached him with a smile, and his nostrils immediately detected a subtle scent of lilac perfume. Her dress was different and of finer material, but still modest. A slight tint of pink rouge accented her porcelain cheeks. He noticed she had pulled her hair back and tied it with a silk red ribbon, which cascaded down her back. No wonder Richard had raised a brow. Erik felt his own lift, as his eyes met her lips, fully plumped with pink lipstick.

He took note of each minuscule change in his student's appearance with great amusement. It was difficult to ignore her obvious attempt to gain his attention by other means. Erik was somewhat flattered, but immediately questioned her motives. He was under the distinct impression she only wished to learn the violin and did not wish to learn the truth of what lay beneath the mask.

"Welcome, Désirée." He finally spoke, taking a step closer. "Shall we begin? I wish to show you the various strings on the violin and help you with the placement of your fingers. Are you ready?"

"I have thought of it all day long!" she exclaimed. "And I have studied my books. I brought them so I could show you how proficient I'm becoming reading the musical notes."

Erik reached for her booklets and placed them on a nearby chair. "Very good. I am pleased with your enthusiasm to learn."

The closer he drew to Désirée, the more prominent the odor of lilac wafted up his nostrils. He hated the fragrance. If he had to breathe perfume during their lessons in the future, he was going to tell her his preference.

"Rose," he blurted out, sneering at the odor she wore. He looked directly in her eyes to make his next point. "If you insist on dousing yourself in fragrance before our lessons, I'd prefer to inhale the scent of rose rather than lilac." There, he had told her his likes and dislikes, and he fully expected her to comply with his request in the future.

She stared at him wide-eyed in return, with a look of shock written across her painted face. Erik stopped, feeling a bit gruff, as he inhaled a deep breath. His eyes watered over the strong scent, but he managed to soften the tone of his voice.

"Forgive me for being so brash, Désirée, but I find certain aromas annoying; lilac is one of them." He wondered if she knew the meaning of the flower when she dabbed the copious amounts on her bodice. "Are you trying to send me a message?" he pried, getting directly to the point at hand.

"What do you mean?" She appeared insulted over his insinuation.

"The fragrance, the lilac flower, its meaning," he sputtered from his lips, flustered over the conversation.

"I have no idea what you're talking about!"

"The first emotions of love," he drawled, half-intoxicated by the smell. "It's not something I think you should be wearing while in my presence. Dispense with the fragrance in the future," he commanded. His voice trailed off with an icy tone.

"And rose?" she spat back, glaring into his dark eyes. "What is it about the meaning and scent of a rose that you find more appealing, might I ask?"

Erik watched, surprised, as she shoved both hands on her hips to posture her irritation. He frowned in exasperation.

"Because a rose, my dear, can come in a variety of colors, meaning anything from a lover's passion, to admiration, affection, friendship, and purity. A rose is a flower filled with both beauty and thorns to remind you that love can be a fragrant experience, but it also can prick and hurt until you bleed."

Erik turned from Désirée. His thoughts from the past threatened to unleash the painful passions he kept reigned within his heart. He spun around and looked at her standing in front of him, wearing her scent of first emotions. Erik wondered if she had dabbed it on her fair skin ignorant of its hidden meaning or if she purposely wished to convey some childish crush on her part.

"Go," he commanded, stepping closer to her in a menacing fashion. "Leave me and wash that insidious odor from your body and return."

"You cannot be serious!" she implored, clearly aghast over his suggestion. "How can a mere fragrance push you into such turmoil?"

Erik lost his temper and pushed over a music stand next to him, spewing the papers across the floor. "Get out! If you wish lessons, I shall teach you, but do not assume that our relationship shall go any further. Do you understand?"

"Are you mad?" she demanded, stepping closer, pushing him to the brink.

Her eyes glared, and Erik saw she would not back down from the tantrum he flung to keep her in her place. It was time to put an end to whatever foolish feelings she entertained here and now. He lowered his head, took his fingers, and slid them underneath the corner of his mask. With one quick jerk, he removed the covering and wig and bore before Désirée his gruesome ugliness. One more thrust of his body a step closer to her face, and he conveyed the frightful message to her unsuspecting heart.

"Now, tell me about the first emotions of love, my dearest. Do you find me attractive and still wish to convey your childish musings?"

His deep voice mocked her intentions. Erik's heart turned cold. He realized his action would end their lessons forever, and the usual reaction of screams and terror would soon fill his ears. Instead, as he glanced sharply into her blue pools, he witnessed no reaction. Her eyes did not blink, flinch, or show an ounce of horror or fear. Her mouth did not open and scream. Désirée's beautiful features veiled her feelings.

Erik felt totally naked and undone in her presence. He had wielded his repulsiveness to repel her intentions and failed. Instead, an eerie silence permeated the air. He glared at her behavior, waiting for her to scream and flee, but her countenance remained blank, unmoved, and unresponsive.

"Well?" he demanded, breaking the silence. "Does your perfume still speak of the first emotions of love?"

"You do not frighten me," she countered, blandly staring at his deformity with little interest. "Monsieur, you are not the ugliest human I have seen in my life."

Erik noticed her blue eyes darken like a stormy sea. An odd sense of defeat flowed through his veins over his inability to frighten her as he hoped. He stood confused and befuddled over the woman before him. Then finally, she responded to his request.

"If you wish not to be reminded that another could perhaps have emotions for you, Monsieur," she stated coldly, "then I shall do as you say. I will wash and return to proceed with our lessons."

Désirée took hold of her skirt and lifted it from the floor, as she spun quickly around. Erik felt the air move about him when she departed up the stairway and out of his sight. For a few moments, he stood unaware that his jaw had dropped open, while he grasped his mask and hairpiece tightly in the palm of his hand. When the shock subsided, he covered his face and the few strands of course sparse gray hair upon his nearly bald scalp.

He looked at the stairs where she left and suddenly felt remorse that he would no longer smell the scent of lilac on her skin.

Chapter 15

Désirée's heavy footsteps thundered down the hall to the bath chamber, driving down the terror and hurt she had endured in his presence. It was merely a dab of her favorite lilac perfume! She had not thought he would catch some hidden meaning underneath the fragrance thrusting him into some emotional outburst that frightened her to death.

She discovered through her foolishness that she had begun to feel something for him; perhaps it was the first emotions of love. Unsure and afraid to pursue the thought that clawed through her mind, she ran to the water basin and poured cold water into the bowl. She quickly unbuttoned the top of her dress from the neck down to her bodice, exposing the skin underneath.

She shoved a wet washcloth down the front of her cleavage to remove the scent between her breasts. Frantically, she rubbed the remnants from behind her ears, wrists, and every place she had dabbed, and then sniffed to make sure every ounce of the fragrance had dissipated.

Désirée's hands shook and her heart pounded. Her legs felt like jelly. She had not anticipated his brash reaction of pulling off his mask and wig bearing everything underneath. Inwardly, she had howled in horror. Outwardly, she stood her ground, cold and determined not to react to the revelation of anguish upon his face. He had attempted to push her to revulsion, but it failed. Yes, it was horrible, but she had seen worse. It was merely one side of his face.

Though it was difficult to look upon, it wasn't as unbearable as she had believed it to be. Where smooth flesh should have, were gapping holes and protruding facial bones. It looked as if nature had molded one side of his face, but had forgotten about the other. The skin looked ghostly white, and sickly in appearance and odor. His scalp was bare, continuing the malformation up into his skull area with hideous gouges.

In spite of his deformity, she knew of his temper and of the rumors that he strangled and killed as well. Nevertheless, no one had told her of his genius, drive, and capacity to play music that poured the balm of Gilead into her soul. It seemed as if the eyes of humans only saw the hideous exterior, which had relegated him to a life of rejection.

His ranting and raving regarding the rose fragrance revealed that his heart still bled. His hand clutched tightly to the thorny stem of the past. The pain remained, and because of this, Désirée knew any plans for a future would be an uphill battle. He would not be an easy man to win over, but she hoped with time and patience, she would succeed in capturing his affections.

The last button slipped through the eyelet and closed the gap. She had donned the perfume long before putting on her dress, so the material held no residue of lilac in the fabric. Désirée owned no other fragrances. Lilac was her favorite; rose was not. She would make the sacrifice. Upon her return, his keen nostrils would not smell anything on her body.

Désirée closed the door behind her and slowly made her way back to the orchestra pit along the dark corridors. When she arrived, Erik was pensively pacing the small enclosure.

As she looked at him, with his mask and hairpiece perfectly replaced, she pondered him with curiosity. He appeared dark and foreboding on one side of his face, but the other side displayed a distinct handsomeness she admired. She wondered if he even realized that part of his appearance was pleasing to the human eye. She quickly concluded, by his obvious brooding, he had never considered it a possibility.

"I've returned washed and free of fragrance," she announced, standing at the top of the stairs gaining his attention. "May we continue?"

Erik turned around and faced her, and she saw his facial features soften.

"Yes, of course," he replied, walking toward her and offering his hand as she climbed down the few stairs to the pit. Désirée felt the coldness of his flesh and quickly dropped his hand when she reached the bottom. He remained quiet and pensive. Erik picked up the violin and handed it to her.

"Hold it while I show you the strings and the various placements of your fingers to produce the notes."

"I'm sorry," she told him, feeling the need to explain herself before they continued. His eyes rose to hers, and she witnessed his shame and embarrassment peering back in return. Désirée wondered if he thought she now perceived him differently, but she did not.

"I will refrain from making any insinuations on my part through fragrance, words, or actions, Monsieur Dante. I'm merely here to learn the violin."

Erik said nothing. He looked at her coldly, which caused a deep sense of frustration. Did he wish her not to feel anything? Suddenly, his demeanor turned serious.

"Your finger placement, on the stem and strings, at various places are the notes. I've sketched this for you," he pulled out a folded piece of paper from his upper vest pocket. "You can learn the placements."

Désirée took the piece of paper and sighed as she thought of more studying that lay ahead. "Thank you," she mumbled.

Erik reached over and took the slip of paper from her. "You may take this with you later," he explained, laying it on a nearby music stand. "Now, place the violin in the position that I showed you before."

Désirée did as she was told. At least the tone of his voice had softened, but her placement of the instrument appeared eschewed. Quickly, his long fingers reached forward and adjusted her hold.

"Wrap your fingers about the stem," he instructed, "and feel the strings beneath your fingertips."

The wire was coarse, stiff, and hard, and she pushed it feeling it dig into her skin.

"You'll get used to it," Erik explained, obviously seeing a flash of discomfort upon her face. "Let's review point by point the finger placement for the notes."

Erik began showing her. She tried desperately not to react to his touch, but still the overwhelming feeling of power flowed through her veins at every glance of his flesh across her own. Désirée attempted to pay attention to her lessons, but it seemed to drag on for an eternity. The emotional tug upon her heart made her feel fatigued, but there was one more thing to do before she retired for the evening. She held out the violin to Erik.

"Will you do a favor before I leave?" She lifted her eyes, pleading. "Play for me." Erik eyed the violin in her hand, hesitating at her request. "Please," she begged. "Please, it touches my soul when you play."

Without another word, Erik took the instrument, placed it under his chin, and then spoke the same instructions as before. "Close your eyes."

Désirée did as she was told, and soon her ears filled with the strains of beauty. The piece he chose was different this time; filled with sadness and laced with painful longing. The strains of music swelled and lowered as she listened. Again, her soul reacted in the same way. He transported her to another place through the anointed tones.

Erik finished, and she opened her eyes to see his hand extended with a handkerchief between his fingers, and a warm smile upon his face. His eyes pierced her soul, as if he knew everything she felt inside—the pain, anguish, and heartache. Embarrassed by his gaze, she grabbed the linen, dabbed her tears, and handed it back.

"I should be going," she declared flustered, standing to her feet, and turning toward the stairway.

"Take this." He was holding out the violin and bow to her. "Take it with you and practice the placement of your fingers."

Désirée looked at the instrument, the wood still warm from his hold. She took it to her chest hugging it as if it were his body. Her hand clutched the bow, as it would his embrace.

"I can find my way back alone," she told him, not wishing for an escort. Before he could protest, her feet swiftly carried her out of the orchestra pit, down the aisle, and out the door. Tears streamed down her face, while her heart raged a battle of good and evil beneath the surface.

❋ ❋ ❋

Left standing alone, Erik bent down and picked up the stand he had shoved over earlier in anger. He felt numb from the past hour they had shared; numb from baring his flesh to destroy her fanciful feelings and from the reaction she had failed to give in return.

Once again, his handkerchief was filled with her wet tears, only he refused to bring it to his bare cheek this time, afraid of the response it would elicit from his soul. His student was stirring him with emotions he did not wish to feel or acknowledge. He always thought any emotions in his life belonged to Christine. She was the one who held the key to his heart. How could he even think of another in his life? Désirée was turning the key and requesting admittance to a place he wanted to keep locked away forever.

When all was in order, he left the pit and returned to his quarters. He headed straight for a glass of cognac. At first, he had no desire to wander the streets of Valletta that night. Instead, he sat upon his divan, raised his feet up on the table before him, and drank in an attempt to relax. When he closed his eyes, he smelled lilacs, remembered the softness of her skin, and gazed into her blue oceans that took him to a place of peace.

He lifted the glass to his lips and sipped the burning liquid, letting it course down his throat slowly so he could feel the pain. It was obvious to him that Désirée Martin wanted more than just violin lessons. What did she see in him, a proficient violinist that brought her to tears when he played? He was a joke of a man she could never love. Erik was unsure, but knew that if he continued with the lessons until the end, there was no telling where his starving heart would lead.

He could not release himself to a place of affection for another woman. He had learned a painful lesson with Christine Daaé and would sooner die a torturous death in one of his former mirrored chambers than from the heat of desire that could consume a man. It was a feeling he loathed; a feeling he wished to release like a hungry animal so he could devour what he never tasted before.

As Erik gulped the remaining drop in his glass and stood to get another, he feared the emotions of love that could be his undoing. It was then the words came floating back in his mind.

"Love you will find . . . "

He set the glass down, grabbed his cloak, and headed out the door. There was no thought in his mind about the late hour. It was time to find out if the woman who enjoyed taunting him years ago was a fraud, or if she had received some message from hell to convey.

Erik strode down the dark streets, remembering exactly where she lived. When he arrived, he saw the lights still on. He had no qualms about making his presence known outside the soothsayer's residence. He balled his hand into a fist and pounded on the door in relentless determination until it opened to reveal Madame Sybelle Renard.

She was clothed in a black dressing gown, but it did not appear as if he had awakened her from slumber. Her face showed no outward shock at his arrival, and Erik thought that perhaps she had expected him to respond to her words one day. A sly smile curled her lips, which he found infuriating.

"Why, Monsieur Dante," she breathed with delight. "What a surprise! After all these years, you've finally come for a visit." She eyed him up and down and then continued her patronizing words. "If you're here for a reading," she intoned, "I'm afraid it's after hours, and you'll have to return another time."

She began to close the door in his face, but Erik thrust his hand against the wooden barrier and shoved it back open. He pushed his body forward until she stepped back into the foyer. Her facial expression spoke surprise over his actions, but also of a satisfied expectation.

"I wish to speak with you," he growled, shoving the door shut behind him. Quickly, he glanced about his surroundings and noticed a parlor to his right. Candles dimly lit the room and embers burned in the fireplace.

"I'd invite you in, but I see you've already decided to invite yourself." She turned and sauntered into her parlor room leading the way. Her hand pointed to a nearby chair. "Please do have a seat."

"I prefer to stand," he noted warily. He wisely used caution, since he did not know whether she lived alone or with a man.

"Very well, whatever you prefer," she replied unmoved. "I prefer to sit."

She sat in a chair and faced him, crossing her legs, and looking more relaxed than he wished. His presence did nothing to rile her apparently, and she displayed a cold, satisfied smirk across her face. He wasn't surprised. If she was steeped into the occult as most soothsayers were, she had danced with the Devil before. No doubt, he presented no threat to her world; hence her unconcerned reaction. Erik sensed evil. It was palpable and sitting in the chair only a few feet away from where he stood.

"What can I do for you?" she asked.

Erik cast his dark eyes at her figure and replied in a menacing tone. "I am here to discuss your fortune over my life, which you were so intent on giving me the night of the masquerade. I wish to know its meaning."

After his declaration, he found himself in an awkward situation, since he told her once he did not believe in fortunetellers. However, her words had eaten at him until he had to discover the truth about her so-called physic skills.

"Was it a vision you saw or simply a ploy on your part to play a ruse?"

Her eyes sparkled at his question, and she tilted her head back and laughed.

"Well, I thought you implied that fortunetellers are merely fakes, out to take the unsuspecting of their money, making up idle fanciful tales of the future to tickle the ears of gullible customers."

Madame Renard stood from her chair and postured herself in front of his body. "Don't tell me, Monsieur Dante, my words are coming true and that has sparked your interest in my abilities?"

Erik braced himself against the witch that stood before him with her arrogant eyes. *Evil against evil*, he thought to himself. He could show no weakness in the presence of this snake attempting to wrap her coils of deceit about his mind. As he stood examining her dark eyes, he questioned his rash behavior for coming to her door.

"Seeking you out was a mistake," he replied coldly. "You are a fake, a phony who enjoys toying with the minds of others."

"Now, now, Monsieur Dante," she drawled, taking a step closer. "You came for a reason, and I know why."

Her finger reached out again and traced itself from the bottom of his neck down to his heart. Erik grabbed her wrist and squeezed it tightly, but she neither yelped nor tried to pull away. He watched her hand grow white as he obstructed the flow of blood to her fingers.

"You came," she continued undaunted, "because an opportunity of love has presented vitself to you for the first time in years. Perhaps Monsieur Dante is not sure what to do with that opportunity? Will it tear your heart? Will it be your death?"

Erik released his grip and flung her hand away.

"You're mad," he snarled. He turned to head for the door, but she followed him and leaned into his ear to whisper her last words. They spilled confidently from her lips in one seductive trail of torment.

"I told you love would come. However, I surmise it's my prophecy that it will be your undoing and death that concerns you the most, eh?" She boldly took a step toward him and placed her hand on his forearm. "You wish for love, Monsieur Dante. Don't we all? It is a risk you will have to take, to fall in love or not. If this woman has caught your eye, then you must make a decision."

Her hand rested on his forearm, and Erik felt a cold chill enter his body.

"Whether you believe that it will be your ultimate end is the path you must walk alone. I only speak what I see in my visions, Monsieur. Take them or leave them."

Her hand slipped off his arm, and Erik stood motionless. His eyes stared at her, trying to sort out the myriad of emotions assaulting his mind.

"You appear speechless," she finally observed. "Au revoir, Monsieur, you know the way out." She pointed to the door.

Erik left without a word, cursing himself repeatedly for having entered her door. He strode down the street back to opera house, clothed in his hooded cloak, pondering the fortuneteller's words.

Already in a weakened state fighting the bewitching presence of Désirée, he felt drawn to a path of seduction he could not avoid. She had begun to touch the core of his hardened exterior. He stopped briefly and pulled out his handkerchief stained by her tears. His heart pounded in his chest. He wanted somehow to mingle the essence of his soul with hers, yet feared the glorious rush of affection for another human being. He thirsted and hungered for an ounce of admiration from her in return, even though it frightened him deeply.

Erik shoved the handkerchief back in his pocket and continued down the dark street. Perhaps it would be his undoing and death; but he was dead already, so what did it matter?

Chapter 16

Erik spent a sleepless night. He should have left well enough alone, but for some odd reason he felt driven to confront his fortune. It only resulted in further confusion, because he could not discern whether he found truth or deceit in her words. He did decide on one thing, though, while tossing and turning in the middle of the night. Fortune or no fortune, he was going to pursue his inclinations toward Désirée, but he needed Andrea's help first.

He found her the next morning at the dining table with Richard, drinking her tea and eating her usual muffin for breakfast. Interrupting the cozy scene between the two, he approached Andrea to convey his wishes.

"I want to speak with you."

"Of course," she replied eagerly. "Richard and I were just having breakfast. Why don't you join us?"

"In private."

"Oh," she responded surprised.

She glanced at Richard. Her expression quickly changed. Erik knew when he used the word *private* with Andrea, she would know he was serious. She placed her napkin next to her plate, scooted back her chair, and stood.

"Excuse me, Richard," she commented, shooting him a questioning look.

"Yes, of course. If privacy is what you need, then by all means. I'll remain here with my coffee and morning news."

Thankful that Richard gave no objection, he escorted Andrea back to his quarters. It was an unusual move, for he rarely allowed Andrea a glimpse inside his world unless necessary.

He sensed Andrea's slight uneasiness as she quickly glanced about his surroundings after entering his parlor. *Nothing much to see,* he thought to himself, except for his usual strewn sheets of music, his violin, and other private endeavors he often amused himself with. Of late, he had taken to reading the history of Malta, and Andrea quickly picked up one the books on a nearby table.

"Reading, I see," she observed, eyeing the title.

"Sit," he commanded. His voice was curt and direct.

Andrea found a nearby chair and did as she was told. Her curious eyes lifted to his face, and Erik cleared his throat in an attempt to convey his unorthodox request.

"I need a favor from you, Andrea, or perhaps two," he admitted. "You'll think I'm mad, but that's inconsequential. I'm just trying to make a point in what I am about to ask you."

"Well, for heaven's sake, what is it, Erik?"

"I need you to purchase a small bottle of rose-scented perfume."

"What?"

The look on her face incited the reaction he expected. "You heard me."

"For goodness sake, why? What on Earth are you going to do with a bottle of rose-scented perfume?"

"It's a gift," he replied, pulling his gaze from her to look at the book on the table. He heard a long sigh escape her lips in response.

"Erik, do you know what you're doing?"

He snapped back. "Of course I know what I'm doing!"

"Is it for Désirée?" she inquired hesitantly over his gruff reply.

Erik softened his exterior at the mention of her name. "She insists on wearing lilac fragrance, and I find it most annoying. I told her if she must douse herself with perfume, then rose is my preference."

Andrea smiled at his explanation. Erik sounded like a youth with a crush. His eyes warily crawled back to look at her, and he immediately saw a mixture of emotions. No doubt, she would be running back to Richard soon to discuss his newest obsession.

"I assure you," he explained slowly to cover his secret admiration. "It's merely a kind gesture on my part. There are no hidden motives. We continue lessons. I am her tutor. She is my student."

"Well," Andrea exhaled, accepting his explanation without outward complaint. "I shall make my way to the nearest perfume shop and make your purchase today. Is there anything else you require?"

"No, that will be all."

Erik looked at his friend, his heart urging him to bear his next confession. He needed to tell someone what had happened. It tormented him with unanswered questions. He couldn't shake her lack of reaction over his unmasked face. Would Andrea have an answer to her strange behavior?

"I stripped my mask and wig off before her, Andrea." His voice hesitated, as he dealt with his embarrassment.

"My God, Erik, why?" She jumped to her feet and came to his side. "What did she do?"

He shook his head trying to compose his response, which he feared would be unbelievable even for Andrea.

"She did nothing. No reaction whatsoever." Erik remembered her words clearly. "She only said, '*You are not the ugliest human I have seen in my life.*'"

At the mention of his appearance, he adjusted his mask and wig, making sure it was in place. He often unconsciously did so whenever he spoke of his deformity, to assure it was out of sight.

"I was stunned frankly. She merely wishes to continue her lessons and apparently can deal with a hideous teacher. I thought for sure she would react as most do, but she did not."

Andrea was clearly shocked and astonished over the revelation. He could tell she was trying to process the strange announcement about Désirée's reaction, but could not come to any conclusions either.

"Well, I must say, that does surprise me," she confessed. "I'm suddenly curious to know what makes her so confident that she did not react."

"Then find out, Andrea," he commanded. "I wish you to befriend her. I'm curious as to what lays beneath the exterior." He paused and then opened his heart to her. "I feel like a bumbling idiot when I'm in her presence. I want to know what she really thinks of me. I . . . "

"Do you have feelings for her?" Andrea reached out to touch his arm, her faced filled with concern.

Erik shrugged his shoulders and turned his gaze from her eyes. "Well, I'm intrigued, but I think she merely has a crush upon an older man. When I play my violin, it seems to have a profound effect upon her. I will admit that much." Erik's mouth curled in a small smile over the thought of being able to touch her so profoundly through his playing.

In an out-of-character move, he reached over and placed his hand upon Andrea's, still resting upon his forearm. "I will be careful, Andrea. My heart is not the type, as you know, to be released so readily to another. Beneath this hardened exterior is a man who still longs to be loved. An opportunity presents itself, and I cannot deny what I crave. I've tried. It's useless."

"We all want to be loved, Erik. There is nothing wrong with wanting to be loved." She patted his hand and removed it from his arm. "I will get you the perfume and will befriend her as requested. Whatever I learn about her, I will tell you. You can be assured."

"Thank you, dear friend." Erik walked her to the door. "As I think about my request, I think perhaps it would make sense for you to give her the bottle. I'd rather not have the gift come from my hand. You may just say her tutor wished her to have it, so he wouldn't gag the next time she came for a lesson." Erik chuckled at his humorous statement. "Perhaps that will make light of it and not encourage her affections unnecessarily."

"Of course, Erik, that sounds quite appropriate."

Andrea departed, and Erik returned to his composition. The remainder of the day he spent locked behind closed doors lost in his music. He would compose a few measures and then play them on his violin. Tonight, if he felt so inclined, he would play his newest movement and see if it had the same effect upon Désirée.

❅ ❅ ❅

Andrea made the purchase of perfume and returned to find Désirée working in the auditorium dusting the arms of the seats. As she watched her go about her duties, she stood for a few minutes observing her movements and paying close attention to her physical appearance. She was a graceful, beautiful young woman, there was no doubt about it, but Andrea agreed with Erik there was much about her that was a mystery.

After she put aside her thoughts, she walked down the aisle and came up behind Désirée, who was bending over a chair. "Might I have a word with you?" she asked.

The young woman whirled around startled by her presence with a look of shock on her face.

"I'm sorry. I didn't wish to surprise you. I hate it when someone does that to me. Forgive me." Andrea smiled and explained her presence. "I have something for you." She held out a small white box tied with a pink ribbon.

"For me?" Désirée asked, eyeing the package.

Andrea watched her confused hesitation before accepting it from her hand, then took a deep breath to fortify her resolve before making what she considered an uncomfortable explanation.

"Yes, your teacher requested that I procure for you a fragrance that is a bit more appealing to his sense of smell." She smiled, pleased with her words. "Sit and let's talk," she suggested, motioning to one of the seats.

Désirée eyed the box. "Go ahead and open it," Andrea encouraged her.

She carefully untied the pink bow around the box and lifted the lid very slowly to see a bottle of Eau de Parfum of Rose inside. A smile spread across her face, and she let out a girlish giggle.

"I guess this means he wishes I throw out my lilac fragrance." She took out the bottle, and squeezed the aromatic ball at the end sending a spray of rose fragrance to her wrist. Désirée lifted it to her nostrils and sniffed.

"A kind gesture indeed, but it's not my favorite scent," she confessed honestly. "I will wear it for his sake, so I don't gag him in our lessons." She replaced the bottle and closed the box. "Will you thank him for me?" she asked, lifting her eyes to Andrea.

"Well, I think, dear, that is something you can do when you see him again at your next lesson." She paused studying the young woman's demeanor, trying to ascertain if she felt any affection for Erik. It would need further prying on her part to find out. "Are you enjoying your lessons with him?"

"Oh, yes," she blurted out, without hesitancy. "He's been very kind to teach me, though I fear I will not be able to play with any proficiency. I only hope he continues to be patient, for I will never make the melodious sounds of his violin." She paused thoughtfully and then confessed her heart. "I love to hear him play. It's very soothing."

Andrea nodded her head in agreement. She noted Désirée's term of love to describe Erik's skill. "Yes, he is a genius, my dear, in many ways. I've never heard anyone in my entire life bring forth such power and feeling from the violin as he is able to do. It's a gift, I believe, to make up for what he lacks. Though, I think Erik would disagree."

"You mean his deformity?" she asked bluntly.

Surprised that she mentioned it in such casual conversation, Andrea continued the discussion to ascertain her true feelings. "He told me you saw him."

Désirée pulled her eyes away and fiddled with the box sitting on her lap. "Yes," she replied, her voice barely audible. "We had a bit of tiff over my fragrance and the meaning of lilac. He accused me of having emotions for him, and then pulled off his mask and hairpiece to discourage me, I believe." She slowly lifted her gaze to Andrea, who sat on the edge of her seat, waiting to hear what she really thought about Erik's appearance.

"I will admit, between the two of us, I found it difficult to gaze upon his face. However, I have seen worse in other humans; much worse. It is only one side of his face too, not his whole body."

"True, but it has scarred him deeply, Désirée. You are aware of the trauma and pain his deformity causes him, correct?"

Her eyes lifted and gazed directly into Andrea's with such certainty it caught her off guard. "Yes, of course, I am aware. That is why I did not react with horror. I've seen other horrors in my life. There are many types of deformities, Madame, both physical and emotional."

"Yes, of course, you are quite right" she replied, surprised by her wise answer. However, it wasn't enough to satisfy Andrea's curiosity. "Tell me, Désirée, about your family. You mentioned you were alone. Is there no one else?"

"No," she replied quickly, shaking her head.

"You said your family came here from France during Napoleon's occupation. Are they all dead and you have no family remaining in France?" Andrea worried she was pressing too hard for information on her little fishing expedition for Erik. "Forgive me," she continued, in an attempt to smooth over her actions. "I don't wish to pry."

"Madame," she replied, sitting up taller in her seat. "If my tutor wishes to know more about me, he may ask me directly."

Andrea sighed over the young woman's insightful observation that she was indeed snooping. "Yes, of course, but he rarely speaks to anyone on a personal level."

"I assure you," Désirée added, "I have tried to open up to him, but he has made it quite clear that we are merely together for violin lessons and nothing more."

Andrea watched her hand clutch the box tightly, as if it pained her to admit he acted as if he had no interest. Before she could respond, Désirée asked a most surprising question in return.

"Does he wish more of me?"

"More?" Andrea asked, clearing her throat of the lump that had formed. "I'm sorry, but I'm not privy to Erik's private intentions or emotions." *Liar,* she thought to herself. "I think perhaps he is somewhat curious about you. However, he doesn't wish to be forward while in your presence by asking you personal questions about your life that you may not wish to discuss."

In a surprise move, Désirée rose to her feet. She placed the box of perfume in her apron pocket. "I must return to my duties. I have at least 50 more arm seats to dust in the pit and then I must do the boxes. The day is nearly over. The doors will open in a few hours for the show."

Andrea stood as well. "Yes, of course, Désirée. Also, might I add, if I haven't said so before, you are doing a fine job with your duties here. We are all very pleased."

Désirée pulled her eyes away and moved over to the next seat with her dust rag. Andrea sensed the discussion had ended, but offered her an open door.

"Please, Désirée, if you ever wish to speak of any matter, I want you to know that you are more than welcome to come to me. Erik can be . . . " She hesitated, trying not to sound cruel in her description. "Well, Erik can be moody and difficult to understand. I'm here if you need me."

Andrea left Désirée's side. It was obvious she had been hastily shut out by refusing to speak any further. She found it troubling, but hoped she would take her offer seriously.

As she walked out of the auditorium and back to her room, the nagging unknown and frequent worry she felt for Erik returned. Something was not right, but Andrea could not put her finger on it. She headed for his quarters to report what she had learned, which was very little indeed.

Chapter 17

Richard called Darius to his office the next day to go over the matter of the lost set of keys. He found the situation most unsettling. There were an insane number of doors in the building, and Richard requested that Darius bring the architectural blueprints in his possession for safekeeping. He needed to go over the plans, write down the exact locations of each door, and arrange for the expedient change of locks.

The cost associated was daunting, but a necessary task. Richard made sure that each night Darius walked the halls. In addition, he placed more crewmembers on watch to assist. They had no idea who could be trusted, which posed a problem. If the keys were stolen and not merely misplaced by an absent-minded Darius, then it was probably an in-house job. The perpetrator could be in their midst. It was troublesome indeed.

On top of the missing key quandary, Richard kept his own secret of sorts buried underneath the piles of correspondence on his desk. It was still too soon, in his mind, to worry Erik over the matter, but there was no indication the current crisis would end anytime soon. Within the last week, written threats had arrived on a daily basis via mail correspondence.

At first, Richard disregarded the first letter as a mere prank, but then with regularity, the postmarked letters arrived with no return address. The handwriting appeared legible, and the first letter was addressed to the Royal Opera House. Then correspondence arrived addressed directly to Erik Dante. Richard took the risk of opening it to read the contents, believing it was another threat.

To his horror, they spoke of death, fire, and retribution. He should have told Erik, but as Darius did, he hid the fact. Richard just did not want to experience the tirade that would no doubt ensue when the man heard the latest news. He was deathly afraid of Erik's temper. His recent loss of control with Darius only solidified the fact he was still capable of the unthinkable when pushed far enough over the edge.

It was time to go to the police with the news of the missing keys and turn over the string of handwritten threats. They would start an investigation. The letters were simple, direct, and carried no clues regarding authorship. Perhaps they would be able to trace something from the parchment or handwriting. All he knew is that he would feel better with a police involved.

A knock came at the door, and Richard called out. "Darius, come in." He motioned to a chair in front of the desk. "Close the door and have a seat."

The man did as instructed and sat down, fidgeting with his hands. Richard's eyes fell upon Darius' open-collared shirt and saw dark marks on his collarbone.

"My God, man, are those bruises from Erik?"

"Yes," he replied, rubbing the base of his neck with his hand. "Had you not intervened, I think he would have dug his nails into my flesh."

"Well, I can't condone Erik's behavior. I'm sorry you had to endure his wrath, but you must admit you were derelict in your duties. How in the world did you misplace the second set of keys?"

"I don't know." His voice was laced with defensiveness. "I kept them in a drawer in my work room, and I went to check on them and found them missing."

"Are you sure you put them there? Perhaps they are in another drawer. Did you look everywhere to make sure you're not mistaken in your memory of placement?"

"Oh, yes. I knew the Master would be angry, so I emptied all the drawers. No keys."

"Well, it's indeed a problem, Darius. It troubles me deeply for a variety of reasons. You should have been more careful."

Darius shook his head in acknowledgement and lowered his gaze to the floor in shame.

"I'll need to go over the architectural plans that Erik gave you for safekeeping. They will indicate where all the doorways in the building are located. We need to have every lock changed and two more sets of keys made. When finished, we're locking the keys up for safekeeping."

Richard stood from his desk chair. "Please go and get the plans and bring them to me," he requested, expecting Darius to comply. However, to his surprise the man sat motionless. The blood drained from his face leaving a pale ashen color, quite unusual for his dark complexion. For a moment, he thought Darius had stopped breathing entirely. He went up to his side and laid his hand on his shoulder.

"Good Lord, man, are you all right?"

Darius slowly lifted his eyes until they met Richard's and then confessed his sin. "I'm afraid they are missing too."

"What!" screamed Richard in horror. "You cannot be serious!"

"I . . . I . . . " Darius stammered nervously. "Someone took the plans too!" He quickly lifted both hands and grabbed Richard. Falling to his knees, he pleaded. "Don't tell the Master. Please, Monsieur Mercier, he will strangle my neck for sure. I just know it!"

"If I don't strangle you first," he growled. Richard unleashed his own temper and grabbed Darius by his collar, yanking him to his feet until he stood upright. Both his hands landed on his shoulders, where Erik's had been the day before, grabbing him hard and giving him a shake. "Have you looked everywhere or have you just misplaced them through total incompetence?"

"I have looked!" he squealed like a pig being dragged to the slaughter. "I looked everywhere. I did! I did! I kept them rolled up and placed inside a closet, but they are gone! Just like the keys!"

Richard was beside himself. The plans told every secret of the opera house. Erik had carefully drawn each architectural change, every new corridor, every secret entrance and exit to his private domain behind the walls. Now they were in the hands of some crazed lunatic no doubt. Even he did not feel safe any longer.

Who would steal from underneath their very noses? It had to be someone on the inside; someone privy to everything going on. An unhappy worker perhaps? Was it the same employees accused of the first fire? Had the disgruntled tenor returned?

Richard released his grip. "He'll have to be told," he groaned in resignation. "Your Master's safety and life are at stake." He looked at Darius, narrowing his eyes. "You do realize now how vulnerable we all are? None of us are safe, and the private entrances that lead to Erik have been exposed. Whoever is doing this has evil motives. I can feel it in my bones."

Spurred by his own fears, he grabbed Darius by the collar and escorted him down the hallway to Erik's private quarters.

"Oh, please," Darius begged. "He will kill me."

"Stand up like a man!" Richard yelled. "He will not kill you, but you will no doubt suffer his wrath for your stupidity."

Darius stumbled the entire way struggling against his pull. They entered through the locked corridor and down to the panel that led to Erik's quarters. Richard's hand felt along the wall for the mechanism, and pushed it until he heard the latch unclick. He would not ask or beg for entrance. The matter at hand was too serious.

The panel slid back, and Richard stepped inside, pushing Darius by his collar through the door. He shoved the servant to the ground, and Erik postured defensively over the intrusion.

"Before he says a word, Erik, I want your word you will not kill him." His knuckles had turned white from his clenched hand on Darius' shirt. "Give me your word!" he insisted, as he lowered his eyes to Darius on his knees, holding his hands up praying for mercy.

Erik eyed Richard and then he looked at Darius. His nostrils flared in anger at the cowering man begging for his life. Richard watched as Erik's eyes changed into blackness. He looked like a tiger ready to pounce upon his prey.

"Promise me, Erik." Richard pressed for a reply, hoping the situation would not turn into a physical altercation between the two of them. If Erik tried to kill Darius, Richard would fight for his life, but knew that in the process he could lose his own by a quick snap of his neck from the skilled executioner.

Erik prowled over to the side of the two men. He circled them briefly and then hissed out a response between clenched teeth. "All right, I won't kill him. Tell me what the incompetent fool has done now."

Richard took his word at face value and pulled Darius to his feet, who fought the entire way. "Stand up, damn it, and tell him what you told me."

Darius' eyes bounced between the two men, looking convincingly as if it were his last confession before death. "The plans, Master, the architectural drawings for the Royal Opera House are gone. They were stolen with the keys."

Erik lifted his hand in the air to backhand Darius in the jaw. Richard quickly reacted and stopped it dead before the blow came across Darius' face. Erik's eyes flashed angrily in response, and for a brief moment, Richard wrestled Erik's wrist.

"You promised you wouldn't hurt him," he protested in defense.

Erik relented and pulled away seething in anger. "You Goddamn fool! I should kill you anyway!"

Richard pulled Darius up by the collar and pushed him toward the door. "Get out now, so I can talk to him in private. While you're at it, go count every damn door in this entire structure and don't come back until I see it written down on paper where they are located!"

Darius nodded his head up and down in agreement and fled from their presence. Richard turned around and looked at Erik. It was still there, the desire to kill. Richard knew if he did not speak wisely in the next few minutes, he might never leave the room alive. Erik was unstable, and this only proved to feed his belief even further that he was still capable of the unthinkable.

"We will deal with it, Erik. We'll find a way to get around these problems."

"And how do you suppose that will happen?" he spat in return. "We are all sitting ducks. The keys and the architectural plans with every secret passageway carefully designed by my hand are in the possession of another! I'm no safer than if I slept on the doorstep at night shrouded only in my cloak."

Richard watched Erik carefully as he paced the room. After a few minutes, his anger subsided, his breathing slowed, and his facial expression relaxed. It seemed the appropriate time to tell him the remainder of the news, now that he was in a calmer state of mind.

"There is something else you need to know." Richard hesitated while waiting for Erik's response.

"What now?"

"There have been threats arriving in the mail addressed to the Royal Opera House and to you personally. They come in short letters, no return address, of course, with threats of death and fire."

"Why haven't you told me this before?" Erik demanded coldly, taking a few steps toward Richard.

"Because of your actions, that is why! My God, Erik, your temper at times is enough to scare the daylights out of me. You bring me here from Italy and give me responsibility for handling the day-to-day affairs. I walk constantly in fear I'm going to be another Joseph Buquet found some day hanging at the end of a rope." He paused for a moment, his voice shaking in blunt honesty. "You scare the hell out of me!"

The confession seemed to soften Erik slightly, as he retreated from his approach in Richard's direction. "I didn't kill Buquet, by the way," he answered nonchalantly. "Not that anyone would believe me. The man was an accident waiting to happen."

"Regardless," Richard commented, struggling to believe his words. "We have bigger matters to handle right now. What do you suggest we do?"

"The locks," Erik decided. "We'll need to change out all the locks as soon as possible. As far as the plans, if they were stolen by someone in-house, we are at their mercy every waking hour."

"Yes, I've thought the same," Richard confessed, sighing in worry at the possibilities. "I'm turning over the threats to the police as soon as possible, asking them to start an investigation."

"Of course," Erik responded, acting as if he had barely heard Richard's comment. "Do what you think is best."

Erik's demeanor quickly changed. It caught Richard off guard, as he watched Erik walk over to his violin and trail the edges of the instrument with his index finger. He appeared deep in thought and suddenly removed from the situation.

"You haven't told Andrea any of this, have you?" he asked.

"No, of course not. You know how she worries."

"I'm quite aware," he responded. "She doesn't need to know, but she'll wonder what's up with the locks. However, the matter of the missing plans and various threats I want left secret at all costs."

"Of course," Richard agreed, approaching Erik by a few feet. "I'm sorry about all this."

Erik turned toward Richard with a distraught face. "I thought," he started, clearly trying to control his emotions, "that coming to Malta would finally bring peace to my life. I was away from Paris, from the past, from the hurt there. I traveled thousands of miles and poured my soul into this endeavor." Turning back to his violin, he picked it up and held it in his hand. "However, it seems as if hell and the Devil follow me no matter where I walk upon this Earth, Richard. I've been unable to flee from the curses of my life once again."

"We'll get past this," Richard told him, trying to offer some encouragement. "Nothing has happened yet and it may not. It could just be all talk and pranks meant to unnerve the new owner. We will discover who is behind this. I feel sure of it."

Richard felt he was offering empty promises. The atmosphere of Erik's quarters turned into one of profound sadness. He felt terrible for Erik. The man was clearly distressed and rightfully so.

"I'll leave you now."

Richard retreated for the door and left Erik standing alone holding his violin, wondering what thoughts he pondered in the darkness of his soul. He could never understand Erik—the Ghost that had haunted and tormented his own life for so many years. It seemed as if now someone was doing the same to Erik by tormenting and haunting him in return. Perhaps it was true that one reaps what one sows in life. Whatever the reason behind Erik's current woes, Richard sympathized over his dilemma.

Chapter 18

Erik did not attend the evening performance. He wasn't in the mood to do anything after the news he had received. However, he was looking forward to his scheduled tutoring with Désirée. He sent instructions for her to meet him on stage that evening, rather than in the orchestra pit, planning to use the acoustics of the auditorium to pick up deeper tones during practice.

She arrived escorted by Richard, who quickly left. Erik noted his obvious troubled demeanor. As for himself, he hid his emotions in front of his student. It was easy with a half-masked face to feign anything, or so he thought.

As soon as Désirée arrived, his nostrils inhaled the scent of roses within a few feet of where she stood. He couldn't help but curl a smile. She noticed his reaction and quickly responded.

"I received your gift."

Désirée drew closer to him than necessary, but Erik allowed her the action without complaint. He made a mental note to thank Andrea the next time he saw her for choosing a decent fragrance that he found extremely pleasurable.

"Thank you, Erik. It was a kind gesture."

"You're welcome."

He cleared his throat. A sense of feeling returned, as he remembered that he held his violin in one hand and a bow in the other. For a moment, he lost himself in her blue eyes glimmering from the illumination of the gas stage lights.

"Have you studied the finger placement for the notes?" he asked, hoping her enthusiasm remained.

"Yes, I have. Can I show you?"

"Of course, the instrument is now in your hands." Erik held out the violin, waited for Désirée to take it, and then stepped back to put distance between them. His eyes crawled lazily from the top of her golden locks down to her petite feet, taking in every inch of the modest dress hiding the curves of her body.

"And which do you find more appealing, sir, the placement of my fingers or the size of my waist?"

Her question embarrassed him. Was it that obvious he was enjoying the view? He shook his head in disgust over his own actions. "I apologize," he mumbled under his breath over his brash behavior. "Show me what you have learned."

"Well, you can't see from over there," she pointed out, enticing him to draw closer.

Erik relented and drew near to her hand wrapped around the stem. Her delicate fingers touched each space, as her voice perfectly recited the placement of each note. She impressed him another time over her ability to learn quickly, so he decided to take a bold step. Hopefully, it wouldn't damage his hearing.

"Take the bow," he instructed. She took it from his hand. "Now place it above the strings and give me a C."

Désirée did her best, but as Erik suspected, it was a total disaster. Horrible screeching filled the auditorium and echoed back in his ears. She looked mortified, and he felt violated.

"Well, this is going to take some doing," he mused, shaking his head. For the next half hour, he gave instructions to Désirée. He showed her how to glide the bow across the string to produce a pleasing sound, but the screeching continued. Erik suppressed every ounce of impatience for her sake. Finally, it took its toll on her too.

"Oh, I must be a fool to think I can learn this!"

A childish stomp of her foot told Erik she was done for the evening. Taking the violin and bow from her hand, he assured her. "Rome wasn't built in a day; neither is the way of a violinist learned in a few short lessons. It could take years to become proficient."

"Years?" she repeated, stepping uncomfortably close to his body. "I don't have years."

"Well, perhaps you'd like to learn another instrument," he offered.

She shook her head no. A pout formed on her lower lip. Erik thought briefly and then asked the absurd. "What about singing? Can you carry a tune?" At that point, he thought any tune would be better than what he had been tortured with throughout the lesson. "Tell me what you know. Do you have a favorite song, perhaps, an operatic melody that you've always liked?"

Désirée shook her head. "No, Erik. It is only the violin I wish to learn."

He did not know what to say. It was still too early in their instruction to determine one way or the other if she truly possessed any musical talent. The fact that she was a quick learner encouraged him to continue with the painful lessons that lay ahead.

"Then the violin it will be. We will start scales soon, which will help. Don't be discouraged. I shall not abandon your endeavor, as long as you study and do your best." His last word barely left his lips before Désirée made her request.

"Play for me."

Her bright blue eyes pleaded, and Erik could not deny her. "Shall I give you my handkerchief before or after, Mademoiselle?" he said, bowing at his waist in jest. To his surprise, he watched as she slipped her fingers up her sleeve and pulled out a delicate lace handkerchief of her own.

"I came prepared," she announced smugly. Désirée threw her head up in the air, making him laugh, and then she waved her hankie in his direction.

"Very well, then, why don't you take a seat in the audience this time, while I do the honors."

He escorted her to the side of the stage and helped her down the stairs. She sat in the front row and looked up at him in adoration. Erik found it difficult to suppress the emotion welling inside his heart, as he gazed into her anxious eyes. She longed to hear his gift, and he could give her beauty.

"Close your eyes, Désirée," he spoke to her tenderly. Erik closed his and embraced the instrument. He had chosen a musical score earlier in the day, anticipating her request, and stood center stage, gliding his bow over the strings. His nimble fingers elicited from the instrument a melodious sound that surrounded his audience. The perfect acoustics picked up each tone filling the atmosphere with the sounds of his genius.

Erik had chosen a romantic violin piece that he composed a few days earlier. It was melodious, slow, sweeping, and unlike the terrible musical scores that he penned long ago in agony over Christine. He wrote the composition for Désirée, weaving his emotions into the music. He opened his eyes briefly while playing to see her own tightly shut, enjoying each note that cascaded and danced about her ears.

When he was through, he lowered the violin from his chin and looked upon her face. Her eyes lifted to him, and she questioned the intent behind the score.

"You wrote that for me, didn't you?"

Erik could not deny the fact. "Yes, I did. Though it seems it has not moved you as my previous scores, for I see no tears on your cheeks." He felt a tinge of disappointment over her reaction.

He watched Désirée lower her eyes. She stood from the seat and carefully took each step back up the stage returning to where he stood. Her blue pools sparkled with radiance and a glow lit her face.

"It moved me to tears in my heart, Erik. It was beautiful. Simply beautiful."

Before Erik knew what happened, he felt her warm lips upon his unmasked cheek. She kissed him and lingered there with her touch.

"Désirée," he whispered, anguishing over the feeling of her lips. "Please . . . don't."

She pulled away, her smile faded as if he had just stolen every ounce of joy from her soul.

"A mere thank you is enough," he muttered, straining for composure. "You should leave."

Désirée's eyes filled with sadness, and her voice spoke of hurt. "Yes, of course, Erik. Whatever you wish."

"Here, take the violin again, practice when you can." Erik hesitated before continuing. He had recently made a decision regarding Désirée. "I'm going to ask Andrea to take you out of the dormitories and place you in a private room. It's the least I can do."

"A private room?"

"Yes, there is one in particular not far from the main quarters. That way you'll be able to practice in privacy without the other workers bothering you."

"I would like that," she admitted.

He was glad she was pleased with his announcement. "Until tomorrow then."

"Until tomorrow."

Erik watched her retreat down the aisle and out the auditorium door. Once assured she had completely departed, he lost all composure and fell to his knees with a thud upon the wooden stage. The feeling of her warm lips upon his cheek still lingered. He lifted his hand and touched the side of his unmasked face where she had kissed his flesh out of her own volition. Did she realize who he was? Did she know he had never been kissed but once in his life?

His carefully woven defenses unraveled. Only one other kiss had had such a profound effect upon his life. It was Christine's, but she had given it out of surrender to save the life of another. It was not the kiss freely given by Désirée out of thankfulness, even if it were just upon one cheek.

The second her lips met his skin, his male urges rose. He wanted to pull her into his chest and claim her mouth with unbridled passion, the way he fantasized in the privacy of his thoughts. He wanted to act like a man! He was a man; a man with needs, desires, and longings like any other! Why had life denied him such pleasures?

Erik waited for an answer, but there were no answers to his cries. There never were. Always silence from heaven and hell. Erik staggered back to his feet struggling with his growing affection for Désirée. She was quickly scaling the protective barrier he had built around his heart. Would it be his undoing? Would it be his death? Only time would tell.

Chapter 19

Andrea opened the door to the single room. "Here are your new quarters, Désirée," she told her, motioning for her to enter and make herself at home. "Erik wished you to have something more private, so that you could practice without being bothered. We'll have your things moved in here as soon as possible."

She watched as Désirée looked curiously around the room. It was modest to say the least, but private as Erik had requested. "There is one other thing," she added, "that I've been asked to tell you."

"He thinks I'll never learn to play the violin very well, doesn't he?" she declared with certainty.

"Oh, no, dear, nothing like that." Andrea reached out her hand and touched Désirée reassuringly. "I promise you he is committed to your studies, even if it will take some time." Erik told Andrea he thought it would take an eternity, but she wasn't about to tell her those words lest she discourage the poor girl.

"What I've been asked to tell you is that Erik wishes for your duties here at the opera house to be scaled back to part-time."

"But I need the money," she protested with concern.

"Well, your wages shall stay the same and your duties will change as well."

"What do you mean my duties?"

Andrea inhaled a nervous breath. She hoped that Erik was not making a mistake, but she would do as instructed.

"He does not wish you to do menial housekeeping, such as cleaning the auditorium and the boxes. He'd like to give you access to our private quarters that will include my own set of rooms, Monsieur Mercier's quarters, and our dining area. You are to be our housekeeper instead."

"And his too?" she asked, her voice rising in hope.

"His?" Andrea shuddered over the thought, raising her brow over her bold suggestion. "I'm afraid *his*, my dear, are never touched by anyone. He prefers utmost privacy in all matters, including his own quarters. I've rarely been there myself."

"May I ask where they are?" she pressed, stepping closer. The move caught Andrea off guard.

"No, you may not!" she retorted in anger. Andrea eyed her from top to bottom. "I cannot disclose such a thing. Erik will not have it! As I said, he prefers privacy."

Taken back by the young lady's insistence on knowing where Erik's private quarters were located, Andrea became defensive. She suddenly felt like a bear protecting her cubs, but did not know why.

As she looked at the beautiful young girl, she discovered the source of her irritation. What would Erik do if they were both alone in his quarters, behind closed doors? Why, he might do the unthinkable! The man was starving for affection and love. If she gave him a hint of impropriety, he might take liberties. The thought sent shivers up her spine. There was no telling where temptation could push him if given enough encouragement.

"I know that you are fascinated with the man." Andrea paused, trying to choose the correct word to describe Désirée's possible affections. "But you must not encourage him in any way, Désirée, or play with his feelings. His heart has been broken into a thousand pieces before. I am quite certain that I will be very unhappy should another woman do the same thing to him!" Andrea was surprised her voice rose to such a loud level. Désirée's eyes grew wide in response.

"Madame, I have no intentions of hurting Monsieur Dante," she responded in defense. "I admire him, yes, but I do not think of anything of the kind beyond that, I assure you."

Andrea wanted to believe her, but the twinkle in her radiant blue eyes spoke otherwise. The woman was definitely enthralled with a man her senior, gushing over the possibilities of winning his heart. She could easily see what Erik saw in her beauty. Her eyes, which Erik mentioned, were mesmerizing. *Mesmerizing indeed*, she thought to herself in a huff. She wanted to discover Désirée's motives.

"Well, I've said my piece and conveyed the instructions. He wishes you to join him this evening on stage one hour after tonight's performance."

"I look forward to it," she replied, with a shade of arrogance.

Andrea reached out and handed her two keys. "Here is the key to your room. I've been instructed to tell you to lock it when you are not inside and to lock yourself inside at night when you return. Do you understand?"

Désirée reached out, took the keys, and eyed them closely, a concerned look spread across her face.

"It's just a precaution," Andrea added. "He wishes for you to be safe, that is all."

"And the other key on the ring, what is that for?"

"That is the key that leads to our private rooms. They are located on the other side of the door at the end of the hallway by the office, which always remains locked. When you are ready to start your duties, let me know. I will show you the set of rooms that should be cleaned on a daily basis."

Andrea headed for the door. "I'd start practicing now," she advised her. "He'll be expecting even more proficiency from you this evening. You'll find he's unrelentingly strict when he tutors, and he can be a bit grumpy when he's not well pleased."

Would she heed her advice? Erik asked her to be a friend, but Andrea felt odd in the girl's presence. She tried to analyze her feelings. Was she suddenly jealous of someone taking Erik's affections or merely being protective? She did not know. Andrea gave her last glance to Désirée, who appeared distraught after her warning.

"I don't mean to be harsh," she added softly. "But I have known Erik for many years. I tend to be protective of him because of the pain he has suffered in life. I only wish him happiness in his endeavors, whether they are personal relationships or tutoring. Can you understand, Désirée?"

"Yes, of course, I can, Madame Giry," she replied, lowering her eyes to the keys in her hands. "I do not want to hurt him in any way. As I said, I've grown to admire him deeply."

"Very well then. I shall take your word for it."

Andrea closed the door behind leaving Désirée alone in her new quarters. She returned to Erik, who she had left in the office with Richard. When she entered, the two men appeared to be in a serious discussion looking over papers on Richard's desk. Upon seeing her arrival, Richard immediately shuffled the mound as if to hide something from her sight. His actions piqued her curiosity, of course, but she had come to report her meeting with Désirée to an anxious Erik instead.

"I've done as you requested," she reported, her voice trailing with a shade of bitterness. In an obvious attempt to try to be pleasant over the matter, she feigned a smile. "Your student has been shown her new quarters, given the keys, and asked to report to you after the performance." Andrea shifted her eyes like an eagle to the desk trying to see what papers Richard was hiding.

"Good!" Erik exclaimed, taking her arm and walking her back to the door in an obvious effort to shoo her away from their discussion. "I appreciate your help, Andrea, as always. Now if you'll excuse us, Richard and I have business to attend to."

Andrea released a puff of air in disgust. "As always, Erik, I get the point when I'm not wanted."

He flashed a warm smile her way, as he always did, to appease Andrea over her dismissal. "They are confidential matters you needn't worry your little head about. I'll see you later."

Before Andrea could protest, she found herself standing in the hallway. The door closed in her face, and a cold ominous feeling crawled up her spine. Something was wrong. Perhaps they were speaking of the changing of locks. She had noticed the locksmith running around in a frantic rush like a headless chicken. Of course, the lock that led to their private quarters was the first scheduled for changing and now a brand new key lay in Désirée's hand.

Yes, it was disturbing that Darius had misplaced the keys. However, Andrea could tell by the furrowed brows of Richard and Erik that there was more to the story than she was being told.

Intent on getting to the bottom of the matter, she flung around and stomped down the hallway to change into something more appealing for the evening. A slight enticement, a little feigned warmth, a dab of perfume, and she might be able to loosen the tongue of her former lover. Women had their ways, even at her age.

* * *

"You've said nothing to her?" Erik pressed.

"No, for God's sake, no, Erik. She'd be inconsolably worried should she know about the threats."

He slipped his hand over the papers he had shoved out of sight earlier. The latest one came in the morning's mail, and he handed it Erik.

"This arrived about an hour ago. It has the appearance of another, but I haven't opened it. I thought I would let you do the honors, if there are any in it."

An awkward silence ensued as the two men held their breath before reading the contents. Erik examined the envelope, flipping it between his fingers from front to back reading every line written by the pen and the seal upon the back.

"Interesting," he drawled. "Whoever it is mocks me with the seal of a skull. Have they all been like this?"

"Yes, I'm afraid so. At first, and I know this sounds ludicrous, I thought it was some type of practical joke on your part, but then after closer examination, I saw it was not exactly like the seal you once used."

"The handwriting doesn't look familiar to me at all," Erik noted, studying it closely.

"Nor to me either." Richard sighed, his brow wrinkled with concern.

Erik slipped his index finger underneath the lip of the envelope and broke the seal. Carefully, he pulled out the folded letter feeling a coldness unleash its contents. His hands hesitated while he examined the grade of parchment that appeared expensive, and then he flipped it open to read the message.

"It is another," he breathed heavily. The threat relayed its intent.

THE FIRES OF HELL AWAIT YOU, ERIK DANTE.
YOU SHALL NOT ESCAPE.

Erik swallowed hard. "Well," he observed with a slight jest to ease the tenseness, "direct and to the point." He handed it to Richard. "Not unlike the others."

Richard took the envelope and letter from Erik's hand and eyed the words. "Yes, penned by the same hand as the others. The writing is similar." He set the document down on the desk. "It looks as if they are veiled threats merely planned to intimidate you, Erik. Perhaps the disgruntled individual who burned it down the first time is upset that you dared to restore the opera house. You've apparently thwarted their intended destruction. It's probably all words."

"All words?" His brow raised in disagreement. "Are you forgetting the missing keys and architectural plans?" Erik took a few steps and shook his head. "No, my friend. The threat is real. Someone intends retribution, and it's directed toward me."

Erik placed the envelope and letter on Richard's desk. "What worries me the most," he continued, poking at the paper with his index finger, "is not that I shall burn in hell! I already expect that for my sins." He inhaled a breath, stifling the horrible thoughts that raged through his mind.

"What worries me the most is that my friends and those I care about may be in danger as well." Erik paused, reflecting on the past and then admitted in stark honesty what he knew to be true. "Madness sees no faces, Richard. It does not care if others are hurt."

He spoke with audible regret, as he remembered his obsession that had brought down the chandelier in Paris. There was no hesitation when he cut the cord holding its weight and freeing it to create the destruction below. Neither was there a thought in his mind of those that stood underneath the monstrosity of crystal orbs crashing about them, or their fate afterward. His mind had fixated on one thing—possessing Christine Daaé. Everyone else he damned, because they stood in his way.

"Whoever is sending these threats is focused upon my destruction. The others around me will be inconsequential casualties of the madness that drives them. Of this I'm sure." Whether Richard agreed with his assessment or not, it made no difference.

"We need to be careful, Richard. Turn this letter over to the police with the others. I don't know what, if anything, they can do. At least they can begin some type of investigation. Ask if they'll increase patrols outside the opera house during the night."

Erik heaved a sigh and walked toward the door. He held the door handle, and turned around to look at Richard before departing.

"It appears my life of peace shall not arrive until I suffer for my sins."

He left Richard alone to his duties and slipped back into his hidden quarters. A brooding darkness filled his mind. He dreaded the days ahead. The entire matter ate at him like a slow-acting poison.

Erik headed for a glass of cognac to settle his nerves. After he poured a stiff drink, he gulped it down so its effects would swiftly flow through his veins and bring an ounce of relief. Before it worked its magic, he lowered his head and his shoulders drooped in despair. There was nothing to do now but wait for the inevitable—his undoing and death.

Chapter 20

Richard was quite surprised to receive an invitation from Andrea to dine in her quarters. He wondered about the motivation behind her request, because up until this time, they had kept their relationship purely on working terms. It was hard to believe that she suddenly possessed a change of heart after all these years.

He prepared by dressing in a casual dark brown waistcoat, matching trousers, and white shirt. In addition to actually spending the time to trim his mustache and his brushy eyebrows, he slicked his hair back with the new hair tonic he had purchased a few days ago, not quite sure whether he liked the new look. Nevertheless, dinner with a lady, even one who had given him the cold shoulder for some time, was worth spending a bit more attention on his appearance.

Though Richard was fifty-two, he was still handsome. His salt and pepper hair gave him an air of maturity, and he was well aware of his strong charismatic presence in the business world.

As far as women were concerned, many had tried to gain his attention, but he found them boring. He missed Andrea terribly. Since the day he left the Garnier and relocated to Venice, he finally admitted to himself she was his only love. She was a feisty woman, but one of strong character that he admired. For years, she had spent serving the Ghost for a mere pittance in return. Richard believed she deserved far better and hoped one day to give her the finer things in life.

He had kept his distance from her since his return, trying not to pressure her into a relationship. They each had had their hands full with the reconstruction, but now the opportunity had arrived to pursue her once again. He wanted to give her the world. While he stood before her modest two-room apartment and rapped his knuckles upon the wooden door, he sincerely wondered if tonight he should make his move.

To his surprise, the door flung open revealing a stunning Andrea, who definitely had more on her mind than mere dinner! He could barely hold back his rather gregarious smile seeing she had gone to extremes in her dress for their engagement together.

"You look lovely tonight," he announced, playing the part of the gentleman, bowing at the waist. He lifted her petite hand and brought it to his lips. "Enchante, Mademoiselle," he added, giving her a wink and a sexy look to elicit a reaction.

"Richard," she giggled, with a *tsk*, "You are a rogue!" He smiled in return as they both played their little game of cat and mouse. As far as Richard was concerned, eyeing her low bodice, perfumed body, and gorgeously arrayed hair, the woman wanted something in return. She was gold digging, as she had in the past, using her wiles to get her way with him.

"You love it when I tease you, Andrea," he noted, entering her room and closing the door behind him. Another surprise awaited with a small table covered in a linen tablecloth, adorned with two tall, lit candles that could burn well into morning, and a plate of food already waiting for his starving stomach.

"My, my," he commented, walking over to the table. "What's the occasion?"

Andrea played her game, fluffing off his question as inconsequential. "Can't a woman invite an old friend to dinner?"

"Of course," he replied, not wishing to express his suspicion of her ulterior motives that she would soon reveal.

They sat down for dinner, and Richard made small talk with Andrea during the course of the meal. As usual, the conversation drifted toward their employer.

"Might I ask how you think things are going between the teacher and his student?" he asked with sincere curiosity.

Andrea's face turned sour. She laid down her fork on her plate, dabbed her lips with a napkin, and swallowed her last bite of food. The unrestrained reaction told Richard everything he wished to know.

"Then it's not going well," he concluded.

"Oh, I suppose the lessons are going well, but I have my concerns about the relationship." She hesitated, staring at her empty plate, as if to serve up the right portion of words as she continued. "I don't have a good feeling about Désirée," she admitted. "As you know, she's been given new duties to clean our quarters and immediately assumed she would be shown where Erik resides within the walls of the opera house. I thought it too pushy on her part. Of course, I immediately put an end to any fanciful thoughts of foolishness."

Richard's face turned pensive. "She probably wishes to see where he lives out of curiosity. He is a bit of a recluse, you must admit, and it must appear intriguing to a young woman such as herself. I wouldn't be surprised if she harbored some type of feeling for Erik. He's a man of mystery who teachers her to play the violin and disappears into the walls at night."

"Perhaps," Andrea replied, shrugging her shoulders. She picked up two cubes of sugar and dropped them into her teacup, swirling them around aimlessly. Richard sensed the conversation was about to change in the direction Andrea had intended.

"So what was it you were trying to hide on your desk today when I came into the office and interrupted you and Erik?"

Her eyes latched on to Richard's, giving him the *look*. He shook his head, surprised at how quickly during dinner she revealed her motives.

"Is that the reason I'm here?" he asked, thoroughly disappointed. He looked at the little nose on her face that so expertly poked around where it didn't belong. "It was nothing. A business matter," he said, dismissing her inquiry.

He placed both his elbows on the table and clasped his hands in front of him. Richard leaned forward with a piercing gaze at the snoop across the table, who he absolutely adored. "Forget about it, Andrea. It was nothing."

"Ha!" she squealed. "You're a damn liar, and I know it."

Richard broke out in a nervous laughter. "Now, now, let's not get ugly. I was so enjoying our quiet time together. It reminded me of old times, Andrea, when you and I were in love. Do you remember?"

Her gaze narrowed, and Richard caught the sparkle in her eyes when they moistened with tears that threatened to reveal her heart. She did care, and without hesitation, he reached across the table and took her hand into his own. The warmth felt wonderful, and Richard wished desperately to return to that place they had once shared.

"Tell me, Andrea," he continued, barely able to release the thought from his throat for fear of her refusal. "Can we start again? I think you know that my feelings for you have not changed. You are and always will be the dearest woman in my life."

Andrea lowered her eyes from his and focused on her hand resting in his palm. He stroked it tenderly, waiting for her reply. Could she sense his love seeping from every pore? His heart beat hard against his rib cage in anticipation. The seconds dragged by painfully, as he waited for her to speak.

"Richard," she answered, her voice barely a whisper.

Her hesitancy worried him, until she reached across the table with her other hand and grasped his own.

"I would like to rekindle what we once had if you'll have me."

He released her hand, pushed back his chair, stood to his feet, and gathered her into his arms in one swoop. "My God, Andrea, at last." His lips claimed hers ardently making up for the years they had been apart. The remainder of the evening they revived their hidden passions. Richard would not tell what he was hiding upon his desktop, but he had no qualms about shouting his love from the rooftop for the entire city of Valletta to hear.

※　※　※

Erik's emotions were on edge as he waited for Désirée to arrive after the performance. He brought a chair and music stand from the orchestra pit and placed it center stage. Tonight would be another session of endurance, but at least he would be in her presence. After all the stress of the past few days, the lessons this evening were a welcome oasis of rest.

Désirée arrived promptly, violin in hand. Erik felt like an inadequate fool. He was nurturing a crush on the petite French mademoiselle, who he knew very little about. However, when he was in her presence, he was at peace and felt alive with purpose.

As soon as Désirée approached, the scent of roses greeted his nostrils. He smiled that she cared enough to wear the fragrance when they were together. When she approached the setup on stage, she appeared confused. Erik began to play his little game for an evening of entertainment.

"On the music stand," he announced, pointing at the score, "you will find measures of scales." He pulled out the chair. "Sit."

The one-word command was obeyed, and Erik turned and headed for the stairs.

"Where are you going," she cried after him, her face scrunched in confusion.

"To my seat in the audience," he yelled over his shoulder. He proceeded to the first row and sat down facing middle stage. Erik lounged in a relaxed position, then pointed his index finger, wiggling it in the direction of the music stand. "Play the scales."

"While you sit there and watch?" She protested loudly.

"Yes, that is what I wish. Do you have a problem with that arrangement, Mademoiselle, or should we just call it an evening?" He yawned, bringing his hand up to his mouth acting tired. He wickedly teased her, while enjoying his little game. "I'd frankly prefer to retire early for I haven't had much sleep lately."

"I'll do terrible with you sitting there looking at me!"

Erik refused to relent and watched in amusement. "Well, are you going to play or not?"

"Your ears will be sorry," she warned.

He had no doubt he would be tortured very soon. Désirée squinted at the sheet music. Erik watched as she brought the bow to the strings and her fingers attempted to find the correct notes. The first few screeches caused him to cringe. The acoustics in the auditorium made it even worse, amplifying the sound. *God, this is painful,* he thought to himself. *The things I do for amusement.*

After a few torturous measures, Erik had heard enough. "No, no, no, Désirée!" He jumped from his seat, stomped up the stairs, and came around behind her body. He lifted her right elbow slightly, tilted her head to a more secure hold of the violin, and adjusted her hand. "Caress it, don't strangle it!"

He wanted to teach her, but as his flesh touched her body, a rush of desire flowed through his veins. Erik lingered longer than necessary to inhale the fragrance that bathed her body and then reluctantly returned to his seat in the front row.

"Again," he demanded.

The bow slid back and forth trying to make music. With each pass, she came closer to making a recognizable sound. After ten minutes, she lowered the violin complaining.

"I'm tired. Can I rest?"

"No." He glared at her. "Practice."

Désirée's eyes shot him a look of irritation in return, and he heard her heave a sigh of frustration. He merely sat stubbornly listening to each note of the scale. He wished to pound them into her memory until she dreamed about them at night. After another half hour, he saw her face express pain, but she made no complaints of fatigue. Désirée was trying to please him, and he admired her tenacity.

"That's enough," he finally told her, not wishing her to come to a point of hating the instrument. She needed to love it, as he loved the violin. Otherwise, it would never bring forth a tune worth enjoying.

"Madame Giry said you were a strict teacher." Désirée sighed in utter exhaustion.

"She did?" Erik stood to his feet and returned to the stage to stand in front of his pupil. "Madame Giry thinks she knows me," he muttered. "But she doesn't entirely, I assure you."

Erik looked at her beautiful face. He wanted to tell her how much he admired her beauty, golden hair, and enticing blue eyes. His hand flexed and itched to reach out and touch her porcelain cheeks and allow his cold fingertips to feel the warmth of her flesh. He pulled his eyes away, cleared his throat, and spoke.

"You should return to your quarters now, Désirée." He hesitated before giving her his approval, but felt she needed the encouragement. "I must admit you are improving, and I am very pleased with your progress." She looked exhausted, but appeared unwilling to leave.

"Thank you for the new quarters and duties," she told him. "It was nice of you to think of me in that way."

In what way? He wondered if she began to suspect his growing affections. "You are welcome." Erik turned around, wishing he could say more, but feared to cross the line of sharing intimate thoughts. "You should go, it's late."

"Of course," she answered, in a tone of sadness.

Erik sensed her disappointment. Désirée turned to leave, but Erik grabbed her arm softly to express one more thing. "There will be no lessons tomorrow evening."

"Why not?"

"I have private matters to attend to," he replied coolly.

"All right."

Désirée made no complaint, which surprised him somewhat. She departed, and Erik dimmed the lights in the auditorium while she returned to her room. His request to move her accommodations satisfied his sneaky intentions. Unbeknown to everyone, including Richard and Andrea, her room abutted against his private quarters and contained a secret panel. When correctly engaged, a mechanism slid the panel back and opened an entrance directly into Erik's parlor. He knew when he designed it years ago that one day it would prove useful.

Though Désirée had occupied the room recently, he had no reason to enter it and fully intended on giving her privacy. There was no reason to tell her or anyone else of the unseen door. As far as he was concerned, some secrets should remain unrevealed and this was one of them.

Her nearness on the other side of the wall gave Erik both comfort and control. He needed to work through the countless emotions he struggled with daily regarding his affections for Désirée. The knowledge that she was merely a few feet away helped to feed his yearnings. He admitted to himself it bordered on a new obsession, but he couldn't help it. Erik enjoyed spending time fantasizing about her every move on the other side of the wall.

He smirked over his little secret and headed back to his quarters.

Chapter 21

Désirée was thankful she finally had an evening alone. Erik's announcement that there would be no lesson came at an opportune time. Her visit was long overdue, but each one needed to be carefully planned to avoid discovery. Since everyone was on edge because of the stolen keys, it became increasingly difficult to come and go as she pleased. New rules for live-in occupants were set that after the doors were locked at night, no one was to leave the opera house. If they did, returning inside would not be granted until the morning.

Since her life had become more restrictive, it called for drastic measures and a bit of ingenuity on her part to bend the rules to her advantage. Darius had chosen another dimwit to help him with security. Désirée used her wiles to bribe the man with a few extra pounds. He would wait at the door until midnight and let her back in after her evening visit.

Tonight she would sneak out at 10 p.m., arrive at her destination, and return without anyone see her come or go. She had taken enormous risks during her tenure as a housekeeper; a job she found most disgusting. However, it afforded her the opportunity to slip in and out of rooms that she would have never otherwise had access to.

Her crafty little missions of thefts and mystery rope cuttings had gone well and the perpetuator remained undiscovered. The recent good fortune of acquiring the key to the most important room in the entire opera house furthered her plans. She couldn't wait to share the happy news with her co-conspirator so they could discuss the days ahead.

Désirée donned her long navy blue cloak, pulled the hood over her curly blond hair, and wrapped her purse cord around her wrist. She quietly opened the door to her room and stuck her head out in the dimly lit hallway, looking to the left and right to make sure it was clear to proceed unseen. She tiptoed down the hall and made her way to the back stage door, where her accomplice stood waiting for her exit. She pressed the bills into his hand and fled outside, with the understanding she would return no later than midnight. He was to wait for her return.

She quickly fled down the street and took the smaller dark side avenues filled with endless steps to her destination. The night was dark and cloudy, without stars or the moon for light. Everything in her path appeared shrouded in chilling shadows. A low foggy mist crawled up the streets off the harbor, which did not help matters. It fueled the ominous feeling in her stomach she had struggled with all day.

The population of Valletta often retreated early in the evenings, spending time in their homes with family. Street traffic at that late hour was very little for the most part. Though she was a self-confident woman, she still was no fool. A female alone at night unescorted was never safe, no matter where she traversed in a dark city. Her heart pounded in her chest with each step she took, and her hands became clammy.

As she traversed the path to her destination, she thought back to her first encounter with Erik Dante. She remembered how frightened she had been afterwards. Her hands shook and her heart thumped wildly in her chest, missing beats. When she ran back to the dormitory, she thought she would faint dead away.

It was purely a chance meeting, but it solved the mystery of finding where Erik resided. Like a fool, she had dared to crawl down in the orchestra pit thinking no one would see her. The violin just begged her to pluck a string. When she fiddled with it, she hadn't expected his dark figure to jump down from above scaring the daylights out of her. He was tall, broad-shouldered, and his eyes bore through her soul like fire. He could have killed her immediately. Instead, she played coy and foolishly asked for violin lessons.

Her request was a ploy to get closer to him, but she really did want to be a skillful musician. Though Désirée possessed mixed motives, she couldn't pass up the opportunity to learn, even if it was a means to an end. She smiled, remembering how she had chewed every fingernail down to a nub in anticipation of her first lesson.

When Mercier left them alone and locked the doors, she was terrified and couldn't breathe. Her airway closed and her eyes bulged out of her head. Then his words came softly to her ears assuring her, *"I won't hurt you."* She was at his mercy, but something in his voice told her of his sincerity. As much as she could, she tried to relax in his presence, but her hands wouldn't stop shaking.

How stupid she had felt when he began to teach her. She listened as intently as possible, but the mere closeness of his body made it difficult to concentrate. Occasionally, she lifted her eyes, looked at his mask, and studied it with curiosity. She wondered what horror lay underneath that would no doubt cause her to faint dead upon seeing the frightful revelation.

After she had repeated the parts of the violin, and he instructed her how to hold the instrument, she tried not to flinch when his fingers grazed her skin. An overwhelming sensation of power flowed through her pores at the touch of his flesh and weakness flowed through her veins. She had never felt anything like it, and she struggled over emotions of hate and admiration swirling inside her heart.

To her surprise, her affections and admiration for the man she once knew as the Ghost had grown over time. It frightened her inwardly and threatened to destroy her future. He held a strange power over her heart when he played his violin. It spoke to her soul, melted her resolve, and left her hungering for more. She squelched the turmoil as she arrived at her destination. If she did not, her weakness would surely be discovered.

Désirée climbed the small stoop of six steps, and knocked on the painted red wooden door until it opened. She smiled at the resident who stood beyond the threshold, waiting patiently for her daughter's arrival.

"Hello, Mama," she announced, slipping inside. The door quickly closed behind her, and her mother walked to the window and pulled the curtains shut. Désirée looked around. Candles burned and embers danced in the fireplace.

"How's business? Told any good fortunes of late?" She smiled at Sybelle and the psychic blood flowing through her veins, none of which she herself possessed. Her mother wore her usual black garb, matching her raven hair and dark features that accentuated the entire look of mystery.

Sybelle gave a hearty laugh. "People are so damn gullible. They pay, I lie, they go. All have itchy ears to hear their wonderful fortunes. If I told them what I really saw, they would never come back! So I tell them what they want to hear."

She reached out and hugged her daughter, and then brushed a lock of her blond hair away from her face. "You have your father's features," she mused, as she leaned in and gave a few sniffs along her daughter's neckline. "What is that fragrance you're wearing?"

"Roses."

"I thought that was not your favorite."

"It's not, but it's his."

Her mother flashed a satisfied smile and then eyed her daughter. "How are you? Is it going well?"

Désirée sighed after her mother's embrace and flopped down on the settee in front of the fireplace. She untied her cloak and flipped it off her shoulders, no longer needing its warmth.

"Yes, I suppose it's going well . . . just like we planned. However, I had to pay my way out of the opera house tonight. I must be back by midnight because I bribed one of the workers to let me back in. There are all sorts of new rules about coming and going, because everyone is on edge."

"Well then, we won't take too long with our visit. Tea?" Sybelle poured a cup of tea from the pot and handed her a cup and saucer. She made herself comfortable in her own seat, and began to sip the brew.

"You look well. They're not working you to death, are they?"

"No," she replied, rather smug over her promotion. "I've been given half-days, new quarters, and new duties."

"Well, that's encouraging. The Ghost set that up for you?"

Désirée narrowed her eyes at her mother. "He has a name, you know."

"Oh, yes," she drawled, "Erik Dante. I wonder where he came up with *Dante*. Fits the devil."

"I don't know why, but I don't like calling him the Ghost." He possessed flesh and blood, but her mother wouldn't understand. She only saw him as the despicable Ghost of the past.

Sybelle sported a smug smile, and Désirée could see the plotting wheels turning in her mother's pretty head. "What's next," she asked out of curiosity, taking another sip of her tea.

"Have they replaced the locks?"

"Yes, just this week." Désirée opened her purse and pulled out the two keys. She dangled them in front of her mother until they jingled. "Look, I've been given a key to the inner sanctum."

"No!" Sybelle quickly set down her cup, reached out, and grabbed the keys from her daughter's hand. "How did this come about?"

"My new duties are to clean the quarters of Madame Giry, Richard Mercier, and their dining area, all located behind the forbidden territory."

"And the Ghost's?" She eyed the keys in her hands as if they were made of gold.

"I'm afraid not. At least we know it's down that corridor. We just need to find the mechanism to open the door."

Sybelle sported a wicked smile of glee and handed the keys back to her daughter. "Take very good care of them, my dear." She stood and walked over to a small desk, opened a drawer, and pulled out a large key ring. "Here, plant these back in Darius' room somewhere to further confuse them."

"God, Mother! The poor man is in enough trouble already," she protested, sighing over her newest orders.

"It's so much fun to play with them all. Don't you think?"

"I suppose," she concurred, taking the key ring. They would certainly rattle in her purse if she was not careful. She took out her handkerchief, laid it open on her lap, placed her two keys and the key ring in the center, and folded the cloth to secure them in one package. Désirée shoved them down to the bottom of her purse and pulled the cord tight to close the opening.

"Are you continuing with the letters, Mama?" she asked, wondering if the threats continued to arrive. "I'm not privy to that information, since no one has mentioned the matter to me."

"Oh, yes, regularly. They vary in words, but I wouldn't be surprised if they are eating away at the man daily. It has to worry him. You know it does. He's not that impenetrable."

"You are probably right. Everyone seems on edge— Madame Giry, the manager, and sometimes Erik appears to brood more often when I see him. I only see him when we meet for lessons. The other times, he hides from the staff, crew, cast, and me. I'm the only worker that knows the owner lives within the walls of the opera house. However, he swore me to secrecy or else!" She placed both her hands around her throat as if to strangle herself, and Sybelle laughed at her impersonation of the Ghost and her bulging eyes.

"Now that we have the plans, and we know where his suite is located, that's all that matters. I suppose we can return those too, but not yet. We just need the time to find that damn panel that releases the lock."

"It's very hard for me, Mother, to play around the walls with Richard and Andrea constantly walking up and down that hallway. They are very careful not to reveal its location. I asked, but was severely reprimanded by Madame Giry for being so nosey."

"Well, when the time comes, he'll either reveal it to you in a moment of weakness, or we'll find it on our own."

"That won't be for quite a while, will it?" Désirée asked, swallowing nervously over her mother's words. It all seemed so dangerous to pry into his private world.

"The sooner the bastard pays, the better, as far as I'm concerned."

Désirée stared at her mother's face as it grew icy cold, her eyes darkened with revenge. The bitterness ate at her mother more than at her own heart. She began to entertain doubts about the sense of their plans to dole out retribution for the Ghost's sins of the past. It had all happened so long ago in Paris. It felt more like a nightmare she had finally awakened from than a real memory of pain and suffering.

She walked a thin line between the two worlds and turmoil brewed over her loyalty to her mother and her emerging affections for Erik. If her mother ever suspected and knew of the doubts she entertained in private, there would be hell to pay at her hand. Désirée's eyes lowered to her purse, containing the keys, and her heart thought of Erik and his good qualities. Unfortunately, she was bound to her mother's will, entangled in a net of lies and evil intent, all because Sybelle Renard wished it that way.

As she thought of Erik, she saw her mother stand to her feet. She must have sensed her internal feelings, because the next she knew, her mother towered over her petite frame. Her eyes met the hatred, and Désirée shrunk underneath her gaze. The hand of the woman who had once raised her in gentleness now grabbed her chin and pulled it upright until her head tilted and their eyes met one another. Désirée tried desperately to suppress her feelings.

"Look at me!" she demanded. "You're not falling for that demon, are you? So help me, I'll . . . "

"No, no, no, Mother! For God's sake, how could I do such a thing? I hate him as much as you do! Haven't you seen me shed enough tears over what happened? My life will never be the same because of him!" Désirée wiggled from her mother's uncomfortable grasp on her chin and stood to her feet to face her accuser. "How could I love that monster?"

Sybelle's gaze bore into her soul, as if she were testing every breath she exhaled to be a truth or lie. Afterward, her demeanor softened when she heard what she needed to know and relented from the interrogation. Her mother returned to her seat, picked up her teacup, and began sipping the brew again, just as if nothing had transpired between the two of them.

"Good," she exhaled.

Désirée felt a chill run down her spine. Her mother's voice sounded like a snake ready to strike with fangs of deadly venom.

"How are the violin lessons progressing?"

Désirée sighed in relief, and sat back down, her body shaking. She rolled her eyes for humorous effect. "God awful! The man is a slave driver, and I doubt I'll ever learn that wretched instrument."

Her mother smiled. "Oh, I have something for you," she announced, standing up and leaving the room.

Désirée watched as she disappeared to her bedchamber, wondering what it could be. She returned with a small-capped glass vial containing clear liquid inside. Reaching out her hand, she gave it to her daughter.

"Here, you'll need this."

Désirée eyed the container. Not wishing to appear hesitant, she reached out, took it, and studied the contents. Her heart skipped a beat over the toxic potion in her hand.

"Is this . . . is this it?"

"Yes. The dosage is correct and will do the deed."

"Mother, I . . . "

"Now, now," she quickly reassured her daughter, "there is absolutely nothing to worry about. It's not enough to kill the man. Only enough to drug him so his surroundings become blurred and his strength incapacitated. We cannot do the deed with the Ghost fully conscious. You know damn well he's capable of strangling us both."

"I know, but it frightens me," she admitted. Her voice shook as she asked the question she feared. "When?"

"Not yet," her mother pondered. "He needs to fall in love with you first, and I hope you're working on that goal, by the way. If you need some tips, I'd be happy to help. He's already thinking seriously about you, as he showed up here a few nights ago."

Désirée clutched the bottle in the palm of her hand, her heart pounding so hard that she felt it throbbing in her throat.

"My God, Mother! What did he want? He came to see you?"

"Yes, I was surprised at his timing, however, not so much that he finally relented and came. Apparently, his fortune is eating away at him already, doing the job that I intended. From what I gather, he's enthralled and intrigued with you, my dear, but you need to encourage him a bit more so he'll take the next step."

Désirée released her grip on the bottle, fearful that it might shatter in her hand. Quickly, she opened her purse string, placed it carefully in the bottom alongside the keys, and then tightened the cord once more. Slowly, she lifted her eyes to her mother, who appeared indifferent and cold over what lay ahead.

"Mother, I'm afraid," she admitted. "Why don't we just leave and forget all this?" As soon as the words left Désirée's lips, she knew it was the wrong thing to say.

"Leave!" she screeched. "Never!"

Her mother stood to her feet, walked over to her daughter, and slapped her hard across the face. Désirée reeled from the blow.

"Don't you ever suggest it again. After all that I've suffered with you! I will not allow him to go unpunished for his deeds!"

Désirée's hand came to her burning cheek and tears threatened to pour in torrents. It was not the first time her mother had reprimanded her with a hard slap across the face. As she gazed back into the icy evil intent that radiated from her eyes, Désirée knew there would be no turning back. Her course was set in stone, and if she did not go alongside her mother's pursuit of revenge, she would take it without her help.

It was true. Her mother had sacrificed everything for her during the past years of suffering. As she remembered her torment of the past, Désirée felt ashamed. Her suggestion showed disrespect on her part. What mother wouldn't wish to protect her daughter? What mother wouldn't wish to hurt the one that had hurt her child? A sad remorse filled her heart for suggesting otherwise.

"You'll do as I say," her mother insisted, softening her voice.

"Yes, Mama, I will," she replied, sounding like a repentant child. "Forgive me." The hesitant obedient words slipped from her lips. The memories of her past flooded back like rivers of pain, and she asked the question that plagued her heart.

"Mama, have you heard from him?"

Her mother pulled her eyes away from her daughter and sighed. "No, nothing. I wrote and told him when we moved to Malta, begging him to reconsider, but . . . " Her voice trailed off, and she shook her head. Désirée knew the answer.

"Do you want me to take the architectural plans back with me tonight?" she asked, changing the subject.

"No, not yet." Her mother pondered momentarily. "Where is your new room, by the way?"

"I can show you on the drawings, if you wish."

Her mother stood and retrieved the plans from her bedchamber and returned. Carefully, she rolled the architectural drawings out on the dining room table.

"Come here and show me," she asked intrigued.

Désirée rose and stood by her mother, flipping through the multiple pages until she found the area of the living quarters. She traced her finger alongside the inner sanctum, past the locked door, and stopped a few doors away. It's here." She pointed at the location leaning over the plans.

Her mother squinted and examined where her daughter indicated. "You mean here?"

"Yes, Mama."

"My God, child!" Sybelle screamed in delight.

"What is it?"

"Have you not noticed? Look where the back wall of your room abuts!"

Désirée bent down her head and looked closer at the drawing. On the other side of the wall was Erik's quarters. She brought her hand to her mouth and gasped. "Oh, my God! His parlor is on the other side of the wall."

Sybelle grabbed a candle and brought it over to the table to give more light. "Yes, and look here. That mark indicates a door."

"No, Mama, it can't be a door. There is nothing there but a wall, I assure you."

"Then it's a secret panel tripped by a mechanism, like the main entrance to his quarters."

Sybelle looked at Désirée with a delightful smirk. "In his heated desire, he's put you right next to him! The damn fool just sealed his fate!" Her mother roared with laughter. "Do you know what this means?"

"He can come into my room anytime he wants?" Her eyes widened with fear.

"No, my child! You can go into his room anytime you want! It's perfect! Absolutely perfect!"

"But I don't know how," she protested.

"Then you must learn. This is our way into his world. Not by the main entrance where you can be seen and heard, but through here."

"Mama, I'm afraid," she confessed again, grabbing her mother's arm.

"There is nothing to fear. Our plan will work perfectly. All we need to do is choose the date to bring his world crashing down upon his head." Sybelle patted her check with the palm of her hand. "It will all work just fine. Don't worry, child."

It's easy for her to say, thought Désirée. In her mother's mind, it was all a rational plan they would soon put into action.

"I should go now," she announced, feeling nauseated from trepidation. "It's late." She retrieved her cape, pulled it over her shoulders, as well as the hood over her hair. Gently, she reached out and embraced her mother.

"I love you, Mama, you know I do." She wrapped her arms around her mother's shoulders, feeling the cruel hatred that permeated from her veins. It sent shivers through her body. She was hell-bent on the Ghost's destruction, and there was no turning back.

Her mother abruptly pulled away and waved her hand in her daughter's direction. "Go now, before you are missed."

Torn over conflicting feelings for Erik and the obedience to her mother, Désirée bid her goodbye and slipped out the door into the darkness of the night. As she walked down the stoop, she lifted her face to the gas light above. The mist that had crawled up the street earlier, wafted through the city shrouding it in a thick fog. A chill ran up her spine as she quickly made her way back to the opera house to continue down the path of deception and revenge.

Chapter 22

Erik walked down the dark streets, slipping in and out of the shadows taking his usual nighttime prowl. It was late, as he found his feet carrying him on the pathway he had taken a few nights before. Perhaps it was curiosity or perhaps it was fate. Whatever the reason, he was about to pass by Sybelle Renard's establishment when the door opened.

Afraid of being seen, he slipped back into the shadows and stopped. His vision fixed upon the form that stepped down gracefully from the stairs, clothed in a dark blue cloak. When her face turned upward and fell under the light of the gas street lamp, the shock drove into his heart like a wooden stake.

Désirée glanced back and forth, as if she were making sure no one noticed her exit, and then speedily walked down the street in the direction of the opera house. Erik slipped from the darkness and stealthy followed her through the thick fog down the small avenue of stairs, confused and angry over where she had been. What was she doing at the soothsayer's residence this time of night? He was determined to find out.

As Désirée approached the perfect place where Erik knew of a dark narrow alley, he glanced about the lonely street to make sure no one was watching and then quickly came up behind her unsuspecting body. In one quick swoop, like an eagle catching its prey within its sharp talons, Erik wrapped his hand around her mouth and dragged her body back into the dark dead-end alley. She struggled the entire way, gagged by his gloved hand pressed tightly against her lips. Her voice screamed in muffled tones, and she wiggled unable to release herself from the death grip he had clamped around her petite waist.

Erik reached the end of the alley where no one could see or hear them. He pushed her roughly against the stone building and clasped both her hands against the wall by her wrists, one on each side of her blond head. His eyes narrowed into cat-like slits in the darkness of the night. As he glared into her face, he knew without a doubt that his captive guest had recognized her abductor. Her blue orbs went wide-eyed, emitting a look of utter horror that crawled across her face.

"Don't scream," he growled underneath his breath. "If you do, it will be your last. Do you understand me, Désirée?" He tightened his grip around her wrists. Erik felt the tremors of fear overtake her body. She nodded her head in agreement and whispered to him in response.

"I won't scream." She gasped between her words, her eyes shut tight, as she pleaded, "Please, Erik, don't hurt me. Please, I beg you."

He looked at her frightened face and toned his anger. However, something in his gut told him to continue with his interrogation, as if her life depended upon giving the right answers.

"What are you doing coming from the soothsayer's house at this time at night?"

"You saw me?" she asked, her lower lip quivering uncontrollably.

"Now why else would I have you pinned against this cold stone wall, Désirée? By all rights, you should be back at the opera house safely locked inside that nice little room I gave you, practicing scales on your violin."

"I . . . I was getting my fortune told, Erik. That's all."

He raised one brow upon hearing her answer and stared into her eyes looking for truth. If it was there, it was hidden by the terror in her blue ocean pools. Even in the dark, they had the power to move him to damnable weakness.

"Does the soothsayer always keep such odd hours? You would think her business would be closed this near to the witching hour of midnight."

"She does," she replied, nodding her head eagerly. "I've come before at this time, and she has read my fortune, my palm, and tea leaves . . . astrology too!"

"For what? Why do you need your fortune told?" Erik breathed heavily along the side of her neck, feeling the palpable terror as he neared her lying throat. "What did you want to know that was so important at this late hour?" He pressed his body against her frame shoving her harder into the wall.

"I . . . I wanted to know, Erik," she stammered, the tears starting to stream down her cheeks, "if . . . if you . . . were going to fall in love with me."

He pulled back and looked into her face studying each line of her features. "Why would you care if I loved you?" he demanded with a menacing voice that mocked her words.

Désirée struggled against his hands still wrapped around her wrists, trying to free herself to no avail. The tears flowed freely down her face, irritating Erik and playing upon his weakness. "Stop your infernal crying," he snapped, "I won't hurt you."

Silence passed between them. Erik pondered the answer to Désirée's question, which she claimed she had posed to the fortuneteller. Before he could say another word, she asked him bluntly.

"Do you? Do you love me?" Her tense voice choked out the words.

Erik pondered how to respond, but baring his soul to another woman was not simple. It was easier to keep her captive, pressed against the wall, and in a state of fear. Then he could command anything he wanted from her with the upper hand of his male dominance. If he confessed any affection, she would weaken him. Then he would be vulnerable to her wiles.

The longer he held her, the more he enjoyed his strong mass pressed hard against her tiny body. Her breasts crushed against his chest, and the warmth of her flesh permeated his linen shirt. His hungry eyes grazed along every line of her face and down to her moist lips. They were plump and full. Erik obsessed over them, wondering what it would be like to force his mouth upon hers and taste the forbidden sweetness.

The thought aroused him sexually. As his lustful gaze lifted toward Désirée, he could see she felt his hardness rise, responding to his thoughts and heated desires.

"Take me if you want," she told him, shaking. "You want to. I know you do."

Erik dropped one hand from around her left wrist and slid it down the side of her body in response to her invitation. He wanted to feel the edges of her curves from her breasts to her hips. His caged lust expelled through heavy breathing, as he moaned with craving for what lay hidden underneath her cloak.

In response, Désirée placed her free hand behind his head and before he could do otherwise, she forcefully pulled him to her lips. Erik dropped his other arm, coiled it around her waist, and then thrust his tongue inside her mouth. The sensations he had dreamed of his entire life flowed through his veins, driving him to a new kind of madness. The blood rushed to hardened flesh, and he groped with his hands across her body, seeking bare skin.

Désirée groaned in return, which only fueled their ferocious kissing. Erik devoured the sweet taste of her mouth, filling the starvation of his soul. Desire burned through his veins, and he realized he was about to lift her skirt and take her in a dark back alley with no remorse.

Swiftly, he withdrew his kiss and pinned her free wrist hard against the wall. Erik pulled away, while his heavy breathing confirmed he was on the brink of losing control. If she refused, he was afraid he would take her by force.

"You do not know what fire you play with, Désirée," he warned, as his hot breath escaped his lips. "I could easily enter you here in this alley and take you like the animal I am inside. I doubt that is what you'd wish from me."

He thought about the pleasures that awaited him, but instead, he dropped his hands and turned away from her body to put distance between them. His anger returned, and he shot her an accusatory remark.

"I don't believe you," he spat through clenched teeth. "I don't believe you came here for a fortune." His demeanor changed to one of dark brooding, as he looked at the young woman he thought he could trust.

"I swear, Erik," she insisted, stepping closer to him. "On my mother's grave! I swear! I only came here to ask about my future."

He studied her with narrowed eyes. "And have you found it?"

Désirée stood speechless. The cool misty fog swept down from the buildings, surrounding their bodies. Erik's ears tuned to the sounds of the dark alley. A rat scurried nearby, and a storm gutter dripped water into a puddle. He listened to the heavy breathing of his lungs, while he waited for her answer. The seconds passed like eternity.

"Erik, I . . . "

Désirée ran toward him and flung her arms around his neck, burying her head into his shoulder with sobs. He stood motionless and stiff, his arms draped along his side, as he inhaled and exhaled the perfumed air about her body. Slowly, he raised each limb and wrapped them around her waist, embracing her with tenderness. It surprised him that he was capable of providing comfort to another human. Emotion welled in his chest until he admitted amidst his own brokenness what he feared the most.

"I am falling in love with you. You have captured a heart, but I fear in the end you shall not truly love the monster underneath."

"Oh, Erik, you are not a monster to me," her words spilled out between her sobs. "You are the world to me." She lifted her head and looked into his eyes.

"We shall see," he replied, releasing her and pulling the hood of her cloak up over her golden locks. He grasped her hand tightly and pulled her down the alley. "It's late."

Erik found it difficult to speak another word in her presence, as he wondered about her visit to Sybelle Renard. She had asked him to take her at her word, but he struggled to do so. It was odd, out of place, and wrong timing. Why would she sneak out at night to get her fortune told? Had she done so before or was this just a random fluke of fate that he had luckily captured her in the act.

Upon returning, he found one of his workers waiting at the door. His surprised face spoke of fear, and Erik pushed him aside. "Lock it!" Now aware of how she weaseled her way in and out of the opera house, he continued to pull Désirée along down the hallway.

Although she did not struggle, he felt a slight resistance over his less than tender treatment.

"We'll talk tomorrow. I trust you'll stay in the remainder of the evening." His icy look replaced the barrier between them that brought a sense of safety to Erik and his vulnerable heart. She nodded and retreated inside her room, while he retreated to his quarters to drink himself to sleep.

❋ ❋ ❋

The door closed and Désirée stumbled backwards into her room shaking uncontrollably. Sweating from the horror of the ordeal, she tried to untie the closure to her cloak but found that it had worked its way into a knot. She pulled and pulled until it gave no release, and then screaming in frustration, she grabbed the fabric with her fist and tore it from the seam. In one hard pull, she ripped it from her body. The cloak pooled at her feet, and she kicked it across the room. She wondered if Erik had heard her frustration but did not care.

Désirée ran to the small adjoining bath chamber to wash. After pouring water in a basin, she splashed the cold liquid on her face repeatedly, trying to wash the feelings away. Instead, she began sobbing.

Désirée grabbed the side of the cabinet and held on tight as the room began to spin. She had to settle down. Her heart was pounding in her chest with such ferocity she thought it would leap to the floor. After grabbing a nearby hand towel, she blotted her face dry.

"Calm down, Désirée," she told herself, taking deeper breaths in an attempt to soothe the mortification clinging to her body. Finally, after the room stopped spinning, she slowly turned and walked back to her bed and sat down.

Kicking her shoes off, she brought her feet up and lay back on her pillow.

Scenes from the alley played before her eyes, and she instinctively brought both palms onto her face trying to make them stop. It was impossible. Erik had discovered her at her mother's no less. She told a boldface damnable lie swearing upon her Mama's grave she was merely there for a fortune telling session. Did he believe her?

Unsure whether he had, she cursed herself for not being more careful. She had no idea he wandered the streets in the dark at night. Did he follow her there? She had been unaware of his habits, but now she knew it was time to draw closer to him or otherwise he would catch her once again in another tall tale.

As the beating of her heart subsided somewhat, she withdrew her hands and ran her tongue across her bottom lip seeking the taste of his mouth. The water had washed it away, but she still felt the residue of where he had assaulted her with his tongue. His kiss felt as if he were searching out a deepness that frightened her to the core. Erik was dark and unpredictable. When his hand crawled down her curves, she shrank in dread from his power.

It was hard to believe Erik had never consumed another woman before. The rumors swelled in speculation at the Garnier about the Ghost who lived underneath. Some said he hypnotized his prey and ravished many women in his lair. Others said he had never been kissed; he was so ugly no one would dare to come near him.

Désirée was sure he was ignorant of the ways of a woman, by the means in which he awkwardly handled her body. He was starving for flesh, but clumsy in his movements. He went about it as if he were discovering the unknown. His kisses and the thrusting of his tongue into her mouth felt like he was devouring her like a meal. It gave her the chills.

As cold and frightening as Erik often acted, he could quickly turn tender at a second's notice. He seemed to stumble over his feelings, acting with cautioned hesitancy. When she ran and put her arms around him to bury her face and sob on his shoulder, he had held her tenderly. In doing so, she heard and felt the thumping of his heart in his chest; and when she did, something broke inside of her own. Désirée clung to the man who had literally destroyed her life. He was falling in love with her, and she feared she was with him.

The realization brought hot tears to her eyes. She rolled over and grasped her pillow, burying her face and shame into the white linen that willingly accepted the moisture between each thread. Had she forgiven him? How could she ever forgive him? How could he ever love her once he knew the truth of her deceit and the pain he had caused? The plan to destroy him was still alive, and she was part of it!

"I'm damned," she cried, sobbing hard, her chest heaving. "I'm damned." Her mother would never let her relent, and now she was tied to the Ghost. The torture and pain would continue. Only this time, another part of her body would suffer—her heart. As she feared the pain ahead, she heard her mother's voice bringing her back to reality.

"My daughter, we are in this together. Do not disappointment me now. Let me have my revenge upon the man who stole everything from you . . . from us!"

Her mother's voice called. She sat up in bed, wiped the tears from her cheeks with the back of her hand, and sniffled a few times. Her eyes stared ahead at the wall, with its hidden door that led directly into Erik's parlor. She knew in her heart what had to happen.

"Yes, Mama, I will do as you say. I promise."

Chapter 23

The weeks passed and the notes continued to arrive with regularity, containing the same threats to irritate and prick like thorns. It was obvious the authorities were useless in their pursuit of the author. Whoever was behind the joke had not acted upon any of their words, at least not yet, for which Richard and Erik were extremely grateful.

To make matters worse, Darius announced his second set of keys had suddenly found their way to one of his drawers in his private quarters. It pushed Erik into another tantrum over the man's uselessness. They had just spent money and hours changing every damn lock in the opera house for nothing. The architectural plans, however, were still missing. Erik wondered if they too would suddenly return from the grave unannounced. Only time would tell.

Erik continued to inspect the riggings above the stage on a regular basis, but nothing out of the ordinary reappeared. Perhaps the perpetuator had given up. All he wanted to do was live in peace. Of late, the only peace he found was in the presence of Désirée.

Their lessons continued, and to his surprise, his student made progress. He mentioned nothing further of the night in the back alley nor did she. There were no more words of love or feelings exchanged between the two of them. It seemed both had barred their hearts, fearful of the possibilities that lay ahead, but her kiss continued to haunt him daily.

Erik built a wall of professionalism once again of teacher and student. If Désirée wished for more, she was concealing it as well. Erik was unsure how long he could continue with the charade, before giving free rein to his desires. Even her name meant desire, and whispering it felt like warm honey dripping from his lips, making him hunger for more.

After a few more lessons, Erik decided that Désirée was ready for a recital of sorts. She balked at first, but he assured her that he would compose a rather simple piece for her to practice before performing. He often listened at night through the walls on the other side as she did so, setting a chair near the panel that led to her room. It was devious, but it satisfied his cravings.

She arrived on the appointed night, violin in hand, and made her way to center stage for her first solo. Erik sat in his usual seat in the front row, placed both his elbows on the armrest, and brought his hands underneath his chin, studying her as she wrestled with her nerves.

Désirée scowled. She looked at the music, placed the violin under her chin, and began playing the score. For the first time, after months of tedious lessons, she played a nearly flawless violin piece. It was raw and elementary, to say the least, but neither the auditorium nor his ears cringed over screeching tones.

When she finished, he jumped to his feet and applauded. "Well done! Bravo!" He took two steps at a time up to the stage platform, clearly excited over the result, and approached her with a contented grin.

"You have been practicing, Désirée, and I am very pleased with your progress. There is still much to learn, but it is a start. I'm proud of you." He wanted to embrace her to show his pleasure but refrained.

She reacted to his praise with a broad smile and a sigh of relief. "I had such trepidation," she admitted. "I'm so glad you're happy with me, Erik."

He took the violin and bow from her hand and set it on the chair. "I promised myself that if you did well tonight, I would reward you with something special."

"Reward me?" she asked, her blue eyes sparkling with excitement over the prospect.

"Yes, come with me. I wish to show you something that I enjoy immensely." He reached out his hand toward Désirée and waited for her to grasp it in return. It was the first time he had touched her flesh since that night in the alley, and the warmth of her palm flowed through his body like a drug. He cleared his throat and decided to risk everything.

"Where are we going?"

"To my favorite place in the entire opera house."

He led the way down the hall, glancing at her curious gaze, until they reached a doorway that opened to a flight of stairs. She followed behind, and when they reached the top, Erik flung open the door. He escorted her outside to the lower roof. The cool fresh night air greeted his nostrils, and he inhaled deeply.

"Perfect," he announced. They made their way to the front of the building and peered over the edge. Every star in the universe twinkled from the heavens above.

"Oh, Erik, it's beautiful up here," she told him. Désirée's eyes darted about the scenery.

"It is, isn't it? If you look to your right, you can see the harbor lights." Erik enjoyed the view. The city streets were lit with gas lamps, illuminating the palace and church domes in all their glory. It was a clear night, with no fog. "You know, Désirée, they say when opera house went up in flames, it could be seen for miles around. They were afraid it was going to catch Our Lady of Victories church nearby and spread throughout the city." The thought of the possible loss of the perfect architecture nearby made him shudder. "It could have been much worse for the city had the flames spread to neighboring buildings."

"I didn't know that," she admitted.

Erik found the statement a bit odd, since Désirée had supposedly worked at the opera house and resided in the city before his arrival.

"I would have thought you'd read it in the news."

She looked at him with a strained look upon her face. "Perhaps I did," she replied, embarrassed. "I must have forgotten."

Erik dismissed the oversight and turned around to look at the city. "I must confess, I've spent many years of my life living under ground. When I discovered the beauty of the roof at nighttime, I started coming here often. The architecture of this city is fascinating. I only wish . . . "

Erik's voice trailed off stopping short of revealing a private thought.

"Wished what, Erik?"

Désirée's voice was soft as velvet and filled with a kindness that broke down the barrier concealing his personal thoughts.

"I often wish that I could be like other men and walk the streets freely in the light of day. You already know that I walk at night. Almost every night," he admitted, his eyes staring at the buildings filling the horizon. "It's too dangerous to reveal myself in the light. I'm a freak in a mask."

"Dangerous?"

Désirée stepped closer to his side and tilted her head, as she looked into his eyes. Erik wondered how much she knew of his past as they never discussed it. He had purposely avoided delving into her own personal affairs, should she press him in return with questions.

"I think you know what I mean," he told her, lifting his hand to the side of her face. His fingertips touched her cheek, grazing her soft skin in admiration. He had opened the door of his desires and stood upon a precipice of possible ecstasy once again.

Désirée responded in a sultry whisper encouraging him further. "I'm not afraid of you any longer."

Erik's ears heard her intoxicating confession, and in response, he inched closer until his body was flush with her own. The night air, the stars, the location, it was all too perfect not to take advantage of a willing woman and their private moment.

She should be afraid, he thought to himself. *She doesn't know the monster that dwells in my soul. The horrors I am capable of inflicting upon others.*

As his finger continued to trace along her jaw line, it found its final destination at the corner of her lower lip. He licked his own while running his finger across the plump flesh of Désirée's mouth. When he lifted his eyes and looked into her blue pools that called him to take what he wanted, he lowered his mouth upon her lips that were parted and waiting. His flesh melted into her moistness.

Once again, the sensation caused a deep guttural moan to escape his throat. Désirée responded by encircling her arms around his neck and molding her curves into his body. Erik slipped his hand around the back of her head and drew her into him, as he thrust his tongue inside once again to search out the sweet taste. She moaned, and he responded.

Désirée's body weakened his arms. His hands began to grope her breasts and around her petite waist, before sliding roughly down the side of her hips. She did not protest his movements, but began responding with her own hands rubbing across his back ardently.

Erik wanted to feel her flesh. He had to feel what lay underneath, what he had never been allowed to touch. His hand reached down and began clawing at the fabric of her dress until his palm filled with the cloth of her skirt. He roughly pulled it up and out of the way and was about to slip his hand up her inner thigh to its ultimate destination, when Désirée recoiled and started pounding her fists on his chest in return.

"No, don't!"

She screamed and fought against him until Erik realized she was refusing to let him experience the treasure of her womanhood. Angry, he pulled away from her lips, dropped his hand from her dress, and stepped back, leaving her trembling body to shake on its own.

"You act as if you want me," he growled eying her up and down in disgust. "Why torture me so?"

"I can't," she screamed in anger. "I can't . . . I won't!"

"Won't what?" he hissed. "Let me take you after you tease?" He stepped toward her and postured over her face. His eyes blazed in anger, as he throbbed unfulfilled and rejected.

"You'll never understand!" she yelled.

Désirée placed both her hands on his chest and thrust him away from her body. Erik was surprised by her rash action and lifted his hand in anger wanting to slap her for her impertinence. Désirée flinched and turned her face away, reacting to the blow she thought would land upon her cheek. His hand stopped short of hitting her.

"Damn you!" He seized her by the wrist and pulled her back inside while she struggled the entire way to escape his grasp. As they traversed the stairs downward, Erik continued to drag her harshly until they arrived at her quarters.

"Erik, please, you're hurting me," she protested, hot tears streamed down her face.

He opened the door and flung her inside. "You say you want my love!" he sneered. "But you deny me!"

"Erik, please," she sobbed. "I want you to love me, but there is so much you do not know!"

"Then tell me, my petite, what it is I should know about you? You are a mystery to me."

"And you to me!" she spat back at him. Désirée ran away and cowered in the corner of her room. "I hate you! I hate you!"

Erik froze in place dumfounded over her words and reaction. Did she think he would rape her? He retreated in anger and slammed her door hard before retreating to his quarters. He pushed the mechanism and disappeared inside. A chair in his way felt his booted heel, as he kicked it across the room sending it into the wall. She probably heard it on the other side, but he did not give a damn.

All he wanted was her! He loved her! Why would she not give him what he wanted? She teased him relentlessly, playing a cruel game with his emotions and desires that burned in his loins. Désirée Martin would be his undoing, he was sure of it.

Erik eyed the crystal decanter off to the side and headed for the alcohol to calm his fury. He poured a full glass and spilled it down his gullet in quick gulps. The glass emptied, and he poured another. Once again, he opened his mouth wide and sent the alcohol burning down his throat.

When he finished the second glass, he felt a fire rush through his veins. Then, without warning, his head began to spin, his vision blurred, and everything in his room grew dark. Something was wrong . . . terribly wrong. Was he having a heart attack or stroke?

Before he could decide which, he staggered, losing his ability to stand. The feeling in his limbs drained away leaving him numb. He grabbed the side table and brought the crystal decanter and silver tray to his feet with a crash. His body fell forward with a loud thud, hitting the floor and falling onto the broken glass. He moaned in pain, and felt an insidious drug course through his body like fire, erasing his conscious mind and eating away at his strength. Someone had poisoned him, and he was sure the angel of death would soon appear.

Barely conscious, he called for help. Unable to raise his voice, the name of Désirée fell from his numb lips in a whisper, as he sank into the pit of unending darkness.

Chapter 24

Désirée's heart pounded and her hands trembled uncontrollably. Why did everything have to happen tonight? She had done despicable things and felt horrible. Erik had tried once more to take her, and she wanted to slap him and embrace him all at the same time.

Her mother's voice kept telling her not to love him, but she did love him and her mother too. She felt torn over what to do and incapable of making a decision. Her mother used the power of guilt and obligation to control her every move. It was her mother who stayed by her through the pain of her own torment and loss. Désirée owed her everything.

The day had finally arrived, and their plot fell into place. Erik had foolishly placed her in a room next to his own quarters; in his weakness, he had put himself within their reach.

She had returned from her mother's that night intent on doing her part. Désirée spent time listening at the wall to learn Erik's habits. If she leaned her ear against the wood, she could hear the panel to his main doorway slide back and forth. When he came and went, she either heard noises on the other side or silence. She noted the times in the evening when he would leave for his walks and when he would return, until she had his schedule down pat. He seemed to be a creature of habit, doing things at the same intervals every day. It all made it easier for Désirée to plot his comings and goings.

One night when he left, she had fiddled with the panel in her room relentlessly. Her hands traveled up and down the wall pushing and pulling at the trim trying to engage it to open. At last, she sensed something odd in one area, a slight protrusion that did not feel quite right. She placed pressure against it, and the panel of her wall slid back. Her heart stopped as she found herself exposed and standing at the threshold of Erik's parlor. She walked inside and quickly looked around. It was then she saw the decanter of cognac sitting on a tray, and the perfect plan unfolded.

She had returned to her quarters, engaged the panel, and it shut. Excited she had breached the wall, she knew they had to move quickly after her discovery. Her mother planned everything down to the very last detail. Tonight would be the night when it would unfurl to perfection. She only hoped nothing would go wrong.

Désirée had waited for Erik to leave for their lessons, and before she met him in the auditorium, she slipped into his quarters. As fast as her feet could carry her across the room, she pulled the stopper from the decanter, unscrewed the vial cap, and poured the entire contents into the alcohol. When the deed was over, she replaced the stopper, returned to her room, and closed the panel. After calming down, she had proceeded to meet him for her recital.

Everything stood ready. She was surprised when he took her to the roof. Désirée hadn't counted on a starlit sky and romance to ignite once again. He kissed her, and she melted her body into his. Then as his hands began to search out her flesh, Désirée thought she would go mad with passion. She wanted him, until his hand lifted her skirt and began its journey up her inner thigh. In another hour, her mother would be at the door. She could not let him; she wanted to, but could not! Instead, she spurned him with beating fists and denial.

It was enough to throw him into a rage. He had dragged her downstairs, threw her inside her room, and stormed off to his. She leaned her ear against the wall and heard him kick something. It became silent. Was he drinking? It did not take long before the sound of crashing crystal met her ears, and she heard the loud thump of his body hit the floor. She closed her eyes, and whispered, "I'm sorry, Erik."

She left her room and made her way to the stage door to meet her waiting co-conspirator. "Mother," she greeted, nervously letting her inside.

"Is everything set?"

"I think so. He retreated an hour ago, and I heard him fall."

"He's made no further noise?"

"No, Mama, I've heard nothing. I'm frightened."

"Don't be," she reassured her. "We are just going to have a long talk with the drugged monster. Take me to him."

Désirée carefully stalked the halls ahead of her mother, making sure everything was clear. She led her to her private room and then shut the door and locked it behind them. Her mother glanced about.

"Where is it?"

"Over here," she answered, reaching her hand to the panel.

"What if he's still conscious, Mother, he'll kill us for sure!"

"I have a backup plan. Don't worry. We will make our demands when he is conscious, but incapacitated. The drug has paralyzed him to some extent, but only temporarily. He will listen. Just do everything I tell you."

Her mother grabbed her hard by the shoulder to make the point. "Do you understand? Our lives could depend upon it."

"Yes, Mama, I will do as you say."

Her hand trembled as she slowly pushed against the mechanism and the panel slid back, opening the door into Erik's domain. Désirée eyes darted around the room searching for signs of Erik, and then her heart stopped when she saw his lifeless form on the floor.

"My God!" She ran over to his prostrate body to see if he was still breathing.

"Did you empty the vial in the decanter of alcohol like I instructed?" Her mother sauntered over to his side and peered over his lifeless body with smug satisfaction.

"Yes."

"Good," she replied, eying him closely. "It was probably more volatile since it was mixed with alcohol. By the looks of it, he must have drunk more than one glass. I'm not surprised he's out cold."

Sybelle wandered around the room looking at his quarters, picking up books, sheet music, and nosing around his world. Désirée worried over how pale Erik appeared.

"Don't worry," her mother reassured her again. "As it starts to dissipate from his system, he will regain consciousness, and we can make our demands."

A few minutes passed, and Désirée heard Erik moan. She glanced over at her mother, who continued to handle his things with curiosity. Her actions irritated Désirée.

"Mother, what are you doing?"

"Enjoying the Ghost's room," she replied, spitting out his nickname. "Aren't you curious what a lunatic like him finds pleasure in, besides you?"

"Mother, please."

"Please what?" She swung around, looking at his body sprawled across the hard floor. She slowly walked to his side, picked up her skirt, and kicked him full force in his ribs with the pointed toe of her shoe. Erik moaned, and Désirée gasped.

"Mama, please don't!"

"He's an animal!" she screamed, kicking him again.

Désirée watched her mother in shocked silence. Her face had twisted into an evil demon, with spiteful eyes and a foul mouth that cursed obscenities at Erik.

The bitterness had always been there, but this . . . this was something different. It frightened Désirée. She wanted to forget their plan. It had already gone too far. It would not change the past or heal her future. She was as doomed as the Ghost, who they had planned to blackmail to pay for her suffering.

She watched Erik groan and struggle for consciousness. Désirée's heart felt like a lead weight in her chest. Her breathing became shallow and labored from remorse. She witnessed his hand twitch and saw him fight against the influence of the drug.

It would not be long now. She would reveal everything to him. As soon as the truth was known and their demands made, she would be gone from his life forever. The thought brought profound sadness to her heart. She did not want to leave him. She did not hate him. Theresa Désirée Hessier loved the man beneath the mask.

❋ ❋ ❋

Erik's eyelids fluttered open. His sight was blurred and his body weak and feeble. He heard voices and strained to recognize who was speaking in muffled tones. To his horror, as his conscious mind drew into focus, he recognized one of the occupants of his room. His half-closed eyelids saw the hem of a woman's dress, and he realized it belonged to Désirée.

Had they noticed he moved? His eyes lifted to the person standing in front of her. He was shocked to see Sybelle Renard. What was she doing here? Why couldn't he move?

Unable to make out the words spoken, his eyes focused on Désirée's shoe. Like a snake striking to bite its prey, he pressed every ounce of strength in his body toward her foot and weakly grabbed her ankle. She screamed and pulled away. Erik's hand dropped like a limp rag to the floor with a thud.

"Ah, the monster lives. See, I told you it wouldn't be long before he'd come around." He watched Sybelle's feet walked toward him. She lifted her foot and kicked him in the ribs. Erik moaned from the pain assaulting his already bruised body lying in a puddle of spilt cognac and sharp glass.

"Mother, please! Don't hurt him like that. We weren't supposed to hurt him. That wasn't the plan."

"Shut up!" she spat in Désirée's face.

Mother . . . mother . . . she's Désirée's mother? Erik tried to process the confusing information swirling in his muddled mind.

"Let's lift him up and lean him in the chair so he can watch," Sybelle directed.

Before he could protest, the two women, one on either side, slipped their arms underneath his armpits and roughly pulled him upright into a nearby chair. They plopped him down, and he fell to the side. His body wanted to roll back onto the floor, but Désirée's hand pushed him back up until he could maintain the position.

He lifted his droopy eyelids and tried to find the blueness in her gaze that always calmed him, but it was gone. Her eyes spoke of sorrowful pain, and her face of fear.

"What . . . what do you want?" He sounded like a thick-tongued drunk mumbling his words. He tried to focus upon the spinning room. After a few more attempts, his gaze rested upon the two women who were watching his every move.

Sybelle Renard reeked of evil. The burning indignation on her face told him things were not going in his favor. His eyes crawled over to Désirée. The room spun, but after a few more seconds, he was able to focus upon her alone. She appeared frightened and confused. He grabbed the arm of the chair to steady himself.

"Désirée, what is the meaning of this? Tell me."

Désirée looked at him with a tinge of pity. "Erik, my name is not Désirée Martin," she told him. "It's Theresa Désirée Hessier. This is my mother, Sybelle Hessier."

Hessier . . . Hessier . . . he had heard the name before in Paris, and tried to remember but could not.

"What do you want with me," he managed to sputter. "Out with it!"

"Retribution," Sybelle replied, slithering over to his side like a snake.

Désirée interrupted to clarify. "We just want you to know what you did, Erik, and that I need compensation for my pain."

"How?" he spat, "By drugging me?" Erik began to regain feeling in his lower limbs and arms, but refused to move, playing their game to bide more time. His hands tingled like a thousand prickly pins, which told him control was slowly returning to his body.

Sybelle walked toward him, her eyes blazing with hatred. She reached down and tore off his mask and hairpiece, flinging it to the floor. He was naked before them both. Her reaction was one of shock, as he had expected from Désirée, who still stood unmoved by his appearance.

"The ugly monster!" her mother roared. "My God, he's disgusting!" She spat in his face, and Erik turned away, feeling her salvia run down his cheek.

Désirée protested. "Mother, please, don't ridicule him."

Her mother turned and eyed her daughter. "I'm sorry, dear." Her mother spoke coldly. "But there has been a slight change of plans."

Erik witnessed horror on Désirée's face, and he braced himself for what lay ahead.

"What do you mean?" she demanded, coming over and grabbing her mother's arm, who quickly tore it from her grasp.

"You'll see, but first let's tell the monster the story, shall we?"

Sybelle's words dripped like bitter bile, and Erik watched stunned as she proceeded to explain the reason for his punishment.

"Well, this is such a wonderful story," she announced, turning to her daughter. "It's almost like a fairytale actually. Of course, my daughter's life would have been a fairytale had it all played out the way it was supposed to in the end. But no, the Ghost had to ruin it all."

Sybelle narrowed her glare and began her discourse, while Désirée stood to the side with her head hanging in shame.

"Once upon a time there was a Ghost who lived under the opera house in Paris, France. He was obsessed with a certain soprano. One night in his selfish attempt to capture the little lovely for himself, he brought down the chandelier on the unsuspecting audience to create a diversion while he dragged her to his lair to have his way with her!"

A hideous laugh escaped Sybelle's lips, as her eyes grew wide with insanity, recounting the story in front of Erik. Désirée wept silently.

"That chandelier fell and it caused a fire. Did you care?" she demanded, drawing near to his face. "No! You were too busy."

"Mother, please, don't . . . " Désirée cried. "I can't go through with this." Erik heard her plea, but it only served to enrage Sybelle more.

"Do as I tell you, Theresa! Don't question me!"

She turned Désirée's body around so that her back faced him. "Show him! Show him!" she screamed. "Show the monster what he did to you!"

Her mother grabbed Désirée's bodice and began clawing at her dress like an animal. The fabric tore, and Désirée fought against her mother's hands, screaming at her to stop. Erik tried to move to protect her, but his body was still too weak to respond.

"All right!" Désirée screamed. "All right! I'll show him."

Her whimpering cries filled the room as she unbuttoned her dress and lowered it off her shoulders. It pooled to the floor and fell at her feet. Désirée continued and removed her corset, which she also let fall to the floor. Then shockingly, Erik watched speechlessly as she pulled her chemise over her head and lowered her bloomers until her naked back was exposed.

His blurry vision focused on her body. His brow furrowed after his eyes finally beheld her grotesque flesh that weaved across the surface. Burn scars laced her back down to her buttocks. The hideous sight caused Erik to glance away in utter shock.

"What's this? The monster doesn't wish to look at you," Sybelle screamed. "I told you he'd be repulsed, didn't I? I told you! He can't look at your beauty now!"

Désirée sobbed loudly when she heard of Erik's reaction.

"You see what you did to my daughter! The chandelier caught the stage curtain on fire and it fell onto her body, pinning her to the floor in a blanket of flames. Thank God, someone had the decency to pull the flaming material off her back and rescue her from certain death. You nearly killed her and perhaps it would have been better to have killed her after all the suffering that followed!"

Désirée wept. Her hands clutched to her face in shame. Erik looked back again at her putrid flesh that sickened his stomach.

"She was engaged to be married to Dom Fernando, brother of the King of Portugal. Of course, as soon as he saw the scars left on her body, after six months of agonizing pain to recover, he broke off the engagement. If that wasn't enough, we were left with debts from hospital bills we could not pay!"

Sybelle looked at her only daughter with compassion. "You stole her future, her beauty, her life. You made my beautiful daughter suffer more than any woman should ever have to in a lifetime."

Erik watched Désirée slip back into her underclothes with trembling hands, still struggling with the horrid revelation. His heart broke watching her sob uncontrollably, devastated over his reaction. He did not notice that her mother was about to make him pay for his sins, until her insane scream reached his ears and he caught sight of her body looming over his head.

"Now you'll pay for what you've done to her and to me!"

Désirée spun around, and Erik's eyes opened wide. Sybelle had drawn a dagger from her cloak and raised it in the air over Erik's heart. He saw her hand start to plummet downward toward his chest, but felt as if weights had him pinned to the chair.

"Mother, no!" Désirée screamed in terror and lunged toward her mother in time to grab her arm. They wrestled with one another as Désirée tried to take the dagger, but was no match for the mad woman's strength.

"Mother, no. I love him! Don't kill him. Don't! Please, I love him!"

Désirée's mother reacted in rage to her confession.

"Love him! You love the monster?" She slapped her daughter hard across her face with her free hand, causing Désirée to stumble backward. Sybelle whirled around and returned toward Erik, once again raising the dagger high above his head, aiming straight for his heart. Whatever strength Erik regained, he had to use now or death would arrive in the next second.

He roared at her like a lion, wobbled to his feet, and grabbed her wrist, pushing the blade away from his chest that hovered a mere inch away.

"I'll kill you!" she screamed! "I'll kill you for what you've done!"

Erik's momentary strength was about to seep from his body; it was now or never. He clenched his teeth, raised his arm, and struck Sybelle in the jaw with his clenched fist. He used every ounce of adrenalin that shot through his veins. The blow sent her flying across the room. She stumbled backward to the floor with a hard thud, the dagger still clutched in her hand. Sybelle landed on top of the blade and it thrust into her abdomen.

Horrified, Désirée ran to her side screaming. "Mama! Mama!" She knelt beside her mother and wailed uncontrollably.

"I did it for you, Theresa. All for you," she gasped in response, wincing from the pain. "I wanted to kill him because he killed your spirit and ruined your life."

"No, Mama," she cried, her hand shaking above the knife, wishing to remove it. "I don't hate him any longer. I've forgiven him."

Her mother curled a knowing smirk across her face. "You foolish girl," she gasped. "Men only wish beauty. He will never love you, mon petite! To him you are only a casualty; a scarred casualty that offers no beauty to his ugly world. He will discard you just like your fiancé did."

Sybelle panted a few times in agony and then closed her eyes, falling limp into her daughter's arms.

Erik fell to his hands and knees on the floor, struggling for breath, still weak from the drugs coursing through his veins. He looked at Désirée, whose scars were visible upon her upper shoulders; he was horrified by their appearance. He was about to speak, when the door to his quarters slid back and Richard and Andrea ran in, horrified at the scene that lay before them.

"My God! What's going on here?" Richard's eyes darted back and forth.

"We heard all the screaming and came running," Andrea shouted. She saw Sybelle Renard bleeding with a dagger protruding from her stomach and clung to Richard's arm.

Erik tried to catch his breath and pointed at Désirée. "Ask her," he groaned contemptuously. Désirée turned and looked at him with profound remorse. Erik's eyes met her blue gaze of sadness, as he blacked out and fell prostrate on the floor.

Chapter 25

Andrea paced the length of the room back and forth wearing out the carpet. No one got a wink of sleep. She stayed by Erik's side waiting for him to slowly recover from his drugged stupor, afraid he would die at any time.

After they arrived upon hearing the ruckus, Richard tended to Sybelle, who was still alive but bleeding profusely. He removed the knife and put pressure against the wound. Darius fetched a physician. Désirée sobbed uncontrollably in the corner like a baby, curled in a fetal position. Erik drifted in and out of semi-consciousness.

The doctor finally arrived, and Sybelle was taken to a nearby hospital for treatment. The wound was serious, but not life threatening. Andrea had heard early that morning from Richard she would survive.

When the police arrived the evening before, Richard and Andrea tried their best to keep Erik's involvement out of it, but it was difficult to do so. Désirée seemed intent on confessing her sins, explaining their scheme of blackmail. Everything had gone terribly wrong when her mother turned into a raging lunatic, trying to kill Erik instead.

Désirée, through heaving sobs, admitted to drugging Erik with some potion placed in his decanter of cognac. Her mother was merely going to blackmail him into paying them a large sum of money for the troubles that

Erik had caused the two of them. Instead, she went off the deep end.

Richard pressed the matter further. By the time Désirée redressed, she showed them some of her scars upon her back, relaying the story of her injuries. She blamed Erik for a number of things, including the reason behind her fiancé breaking off their engagement.

Andrea had no sympathy for her after the diabolical plan the two women had perpetrated upon Erik for revenge. Désirée knelt by Erik's unconscious body, telling him repeatedly that she loved him and was terribly sorry. It sickened them both. Richard would hear nothing of her ranting about love, thinking she only said such words to keep from getting in trouble.

He insisted on pressing charges against her for whatever reason they could drum up. The police cuffed Désirée and led her away to jail, sobbing hysterically and pleading to stay by Erik's side. The authorities decided to charge her with conspiracy to commit murder, since she admitted that her mother had attempted to do just that. Richard and Andrea did not protest one bit. In fact, they were thankful to see her hauled off to receive her due punishment for her actions.

Beyond what she had told them, everything else was speculation on their part. Andrea anxiously waited for Erik to come back to life, so they could ask him what had really happened. When he finally moaned and brought his hand to his head, she ran to his bedside.

"God, Erik, are you all right?"

"Yes," he mumbled, trying to sit up as he held his head with his hand. "I feel like I've been hit with an iron rod," he admitted. He squinted when the light hit his eyes, realizing he was still unmasked and without his hairpiece. "Have I been lying here like this all night?"

Andrea shook her head, but his deformity was nothing she had not seen before. It did not bother her, but she knew that Erik always felt profound shame when uncovered. She handed his mask and hairpiece to him, and he quickly slipped them both on before speaking with her further.

Andrea watched compassionately while he struggled to regain his senses and composure. "Where is she?" he finally asked.

"Which one?"

Erik's eyes shifted his gaze toward Andrea. "Both, I guess. Is Sybelle dead?"

"Dead? No, she's in the hospital. The witch will live."

"I suppose that's good news," he answered, with a half-hearted drawl. "At least I won't be accused of that murder."

Erik tried to stand to his feet, and Andrea reached out to help him steady himself. "I can do it," he told her, pulling away from her. "Don't drink the cognac in the decanter, by the way," he added, with a slight chuckle. "It's a bit deadly."

"Don't worry. It shattered to the floor in a million pieces. I'm surprised you have no cuts on you from the glass.

"Yes," he noted, "but I reek of alcohol apparently."

The poor man looked horrible, and Andrea sighed. "Désirée confessed to drugging you." She wanted to make it perfectly clear who was responsible for his horrid condition.

"I wish to see her. Bring her to me."

Andrea pulled her eyes away from him, not wanting to look at the displeasure that would follow. "She's not here, Erik. She's in jail awaiting trial."

"What? What do you mean in jail?"

"Well, the authorities came to the scene last night. She admitted to everything from the beginning. She cut the rope on the rigging, and stole the keys plus the architectural plans. Her mother sent the death threats through the mail. Their last plan of action was to drug you and then blackmail you for money by threatening to turn you over to the Parisian authorities. Of course, when her mother tried to murder you, the charges quickly turned into conspiracy to commit murder. I'm afraid the police were not too lenient and hauled her off rather roughly in handcuffs."

"Damn it, Andrea! Why did you let them do that?" he demanded. He brought his hand back to his pounding head.

"Are you crazy, Erik? Her mother just tried to cut your heart out with a dagger. Désirée poured a drug in your alcohol, and you wonder why she's in jail?"

"Did you see?" he asked, his voice laced with remorse. "Did you see the burn scars?"

"Yes."

"I did that," he remarked coldly. "One moment of madness on my part. How many more did I hurt that night, Andrea?"

She grew silent as her memory filtered back to that night and his reign of terror that she wished to forget. "A few suffered injuries, Erik. Then there was the one poor woman that died. I didn't even know of Désirée."

"Her name is Theresa."

"Yes, she told me. She was, as I recall now, a dancer who only performed periodically as a backup, but I didn't recognize her when she came here to work. There were so many that worked at the Garnier. She happened to be in the chorus that evening, and her fiancé was in a box with her mother watching when the chandelier fell. They escaped unharmed, but she did not."

Erik looked at the clock. "I want all the charges dropped, Andrea. Tell Richard that I am not pressing charges against her. She's innocent. In fact, she tried to save my life while her mother tried to take it."

"You cannot be serious! She drugged you and was going to blackmail you!"

He growled at her, emphasizing each word slowly. "I want Richard to see that all the charges are dropped! If I must, I will go to the police myself and testify what happened and her attempt to save my life."

Andrea sighed, giving in to his demands. "Very well, I will tell him what you have suggested. However, going to the police yourself will only put you in even more danger. Have you thought of that?"

"I don't care. I can no longer hide like a rat. The police already know I exist after last night. Whether they put two and two together as to who I am and where I came from, only time will tell."

Erik turned and looked at Andrea. He still felt as if weights were tied to his limbs from the drugs, but he wanted to return Désirée to the opera house. "Go get Richard and tell him I wish to go to the police station within the hour." He wrinkled his nose over the stench of his clothing. I need to bathe and change first."

"As you wish, Erik." Andrea relented and left to carry out his request.

❄ ❄ ❄

Finally alone, Erik tried to recoup his thoughts. He stripped his clothing and noticed his suit coat had jagged tears from the shards of glass upon which he had fallen. It was a miracle his face missed the pile of broken crystal. They could have easily dug into his exposed flesh leaving him scarred on the other side of his face. He shuddered over the thought.

He threw his cognac-stained clothing in a heap and drew a hot bath. He wanted to take time and soak his stressed muscles. Erik took advantage of the quiet moment to sort out his torn heart filled with shock and remorse. He struggled with the revelation, as his vivid memory brought back the vision of Désirée's scars.

How could he not react to what he saw? It was hideous. He had worshipped her beautiful face, hair, and eyes. Her appearance had been a facade. She was like two different people—gorgeous on one side and ugly on the other.

The thought stabbed his conscience with a sharp thrust of realization. For the first time in his own miserable life, he had experienced the horror others felt when they looked upon his deformity. He could barely control his own shock with Désirée. The sight sickened and repulsed him. He was mortified and deeply ashamed over his reaction to her scars. The Phantom was no better than the rest of humanity, void of compassion.

Erik's entire life had been spent seeking only one thing, which was beauty. He worshiped beauty. He hungered for it. It was an insatiable need in his life to counteract his own grotesque appearance. That was why he had obsessed over Christine. In his mind, she represented the epitome of beauty in her voice, face, and body. Erik wanted to possess her heart and soul, and become one with the beauty of her flesh and spirit.

As he soaked in the bath, his chest grew heavy with grief. Désirée posed the greatest challenge of his life. He struggled with profound shame. He had fallen deeply in love with the Désirée he thought he knew. She had appeared to him as a beautiful angel, with blue eyes, and a body that he worshipped in his imagination. Underneath the veil of her clothing lay the truth hidden from his vision. He couldn't imagine loving the ugliness he abhorred.

No matter what he felt, he had to rescue Désirée from further suffering. It wasn't right to make her pay for her mother's sins, who no doubt like a crafty witch had poisoned her daughter's mind into seeking revenge. Erik remembered her last words when he had returned her to her room. *"I hate you! I hate you!"* It was a lie, for he had heard her words while in a semi-conscious state, as he lay prone on the floor. *"I love you! I love you!"* Somehow, he knew it to be the truth.

Erik rose from his bath, dried, and dressed in clean clothes. He worried over how he would react to seeing Désirée again, but he had to. He alone was the reason for her suffering and the scars on her back. One moment of his madness had turned her beautiful life into a thing of ugliness. He had to make restitution, and this was the only way he knew how. He had to free her from jail and see that the charges were dropped.

※ ※ ※

Désirée crawled into the corner of her cell and sat against the stone floor and wall, bobbing back and forth in uncontrollable wails. Her charge was conspiracy to commit murder, and as far as she knew, her mother was probably dead. Everything had come crashing down around her at an unprecedented rate. Things had gone terribly wrong.

It had all seemed so rational when they hatched their scheme. They were going to tell Erik they would inform the Parisian authorities where he could be found unless he paid restitution. One way or the other, they were going to make him pay for his reign of terror in Paris that had so terribly scarred their lives.

Désirée had spent nearly six months in a Parisian hospital recovering from burns and subsequent infections. The pain could only be killed by morphine; but she had taken so much that by the time her recovery came, she needed to withdraw from her addiction. Her life had turned into a living hell of a broken engagement, a broken body, and a broken spirit. Désirée's mother swore every day that the Ghost would pay for what he had done.

Sybelle was a resourceful woman and stood by her, daily encouraging her to recover when she often wanted nothing more than to die. Everyone knew the Ghost of the opera house was responsible for the horrible night of terror. The police were looking for him, and so was Sybelle.

She had heard rumors that Madame Giry had been his friend and confident over the years. She hired a private detective to follow Andrea because she was the Ghost's friend. When she received a report that Andrea left France for Malta with two other men, it piqued her interest. She had followed an unknown investor who purchased a defunct Royal Opera House.

Convinced they were on the trail of the monster that had destroyed their lives, Sybelle had convinced Désirée to travel to Malta, so they could infiltrate his world. Désirée applied for work feigning lies of having worked at the Royal Opera House before it burned down. Madame Giry hired her without blinking an eyelash. It was all too easy. Suddenly she found herself surrounded by his world, but unable to find him as he continued to hide behind his secret doors, until that fateful night in the orchestra pit. The next she knew, the Ghost was in front of her, and she was face-to-face with the man who had caused all her pain.

It was easy at first. Désirée wanted him to pay as much as her mother did, so she played upon an opportunity to continue seeing him. Everything fell into place like a well-dealt hand of cards in her favor. She fed off her own bitterness to continue the façade in front of the mysterious man. Her only struggle was the profound way his violin playing made her burst into tears teach time her ears heard the glorious strains of music. It was hypnotic in its own way, filled with power and longing. She tried to resist, but quickly fell under its spell.

It was after she met Erik and spent time with him night after night that she discovered his attractive genius. At first, it was mere fascination, but then a hook drove through her heart and would not let go. Seeds of doubt sprouted over the wisdom of their plans.

However, her mother was determined. Désirée feared disobeying, even though she tried to talk her out of it more than once. Blackmail after all was just extortion of money, so what they had planned really wasn't that bad, was it? She would never have imagined her mother intended to murder him instead.

As she continued to rock back and forth, oblivious to the world around her, Désirée struggled with her mother's parting words. She wondered if Erik loved her. Could he love her now? He had loved her beauty, but it was all a lie. She was a monster inside and out; just like him, and he now knew the truth of what lay underneath her clothes. Désirée lowered her head into her knees, dealing with the crushing weight of painful regret.

A key inserted into the steel lock, and her head shot up to see if they had come to hang her without a trial. To her surprise, the jailer opened the door, and Erik entered her cell. Désirée's lip quivered at the sight of him, longing to hear a word of forgiveness fall from his lips. He stood silently studying her tear-streaked face showing no emotion whatsoever, but only a cold steel-like glare from his dark eyes that bore into her wounded heart. He reached out his hand and spoke.

"You're free to go, Désirée. The charges have been dropped. I want you to come with me back to the opera house."

She looked at his resolute face and his outstretched hand that stayed firm and unshaken before her. Had he forgiven her? She wobbled to her feet and took a step forward. "Please," she pleaded in a forced whisper. Her voice shook as the words fell from her lips. "Forgive me." She put her hand in his and his fingers wrapped around her own, clutching them tightly.

"We'll talk of it later," he responded in a non-committal tone. "It's time to go."

"And Mother?" she dared to ask.

"She lives."

Chapter 26

Sybelle opened her eyes and focused on the white ceiling above her head. A searing pain in her abdomen caused her to wince and told her she was alive. The flames of hell had not engulfed her yet. The last thing she remembered was Theresa bending over her body with her own dagger sticking out of her stomach. Anger flooded through her veins over their failure. Years of planning had ended unsuccessfully, and all she had to show for it was a hole in her stomach and a hospital bed.

She glanced around at her stark white surroundings, having difficulty focusing on any one object. Instead of struggling in her weakened state, she decided to conserve whatever energy she had left to flee the hospital as soon as the opportunity presented itself.

Sybelle wondered what had happened to her daughter. She was still mad at her foolish confession of love. Her own daughter, who she had cared for through her pain and suffering, had disrupted the dagger's plunge into the heart of the monster Sybelle so vehemently hated. She was so looking forward to taking the knife and pulling it down his chest cavity to exposes his heart underneath. Such pleasure it would have been to stab it repeatedly until it ceased beating and his heart turned cold. Sybelle had played the scene over in her mind a thousand times before that evening. Her daughter had spoiled everything by falling for his wiles.

For three long years, she had devoted her life, money, and time to seeing her daughter restored to some semblance of normalcy. She was so proud of her when she had caught the eye of Dom Fernando, the prince of Portugal. He was next in line for the throne. Her daughter would have been a princess—a beautiful princess.

Sybelle was as surprised as anyone that a dancer at the Garnier had intrigued a handsome prince. Obviously, it was her beauty and grace that enticed him, and with Sybelle's coaching, she had won him over quickly. She was elated to think they would be part of a royal family, living in wealth for the remainder of their lives. A date for the wedding had been set and all was in place until that night; the one night that changed the course of their lives forever.

Désirée was filling in for an absent dancer that evening. Dom Fernando was in the audience drooling over his talented fiancée. Sybelle had accompanied him that night, and they sat above in one of the boxes to the right. Then all hell broke loose. Pieces of plaster began tearing from the ceiling and falling upon the stalls below. Then a loud snap occurred, and the crystal orb started its descent. It crashed into the seats, and one poor woman underneath was crushed to death. Others were injured trying to flee the disaster as the candles began their hellish job.

The lit candelabra quickly ignited the seats. As soon as it hit the carpeted floor, it crawled up the stairs to the stage like a monster from hell, catching the corner of the curtain on fire. Everyone on stage panicked and ran, but Désirée stood frozen looking up at their box to make sure they were all right. She was shocked like everyone else, watching the horrible scene unfold before her eyes. Too engrossed to notice that the flames had spread upward and burned the ties of the curtain, it suddenly gave way, falling upon Désirée. The heavy weight of the fabric pushed her face forward onto the stage floor.

Sybelle would never forget the screams of her daughter trying to wiggle herself from underneath the burning fabric that pinned her into hell. A stagehand ran to her aid and pulled the heavy brocade cloth away, trying desperately to stomp out the smoldering flames. When Sybelle saw Désirée's exposed back, she nearly died.

The hours that passed after that moment were branded into Sybelle's mind like an etched painting. It would never leave. She fled to her daughter's side. Désirée lay on the stage floor writhing in pain, her shrill screams filled the auditorium. Her clothes had been burned off her body, and Sybelle was helpless as she gazed upon the horror that remained. She looked up at Dom Fernando, who stood in the box emotionless. He made no move to come to her side, but merely lowered his head and turned and left. The smell of her daughter's burnt fleshed filled Sybelle's nostrils. She would never forget it as long as she lived.

The weeks that followed were pure hell. Désirée lay drugged in a morphine stupor, unable to bear the pain when awake. The doctors seemed helpless to heal her charred flesh and prevent infections. Finally, six months later, her skin began to scar over into a hideous landscape. Dom Fernando visited her once in the hospital and then never returned. He broke off the engagement. Sybelle never had the heart to tell her daughter he had wed another before her recovery. She lied each time Désirée asked if they had heard from him.

Months passed and Sybelle used the time to her advantage while her daughter recovered. At first, speculation was rampant about the cause of the disaster. Somehow, the metal hook that held the chandelier in place either bent from the weight or snapped, causing the crash. After further investigation, it was discovered that the safety rope had been cut, and everyone blamed the Ghost.

Everybody who worked at the Garnier knew about the Ghost and his pranks. Désirée had told Sybelle the horror stories the girls passed around in the dormitories to frighten the daylights out of her. He was hideous and routinely captured unsuspecting women to drag them to his lair and have his way with them. Sybelle at first thought it was nonsense, but after further investigation and pressuring of the managers after the disaster, she found out the Ghost truly existed. He used the catastrophe as a diversion to haul off one of the singers, a soprano named Christine Daaé, who he later released.

After the fiasco, he disappeared when the authorities began questioning his involvement in the mysterious death of the infamous Comte de Chagny. Others thought perhaps the Ghost had died too.

Sybelle's psychic instincts told her otherwise. She knew the monster lived, and she was determined to make him pay for their pain and suffering. It did not take long for her hatred to turn into a bitter obsession for revenge. Nothing would satisfy her hunger for restitution, except holding his dead heart in her hands.

She had hired a private detective and everything fell into place. After her own investigation, it did not take a genius to put two and two together. The box-keeper, Madame Giry, had been his assistant. When he supposedly died, she mysteriously left for Malta a few months later with two male traveling companions. Désirée and Sybelle were not far behind.

Sybelle had carefully planned her revenge. It irritated the hell out of her that he was free, and she was confined to a hospital bed. The thoughts of the past and her unsuccessful outcome stirred her insane anger. She had to get up and leave. Her work was not finished! He still needed to pay for his transgressions, and Sybelle Hessier would never rest until she made sure he was dead. This time, she would burn the opera house down with him inside. Erik Dante would feel the pain of flames, experience the smell of burning flesh, and wail in tormenting pain.

Sybelle needed to reclaim and deliver her wayward daughter too and bring her back to her senses. She had to get out of bed and leave. Sybelle tried to move, but when she did the searing pain in her abdomen returned. A nurse came to her side after hearing her moans.

"Madame, you need to lie still or you will start to bleed again. You've lost a lot of blood."

"I need to leave," she spat. "I have things to do!"

The bitter words filled the room and swiftly another figure drew near to her bedside. It was a uniformed police officer. Her eyes shot wide open.

"Madame Hessier, I'm here to inform you that you are under arrest for the attempted murder of Erik Dante. As soon as you recover, you will be transported to the city jail where you will await trial for your crimes. Do you understand?"

Sybelle's eyes grew wide in rage. "You stupid fool! You should be arresting him, not me! Don't you know who he is?"

"He's the owner of the Royal Opera House, Madame. Yes, we are aware of who he is."

"You idiot! He's the Ghost!"

The policeman's brow rose over her incoherent ramblings. "Madame, he is no ghost, I assure you."

Sybelle hated feeling helpless. She tried to move and sit up, but groaned in pain. The nurse pushed her shoulder back down on the bed.

"Madame, Madame! You must listen or we will have to restrain you."

The policeman cleared his throat. "You will remain here until you are recovered. A guard has been posted outside your hospital room door to make sure you stay put. Though I doubt in your condition, Madame, you are able to go anywhere."

"Damn you! Damn you!" she growled at him.

He turned and left her bedside, and she looked at the irritating nurse giving her orders. "I will do as I please!" she announced.

"I'm afraid not," the nurse retorted. She picked up a syringe and motioned for an orderly to help her inject the needle. The man held Sybelle's arm and shoulder in place, while she struggled against the assault on her body. The nurse found a vein in her arm and shoved the needle through her flesh, causing her to scream in pain. The contents were injected, and Sybelle felt the quick rush of morphine coursing through her blood. The bitch had sedated her with enough painkillers to incapacitate her for hours.

"You'll be back asleep in no time," she reassured her. "And if you continue to fight your recovery, we will bind you to the bed. Do you understand?"

Sybelle looked at the policeman who stood nearby with a smug look of victory across his face. She wanted to spit at him, but did not have the strength to form the spittle to eject from her mouth. *Next time, you bastard,* she thought to herself. A moment later, everything went black.

Chapter 27

"Has he seen her yet?" Richard asked, as he sipped his cup of tea in Andrea's sitting room.

"No. He's secluded himself away and only comes out at night to wander the streets again. He refuses to speak with her."

"She seems no better," Richard replied thoughtfully. "I see she's returned to her duties, but her face is filled with remorse and sadness."

"Her mother is recovering well, but has no future with the trial looming over her head," Andrea added with a hint of satisfaction in her voice. "I still can't believe she tried to kill Erik, but I suppose we must be thankful Désirée attempted to wrestle the dagger from her hand giving Erik time to defend himself."

Richard set down his teacup and stood to his feet. "I'm not sure what we can do about it, Andrea, but it's clear they both have deep feelings for one another. However, Erik cannot handle the obvious."

"You mean the scarring?"

"What else?"

"No, no, I don't believe that's the entire reason" she countered, standing to her feet and walking over to Richard's side. "I'm convinced his heart is wounded over her betrayal. What else could it be? I think it brought back painful memories. He allowed himself to love another woman, and once again, she turned against him. He has every right to sulk if you ask me."

"Well, I have no answers to the dilemma," he confessed. "I better get back to the office. Perhaps you can talk some sense into him. He's always listened to you."

"I will, when he's past the irritable stage."

Richard smiled and bent down to kiss Andrea. "Well, I'm never irritable," he teased, as their lips met. Their relationship had been going very well, in spite of all the stresses that surrounded the two of them lately.

"No, you're never irritable, my dear."

Andrea, consumed with Erik's wellbeing, struggled with feelings of disdain toward Désirée. Perhaps it was time to at least approach her and see what she could do about her broken heart. After Richard returned to his office, she wandered down the hallway to Désirée's door and knocked softly. A meek voice on the other side of the barrier replied, "Come in." Andrea did and found Désirée sitting in her chair with the violin in her lap. She looked as if she had been crying and a gloomy look shrouded her face.

"I thought I would check on you, Désirée, and see how you are faring," she explained. After seeing her appearance, Andrea felt a twinge of compassion as she walked closer. She examined the girl's countenance and was shocked at how pale and sickly she appeared.

"You don't look well, Désirée. Are you all right?" The back of her hand reached toward Désirée's forehead to feel if it was warm. "Well, you have no fever." She sighed in relief.

Désirée sat quietly, her eyes avoiding a direct gaze into Andrea's as they darted around the room at everything except her face.

"He hates me, doesn't he?" Her defeated words fell from her lips. "Why does he allow me to stay here if he doesn't wish to speak with me any longer?"

The brutal reality that Désirée spoke rang true, but Andrea did not wish to discourage her completely. "I do not think he hates you, my dear. He's merely struggling over being betrayed again. This is the second time that he's given his heart, and the second time the woman he loved turned against him and betrayed that love. For him, love doesn't come easy. He's been rejected so many times in his life that I'm sure he still doesn't understand the entire concept of true love."

"I know he has every right to hate me," Désirée admitted, brushing her hand across the violin in her lap. "At first I wanted to hurt him, I really did, and Mother had such hatred in her heart. I wanted to see her satisfied for what she had endured on my behalf. When I discovered the Ghost was a man I admired, my feelings grew to love, but I was bound to Mama's wishes."

Andrea watched her hand stroke the violin. "It's all you have left of him now, isn't it, Désirée, the violin?"

She nodded her head up and down.

"Are you still practicing?"

"No. I have no heart to practice."

"Well then, I think you should. If anything, I know Erik would be pleased that you still show an interest in what he loves the most, Désirée." She bent down and patted the girl's hand, offering her reassurance. "Give him time. When he is able, he will come to you, and then the two of you can talk about the feelings you have bottled inside."

"Do you think so?" Her voice raised in hopefulness.

"Yes, I do." Andrea watched Désirée struggle. She looked as if she wanted to say something more, but couldn't bring herself to speak the words.

"I still love him, Andrea," she finally mumbled, her eyes welling in tears. "My own body repulses me more than his deformity, but I'm afraid he cannot accept the way I look."

"Time will tell, though I think it is more of a matter of trust than anything else."

Andrea bid her goodbye and left her room. Her heart was touched over the girl's honesty. Though she was in no mood for Erik's irritableness, it was unavoidable. Andrea headed toward his quarters next.

※　※　※

While in her cell, Désirée had begged him for forgiveness, but Erik did not possess the strength to grant mercy to his betrayer. On the other hand, he did not want her to suffer any longer either. She had gone through enough.

Désirée had returned to the opera house and her duties, and Erik returned to a deep depression. His life sunk into a pit of despair, and his self-hatred reached to new depths. All he wanted to do for weeks after the incident was hide in solitude and avoid all human contact.

Richard and Andrea were intelligent enough to leave him alone while he sorted through the emotions. He kept his days filled with composing a new operatic tragedy, which was quite appropriate in his mind. His life had been a continual tragedy of both outward and inward pain, so the inspiration freely flowed through the musical score. Whether he would ever perform the opera was another matter entirely. For now, it served a greater purpose, as he penned the pain of his heart through notes, measures, and beats.

He purposely refrained from seeing Désirée. To him, she would always be Désirée, not Theresa, and he found it difficult to accept her real name. The haunting images of her back never left him. He would close his eyes and the grotesque flesh would appear. Erik could only imagine the shrilling screams of pain that followed while her body burned. He cringed at the thought he was to blame. A woman who had once been a picture of perfection and beauty was now clothed in scars that she would take to her grave, because of his insane obsessions.

Though Désirée confessed her love, he would not allow her to love the man who was to blame for her misfortune. He should be hated. If only they had killed him while he was drugged, then retribution for his sins would have been served.

A knock at his door drew him out of his depressing thoughts, only to elicit a growl from his throat. "Go away! I don't wish to speak to anyone."

"Erik, please, it's me, Andrea. Open the panel."

He hesitated mulling over what she had come to talk about, angrily wishing to gag her nagging mouth. The entrance opened, and Erik stood tall over her with a piercing gaze relaying his displeasure. "I don't wish to talk, Andrea, now go away."

"Well, that's too damn bad," she boldly snarled in return. "You're going to do just that!" She pushed past Erik and entered his sitting room with an air about her that he found most irritating. Andrea always knew he would never physically harm her, but Erik was in no mood for a discussion either.

"Fine," he spat, slamming the panel shut behind her. "Get on with it then get out!"

Andrea glared at him over his rash words and stuck both her hands on her hips. She walked up and postured herself before him looked into his eyes without flinching.

The woman was serious, and sparks were about to fly between the two.

"How long do you intend on sulking in here? Another week? Another month?"

"As long as I damn well please," he spat. "What's that to you?"

"I could care less," she retorted, flipping her hand in the air. "I've watched you brood on and off for years and know damn well you don't come out of your seasons of depression until you are damn well ready. However, this is not all about you, Erik! You're being selfish, terribly selfish. There is a young woman who is pining for you even now with a broken and repentant heart. How long are you going to ignore her before you speak and settle whatever it is between the two of you that needs to be settled?"

Erik turned away from Andrea's glare. "I don't know," he admitted. His voice sounded broken and weak. "I cannot forgive myself for what I have done to her. She should hate me, not love me."

"Well, she is a remarkable woman then, because she completely forgives you for the past, Erik. I can assure you that woman loves and accepts you completely. She holds no more resentment for the fire or her scars, but she does hold in her hands a broken and bruised heart. She fears you will never speak to her again."

The words caused Erik to turn and look into Andrea's face. Was it the truth? "I find it hard to believe," he admitted.

"Do you love her, Erik?"

Erik smirked. "Love? What is love, Andrea?" He walked over and pushed around the musical scores he had penned recently, pondering love. "I write scores of love, wish for love, dream of love, and want to be loved for who I am. All I feel is lust in my loins when I'm with her. Is that love?" He chuckled knowing his admission shocked Andrea by the look on her face.

"Have you . . . "

"No, but I can assure you I came close."

The room grew silent, and Erik watched Andrea closely, wishing for an explanation from her to make sense of it all.

"Love, Erik, is more than physical desire, which is apparent you feel for Désirée. I know all you've ever wanted in life was to be loved for yourself, and from what I hear from Désirée, she looks far beyond your deformity and loves you wholeheartedly."

"The monster?" he retorted in disgust.

"She doesn't see the monster; she sees the man."

Erik couldn't resolve the disparity that she could love the madman who had taken her beauty.

Andrea continued to encourage him. "What you feel right now are the same struggles inside Désirée. She fears you no longer care because of what she did to you and how she looks with her scars. It sounds to me as if both of you are afraid of the same things."

"I don't know," he responded, exasperated.

"Well, I think you have a difficult decision. It's time, as far as I'm concerned, for you to stop your brooding." Andrea raised her voice to a demanding tone. "Go and see that girl! What if this is your chance for happiness, Erik? Don't throw it away."

"I'll think it over." Erik knew that wasn't the answer she wanted to hear, but it was all he could say for now.

"Good, that's all I can ask. Will you start having meals again with Richard and I? We miss your presence."

"Perhaps."

Andrea's eyes roved over Erik's quarters that were in an absolute shambles. "You need housekeeping service in here terribly. It's an absolute mess. Shall I . . . "

"No," he countered, quickly cutting her off from suggesting that Désirée be allowed to enter. "I don't want her in here."

"Very well. Then I won't scold you like a little boy with a dirty room," she joked as she headed for the door.

"You've scolded me for years, Andrea, and I doubt you'll stop any time soon." They both exchanged warm smiles. Andrea left, and Erik found himself perched upon an emotional abyss, wondering if he should jump in or run the other way.

Chapter 28

Désirée's emotional heartache grew exponentially hour by hour when the days stretched farther away without a word from Erik. Richard gave her regular updates on her mother's progress. She had recovered from the stab wound, but the authorities and physicians decided she was mentally unstable and not able to stand trial for her crimes. They transferred her to Mount Carmel Hospital's mental ward for further evaluation and treatment.

Désirée had not seen her since that horrible night, afraid to visit a mad woman. She felt guilt-ridden for partaking in her mother's sick desire for retribution. She should have put an end to it quickly and convinced her long ago to end her scheme of revenge. If she had, all this woe could have been avoided. Instead of her being prisoner in an insane asylum, they could be living elsewhere happy and content.

To keep busy, she asked to return to full-time work to take her mind off her woes. In her own attempt to deal with her sadness and pain, she went about her chores, cleaning for hours. Like Erik, she had taken to a life of solitude, avoiding communal dining with the other employees or even speaking to anyone else. Each day she would work. Each night she would lock herself behind closed doors and sulk.

The violin remained silent, but not untouched. She often caressed it in her arms as the only part of Erik that remained with her. Her hand rested where his did, and she found it comforting to place her fingers in the same place. Désirée missed hearing him play. Though she knew he was on the other side of the wall, she never heard any strains from his violin either. They both had lost the song in their souls apparently.

One night, to deal with her loss, she thrust the violin under her chin and released her sorrow through music. The small score she had played the night of her recital was still in her memory. It flowed like healing water, and to her surprise, she was able to play it again to near perfection. Her eyes shut tight, like Erik when he played. She released the music within, and her arm caressed the violin like a lover.

A sudden rush of fresh air entered the room, and her eyes shot open at the sound of movement from the sliding panel. She quickly glanced at the doorway and saw his tall form at the threshold. Her heart stopped.

"Erik!" Désirée jumped to her feet, surprised that he had dared to enter her room. His eyes bore into hers silently, and she tried to find an ounce of compassion in his face. He said nothing but stood motionless just looking at her until she felt naked before him.

"I . . . I'm . . . " she stuttered, trying to explain her actions.

"I heard you play," he finally whispered from a raspy throat. "You did well."

Désirée set the violin on her bed and took a step closer. No words were exchanged as they looked in each other's eyes, searching for answers. Finally, Erik offered his hand. "Come with me," he commanded softly. "It's time we talked."

With no hesitancy on her part, Désirée responded. She gently grasped his hand, letting him lead her into his private quarters. The panel closed behind them. A rush of fear coursed through her body at the thought of being alone with him. He could burn his anger against her, and she could pay for her sins too. Her eyes narrowed with concern.

"It's all right, Désirée," he told her, releasing her hand. "I won't hurt you." Stopping his stride, he looked at her and asked, "Do you prefer Désirée or Theresa?"

"I prefer Désirée, Erik, but you may call me whatever you wish."

He let out a half-hearted chuckle with a huff and walked into the center of the room. "I'd offer you a drink, but I have a hatred of crystal decanters with alcohol these days. You never know what's inside of them, do you?"

Désirée's heart sank over his snide remark that confirmed the hurt and distrust still brewed inside. "You'll never forgive me, will you, Erik." It was more of a statement than a question.

She walked over to the empty divan feeling the need to sit down. Erik crawled like a preying cat over to her side, unsettling her nerves. He stood over her briefly, gazing into her eyes so intently that she melted under his power. The intensity made her uncomfortable, and she pulled her gaze away from his and began to fiddle with the folds of her skirt. What she heard next from his lips shocked her to the core.

"I should think, Désirée, that it is you that has much to forgive me for," he confessed remorsefully. "I am tortured daily by the pain I caused you and the responsibility I share in your scars. There is no forgiveness from heaven or hell for my sins against you."

Her heart melted inside her chest, and Désirée jumped to her feet and clutched both his upper arms in her hands.

"Oh, no, Erik, no! I do not want you to suffer as I have. Truly, I have forgiven you. You had no way of knowing this would happen to me. It was purely an accident and nothing intentional on your part."

"Oh, but there was intention," he told her, as he remembered that night. "When I took Christine Daaé, I hated everyone and didn't care if they lived or died! All I wanted was her, and I damned those who stood in my way. Without a second thought, I cut the last cord of the chandelier and brought it down on the audience. They gave me no compassion, and I gave them none in return. I wanted them to die! I . . . I . . . "

Erik's voice trailed off as he brought his hands to his eyes, trying to stop the visions of that night that painfully taunted his soul. "I just didn't see their faces. I didn't see you. I only wanted her."

Désirée's eyes filled with burning tears that quickly spilled down her cheeks. He dropped his hands from his face. When he saw her tears, Erik took his handkerchief and dabbed them away with such tenderness she felt weak from his touch.

"If I forgive you, Erik, you must forgive yourself," she gasped between each word. "All I want is your forgiveness for trying to hurt you."

Désirée could no longer stand the distance between them. It felt as if a large canyon separated their lives. She had to breach it now, or both of them would fall into an abyss and be lost forever. Without further thought, she flung her arms around his waist and clung tightly to his body with a relentless hold. She leaned her head against his strong chest and listened to the beat of his heart. She would not release him until forgiveness flowed.

Her sobs begged him again. "Forgive me, Erik. Forgive me! I have forgiven you."

Erik remained stiff for a few seconds, but then responded by wrapping his arms around her waist. He bowed his head. A drop of moisture hit her upper cheek, and Désirée felt Erik convulse with guttural sobs leaving his throat. She tightened her grip around him, wishing she could melt her entire being into his and never leave his soul.

"I love you," she whispered.

She held him close until his convulsing waned, but dared not gaze at him until he was ready. Désirée feared the raw emotions he expressed would cause him embarrassment. She stood upon a thin line, and she knew one wrong move might break the tie they had forged.

Finally, the words she longed to hear from Erik were released in a breathless whisper of emotion from his lips.

"I forgive you, Désirée." His hand lifted and gently stroked the back of her head, and he lowered his mouth close to her lips. "I love you."

His words melted into Désirée's wounded heart like warm oil. She lifted her head to look at him, and his lips tenderly met hers. There was no thrusting of desire behind the kiss she received. Only a tender longing for acceptance that felt hesitant, as if he was worried she would not respond.

Désirée gave back to him the same and drank in her first taste of the man she loved, not the lustful monster that had twice tried to take her for his sole satisfaction. He opened his heart, and Désirée was more than aware that she held in her hands a precious gift.

As they continued their tenderness together, his kisses became more intense. The fire of desire ignited in her body until she ached for release. She felt Erik respond to the heated chemistry, and she threw all caution to the wind.

She stood before him and began to unbutton his black velvet vest, but after the first button fell loose and slipped through the hole, Erik grabbed her hand and shook his head no.

"Please," she begged. "Please."

Her blue eyes met his anxious gaze, and Erik relented, dropping his hand while he watched her proceed with each subsequent button. She slipped her hands underneath his suit coat and shoved both the vest and jacket off his shoulders until they slipped down his arms and fell to the floor.

She eyed his white linen ruffled shirt, and then Désirée molded her lips to his mouth sensuously kissing him until he moaned in anticipation. Her fingers played with the buttons on his shirt. One by one, they released until his chest was exposed. She shoved the shirt over his shoulders and pulled it down his arms until the naked flesh appeared before her eyes. When she saw the taunt lines of his toned body, it sent shivers of desire coursing through her blood like fire.

Désirée, unbeknown to Erik, was not a virgin. Her former fiancé, who could not wait until their wedding night, had deflowered her long before the accident devouring her perfectly beautiful curves that later turned him away in disgust. She feared once she exposed herself, that Erik would recoil from her in the same way. It was then she knew, as she gazed into his eyes of desire, that what was about to transpire between lovers had to be on common ground.

"Take your mask and hairpiece off," she pleaded, imploring him in love. "I shall not allow you to look upon my scars and make love to me unless I can look upon your deformity." She lifted her hand to the corner of his mask, and he quickly grasped her wrist.

"Are you sure, Désirée?"

"I love you, Erik. All of you. I only wish the same in return, but I cannot give you my body wholly in love unless you give me yours."

Erik released her hand, and she slowly removed his mask and hairpiece revealing the man underneath. It was horrible, yes, but it was Erik. His half-face was no worse than her half-body. She placed his mask and hair on the table and then returned to embrace him. "Make love to me, Erik."

He scooped her up in his arms, carried her into his bedchamber with long determined strides, and set her upright before him. Her passionate desire pulled him against her breasts, and Désirée led Erik on the journey she knew he had dreamed of his entire life.

❊ ❊ ❊

Erik's denial ended. He had waited for what seemed like an eternity to feel the thrust of his body enter a woman. There was no turning back now and no doubt in his mind that Désirée had captured his desire in every way imaginable. She was willing to let him bare himself before her to the deepest core of who he was as a man, as long as he was willing to accept her on equal grounds. The choice, Erik discovered, was an easy one.

Désirée continued to play with his flesh, and he had no doubts she had already experienced the pleasures that awaited him. At that point, morality for either of them was the farthest thought from his mind. He needed a proficient teacher; who better than his heart's desire to take him toward the ultimate satisfaction and undiscovered place of sexual bliss.

In like manner, he began to unbutton the bodice of her dress while she fiddled with his trousers. They acted like two heated animals that couldn't devour each other fast enough. It wasn't long before he had pulled her dress over her shoulders and let it pool at her feet. With each breathless kiss they exchanged, Erik's arousal increased tenfold.

Finally, after their ceremonial undressing, Erik felt every inch of her flesh with his palms. The smoothness of her breasts and the toying of her nipples brought heated surges coursing through his veins. At first, he enjoyed the untouched and unscarred portions of her lovely curvaceous frame and curiously eyed everything that made her a woman.

"You are so beautiful, Désirée. He wanted all of her to be beautiful, and he was determined to see her as such.

"Turn around," he told her tenderly. She obeyed, but he felt the slight trembling of her body over the thought of what he was about to see. He examined the burn scars that weaved an ugly pattern of pain and sorrow across her torso. With his fingertips, he touched the edges. "Does it hurt?" he asked, afraid of what she would say.

"No, Erik, there is no more pain. It only feels coarse and tight, not like my skin that is soft and supple."

"I'm so sorry, Désirée. So sorry." He lowered his lips and began kissing her back. She flinched at first, and then softly sobbed in response while he accepted and loved every part of her body. "Don't cry," he begged. "You are still beautiful to me."

When he finished embracing her scars, he turned her around, lifted her up, and took her to the bed as she clung tightly around his neck, burying her head in his shoulder.

Erik stood naked before her, unashamed for the first time in his entire life. No mask covered his face, no hairpiece covered the lack of strands, and no feeling of rejection came from her gaze. In response, she held out her arms lovingly.

"Come to me, Erik, and let me love you."

He gently lowered himself on top of her body and their lips met. The sensation of warm flesh against his own surged through his body, fueling his desire. He was about to play the music of love. Their kissing became heated, their moans pronounced. Before Erik thought otherwise, he slid himself into the warmth of her body and felt the glorious oneness with a woman.

Désirée encouraged every rhythmic movement and like a perfect musical score, they moved in heated unison and desire until at last Erik released the grunts of a satisfied man. She responded in like manner, clutching his back tightly grazing her fingertips into his flesh with a satisfied cry of her own. He wondered what she felt to make her writhe with such a glorious response that was pure music to his ears.

When they finished, Erik could not stop kissing the desire of his life and telling her repeatedly of his love. Finally, he had become a man accepted wholly by a woman. Nothing could take away the bliss he felt at that moment of his completion. He rolled to his side and cradled Désirée in his arms.

"Did you enjoy it?" she asked, sheepishly.

Erik smiled. "It's difficult to put into words," he admitted. He stumbled over his thoughts, trying to grasp the right phrase. "Immensely," he finally breathed, leaning over to kiss her again. "For the first time in my life, Désirée, I feel whole. The monster has become a man."

"And I a woman." She chuckled with glee. "A perfect pair of half-bodies blended together to make one."

"That's right," he pondered. "All my life I've sought for beauty to compensate for my ugliness. But I never understood true beauty, Désirée, until you came into my life."

Her flesh pressed against his body, and he held the warmth closely, letting each pore encapsulate the essence of the woman in his arms.

"I will never let you go now," he warned her with a stern and determined voice. He had found a new obsession to replace the old; the obsession of expressing love through sexual means. Désirée had succeeded in drugging him with the most potent of aphrodisiacs, and he embraced the new addiction willingly, already contemplating the next time they might share flesh.

"I don't wish you to let me go, Erik." Her arms tightened around his body, giving him the encouragement that she wished for the same. "I'm yours in every way . . . forever."

"Good," he told her, rolling her underneath him one more time to feel the rush of his body pressing against her. "I'm not ready to let you leave my bed," he added, a wicked grin curling his lips. Erik knew she looked back into his eyes, his ugliness greeting her in return. He had never felt such joy of total acceptance as she clamped her arms around his neck and brought him forcefully back to her lips. This time, her tongue thrust into his mouth searching out the treasure, and he responded willingly in return. Erik did not care if he ever came up for air again.

Chapter 29

Désirée returned to her room to do as Erik asked. She would no longer stay within the small four walls of one bedroom; she would live with him in his private quarters. There would be no more work or labor in the opera house. Her life belonged to him, though Erik made no mention of marriage. At that point, she did not care. She only knew that they had accepted each other with their flaws and had solidified their relationship with the most glorious intimacy she had ever known.

He seemed to have changed. His harshness disappeared and the anger dissipated. Forgiveness was exchanged freely between the two of them, and the bitter roots they had harbored died unfed. Whatever lay ahead, Désirée was more than willing to accept, as her heart wove its brokenness into his own, making them one on every level.

She quickly emptied her room of her meager belongings and closed the panel behind her to stay with him alone. Like two crazed lovers, neither of them could keep their hands from one another as they continued to explore each other in heated passionate displays.

Désirée knew that once discovered missing from her quarters and derelict in her housekeeping duties, inquiries would come knocking on his door. Erik did not attempt to tell Andrea or Richard about their arrangement, wishing to wait until they inquired. It did not take long, when the next morning Andrea stood outside asking for entrance.

"Let me handle this," he told her.

He opened the door and greeted the concerned faces of Andrea and Richard, who pushed their way inside.

"I assume you're here about Désirée," he stated, playing coy over the situation.

"Yes, we are! Her room has been emptied and she hasn't . . . " Andrea's words abruptly ended when she saw Désirée standing in Erik's parlor.

"Désirée will be living with me in my quarters from now on," he announced, signaling her to come to his side. In a surprising move that caused the jaws of Andrea and Richard to drop simultaneously, he slipped his arm around her waist affectionately. "We have made peace with each other," he announced.

Désirée responded by holding him close, her hand slipping over his heart.

"We have," she agreed, looking up with a girlish expression of love across her face.

"I see," replied Andrea, surprised. "Might I ask . . . "

Erik abruptly interrupted her. "No, you may not ask. This is our decision and both of you are kindly requested not to comment about our living arrangements. We're both consenting adults."

Andrea huffed in disgust, and Désirée knew she was posturing disapproval for both of them to take note.

"Now if you'll excuse us," he told them, tickling Désirée playfully causing a giggle to escape her lips, "we'd like to be alone."

"Come along, Andrea," Richard suggested, tugging at her arm. They both left without further word, and Erik closed the panel door behind them.

"There! Taken care of," he announced, pulling Désirée to his lips. "Now," he added with a wicked grin, "where were we?"

Désirée smiled.

❈ ❈ ❈

"Oh, Richard, I can't believe what's happened!" Andrea raced back to her room with Richard in tow to expel her obvious disgust over the turn of events. "This cannot be good," she declared, flinging the door open and stomping over to her settee where she flopped on the cushion. She grabbed a nearby program from *Faust* and began fanning herself to cool down the heated blush bursting from her cheeks.

"Did you see them?" she exclaimed. "Clinging to one another as if they had just . . . " Andrea felt as if she were on the verge of fainting. All these years, Erik hadn't dared to touch a woman and now this!

"The nerve of her!" She shook her finger at Richard. "Why, that hussy has drugged him again and has him in her clutches! We much save him, Richard!"

Richard flashed a smile of amusement that angered Andrea. She knew he was about to lecture her for the next ten minutes, so she braced herself, sending him a glare of warning. He walked over, sat next to her, and gathered her up in his arms to soothe her incessant worry. It was more than worry though, but Andrea couldn't put her finger upon the feelings churning in her soul.

"Calm down, Andrea. They are consenting adults, as he said. We cannot judge them, and I for one am quite happy they have forgiven one another. What a monumental step for both of them if you think about it rationally."

"Rationally," she protested. "I cannot think rationally about this matter at all!" She stewed while Richard held her, thinking thoughts of impropriety between the two of them that sent shivers up her spine.

"Did it ever occur to you that you might be jealous?"

"What!" Andrea pulled away from Richard's embrace and jumped to her feet in protest over the horrendous innuendo he just flung her way. "Why, Richard Mercier! How could you suggest such a thing?"

Richard burst out laughing hysterically over Andrea's interpretation of his statement. "No, no," he protested, trying to stifle his laugh. "I am quite aware you have never looked at Erik in that way, but you have in other ways."

"Such as what? What are you suggesting?" She took an angry stomp in his direction.

"You're almost a mother to the man, Andrea. You have sheltered and cared for him for years. Like a parent, you've watched over him, worried about his welfare, cared for him when no one else would. Now that he knows a woman in the Biblical sense, if you'll forgive my analogy, he is doing what is most natural to him as a man."

Andrea softened her tone, trying to understand what he was saying. "And what is that?"

"He's clinging to her and leaving you. Désirée is taking that intimate place you've held for years. She is now his confidant and much more. If they have shared a bed, they are more attached than ever."

Andrea did not want to think of Erik sharing a bed with anyone. She quivered at the thought, but as she pondered Richard's words, they rang true and she realized she did harbor a great deal of jealousy toward Désirée. She pulled her eyes away from his in shame and exhaled a long sigh of defeat.

"Am I correct?" he pressured.

"Yes, as usual. I do wish him happiness though I think their morality is a bit distorted."

"I doubt Erik has any moral compass to pain him like it does us. After all, Andrea, he has murdered, so the lines for him are blurred. His conscience is seared."

"You are quite right," she admitted with a tinge of remorse.

"Speaking of morality," he added, quickly changing the subject to her surprise. "Marry me."

Andrea gasped and brought her hand to her mouth. "Good God, Richard Mercier, have you lost your mind?"

He inched his way forward and pulled her into his chest. "No, I have not. This is the perfect time to claim you. Erik is now in the hands of another, and you are in my hands. Marry me."

Her stoic face relaxed, and Andrea allowed her pent-up love for Richard to release unabashed. "All right," she replied. "I will marry you."

"At last!" he shouted. Richard kissed her fervently and then pulled away. Andrea looked at him with great joy, feeling as if the weight of the world had slipped from her shoulders. No longer did she need to feel responsible for Erik's happiness, it now belonged to another; she finally could find her own.

❊ ❊ ❊

"Married?" Erik questioned, surprised at the news. "Well, I'm happy for you," he frankly admitted. Of course, he had played matchmaker by bringing the two back together, so he had to show his smug approval over the outcome. "I wish you happiness. When is the day?"

Andrea spoke for both of them. "We're leaving for Rome in the morning, Erik, and will be back in two weeks, if that is all right with you. We shall marry there, honeymoon, and return."

"Yes, yes, of course. I'm sure I can handle things here." He had seriously thought of becoming more involved in the day-to-day operations anyway. Everyone still wished to know the genius behind the Royal Opera House, and his relationship with Désirée infused in him a new boldness to step out from behind the shadows without fear.

"Well, I'm sure Désirée wishes you happiness as well."

"Where is she, might I ask?" Andrea looked confused at her absence.

"She's gone to visit her mother. I've encouraged her to make amends for both our sakes."

"That's good," interjected Richard. "Perhaps she will recover from the insane bitterness that keeps her captive once she realizes the two of you have passed that point of forgiveness and restoration."

Erik nodded his head. "Yes, I hope so." He sighed. "I feel partially responsible for her mental instability. She was only protecting her daughter and suffered much because of my own insanity that I once harbored in life."

"Are you happy?"

Andrea shocked him by the question. His eyes sparkled, which he knew she had rarely witnessed in his life, as he confessed his joy.

"She accepts me wholeheartedly, Andrea, my true man; deformity and all. We are much alike, she and I. Both filled with scars and pain, but both able to embrace each other for who we are." Erik smiled in satisfaction. "I couldn't be happier."

Richard approached Erik, moved with emotion, and patted him on the shoulder. "I'm happy to hear that, Erik. You have no idea."

"Take care of Andrea, good man, or you'll have me to answer to!" Erik gave him a look, and Richard smiled in return.

"I wouldn't think of crossing the Phantom of the Royal Opera House," he replied with a chuckle. "You have my word as a man. I shall cherish her until my dying breath."

Erik looked at Andrea feeling the need to do something he had never done before in their entire relationship. He took a step toward her, embraced her tenderly, and kissed her on the cheek. "Be happy, dear friend." He quickly released her and saw her eyes fill with tears.

"I will," she promised, wrapping her arm around Richard. "I will."

He was about to turn and leave when Andrea asked the one question he feared. "Will you marry Désirée?"

Erik halted and did not turn around immediately to face the question he held no answer to. After a strained minute of uncomfortable silence, he turned toward Andrea and answered truthfully. "I don't know. I've always dreamed of having a wife and being like everyone else. I'm fearful of that commitment right now, and I'm not sure why."

"She may wish for more, Erik, and what if . . . "

He raised his hand quickly in protest to the words. "I'll face the *what if's* if they ever arrive," he told her. If he could not think of marriage, he certainly did not wish to entertain the thought of siring a child. "One thing at a time."

"Of course," she replied with understanding.

Erik turned and left the two lovebirds alone to pursue their marriage and honeymoon. He missed Désirée and hoped she would return soon, but dreaded the news regarding her mother's health.

Chapter 30

Désirée had heard of mental institutions, but had never dreamed the horrors her eyes beheld or her ears heard. Mount Carmel Hospital's ward for the insane was unlike anything imaginable; a madhouse of screaming souls.

Before they allowed her to visit her mother, the physician led her to his office and closed the door behind them. He offered her a seat in front of his desk, and she sat nervously in the chair, bracing herself for bad news.

"I'm afraid that your mother has not responded to treatment. I don't want you to be shocked upon what you see," he warned her, pausing briefly before continuing. "But I should caution you we have had to keep her restrained for the majority of her stay her with us."

"What do you mean restrained?"

"When you visit her, you'll see her tied to her bed with arm and leg restraints. It's for her own good, as she often becomes violent with the staff, acting like she wishes to stab them repeatedly in the heart."

"My God," Désirée gasped, bringing her hand to her mouth as tears welled in her eyes.

"We have sedated her somewhat, so when you see her she will be more subdued for your visit, but a bit groggy, I'm afraid."

Désirée nodded her head in acknowledgement. "May I see her now?"

"Yes, of course."

Désirée followed the doctor down a long white corridor, hearing the screams of men and women behind locked doors. Occasionally, a face would appear in the small window with glaring mad eyes watching her as she passed by, often yelling obscenities as the demons inside enraged their actions. She wanted to clamp her hands over her ears to stop the sounds, but before she could respond, an attendant took out a ring of keys and at the doctor's instructions, he unlocked the door.

The doctor paused before entering. "We are doing our best to bring your mother back to health, but the prognosis is not good at this point. The attendant will stand in the room with you for your safety should she attempt to harm. "

"She won't hurt me," she reassured him, even though she remembered her hand slapping her across the room that night she had lost all sense of reality.

"It's merely a precaution and a safety measure we take with all family visitors. Patients in this state of mind are often unpredictable in their behavior."

The doctor nodded and the attendant released the latch. He pushed it open, and Désirée slowly entered the stark white room with bars upon the window. She glanced at the hospital bed that held her mother bound in a prison of cruel leather straps and encased in white sheets. Her heart broke into a thousand pieces.

Tears welled in her eyes as she walked to her bedside. Sybelle's eyes were shut tight and a grimace outlined her jaw. Désirée wondered if she was in pain from the tight restraints.

"Mama," she called in a light whisper that failed to rouse her from slumber. She lightly placed her hand upon her arm and called again. "Mama, it's me."

Sybelle's wild eyes shot open, and she turned her head in the direction of her daughter. A sickening wicked laughter escaped her mother's mouth. Désirée had thought she would be groggy, but suddenly she appeared awake.

"Ah, my daughter, Theresa!" she jeered. "You've come to visit your insane mother at last, have you? How long has it been? Weeks? Months? I've lost count."

"Mama," Désirée cried. "You're not insane, just ill. I want you to get well, Mama."

She turned her head away from her daughter in anger. "You left me to rot in this hospital and now you come."

"They arrested me too, Mama. They were going to charge me with conspiracy to commit murder, but Erik—"

"Erik!" her mother interrupted. "You dare to say that name in my presence! He's the Ghost."

"All right then, the Ghost," Désirée relented. "He made sure the charges were dropped."

"Did you return to my home?" she asked.

"No, Mama, he brought me back to the opera house."

"You're still there? Now you are the insane one! Why haven't you killed him yet?" she shot back at her with glaring eyes. "You should have taken the dagger from my gullet and thrust it into his heart! But no, you stayed at my side like a weakling and watched me bleed to unconsciousness."

"Mama, please, don't . . . "

Her face turned to a sneer that sent a chill up Désirée's spine. "He's put you in a trance, hasn't he? Just like the other women of the Garnier he put into trances and dragged to his lair to rape their bodies."

"Mother, that's ridiculous. Those rumors are utterly untrue."

Her mother's hand tried to move to grab her daughter's but she could not reach her. "Did he rape you, Désirée? Did he? Tell me, so I can kill the bastard when they let me out of this insane asylum!"

Sybelle's body began to thrash against the restraints with such intensity that it enhanced the bruising already on her arms from her previous struggles. "They try to sedate me," she screamed in an evil laughter. "But my hatred keeps me alive and strong!"

"Mama, please," Désirée pleaded. "Erik has not hurt me. We have forgiven one another, Mother! Forgive him, please! It will make you better."

"Forgive him!" She spat in her daughter's direction. "You are no daughter of mine if you have forgiven the monster for what he did to you! I'll see him burn in hell, so he can feel the pain and smell the odor of burning flesh, as I did with you!"

"That is enough," the orderly commanded, pulling Désirée away from her bedside. "You must go now. Your visit here is clearly upsetting the patient."

"Mama, I love you," Désirée sobbed. She wanted to kiss her but was afraid to touch the madness seeping from her soul.

"He'll hurt you, Theresa!" Her mother's words followed her down the hallway as she fled from her presence. "He'll hurt you! Mark my words; he'll rip your heart to shreds! Theresa . . . Theresa."

Her voice trailed away until she could not hear it any longer. Désirée's feet ran down the tiled corridor passing the white walls until they reached the door. She begged the guard to let her out and he did. She thrust the door open with both hands, ran down the stairs to the exit, and into the street. Hot tears streamed down her face.

Her mother's words rang in her ears like a prophetic omen. *"He'll hurt you . . . He'll hurt you . . . "* With each pounding footstep, Désirée cursed the words spoken over her life to break the bondage she felt curling around her heart like chains.

❊ ❊ ❊

Erik was broken over Désirée's news regarding the visit with her mother. The responsibility of her insanity rested entirely upon his shoulders, whether it was his or not. The consequences of that night still followed him, even though Désirée offered forgiveness. He wondered if she still harbored anger for her mother's inability to release him from the past.

"Do you blame me?" he asked, as he held her sobbing body in his arms.

"No," she replied quickly and firmly. "She makes herself ill because she cannot let go of the bitterness. If she only knew you, Erik, like I do."

"The chance that will happen is a long way off," he admitted with regret. "If I could take that night back, I would, but then we . . . " He stroked the side of her face tenderly with the tips of his fingers. "I wouldn't have you here in my arms."

Désirée lifted her eyes and spoke her heart. "I would suffer the pain of it all again in a heartbeat if that was the price I needed to pay to be with you," she confessed soulfully.

Erik was shocked. How could she say such a thing? How could she love him with such unbridled conviction and forgiveness?

"Perhaps fate would have been kinder to us and brought us together through other less painful means."

"But we wouldn't have the kindred spirit we do now," she protested. "The two halves making a whole."

Désirée reached up with her hand, as she had done multiple times before, and tenderly removed his mask and hairpiece. He always flinched. It was difficult to entirely eradicate the residue fear of possible rejection when he bared his deformity in front of another human being.

She pulled herself into him, kissed him deeply, and then pleaded for what he knew she wanted. "Comfort me, Erik," she begged. She clung to him as if it were her last dying breath. "Comfort me."

Erik never resisted her pleas and with nimble fingers, he assaulted the buttons on her dress while she clawed to undress him. In a profession of acceptance and love, they stripped naked before each other. Their own bodies they loathed but found comfort in each other's.

Their ritual culminated in erotic lovemaking until they spent each other completely. Nothing could compare to the beauty they found together, or the contentment their souls enjoyed as they knit and intertwined their bodies through intimacy.

When they finished, Erik held the woman he loved and comforted her with his words. "She will get better, some day, Désirée. Do not give up hope."

Désirée responded with small weeping sobs. "I love you so much, Erik. You would never hurt me, would you?"

"Hurt you?" he asked, confused over her question. "Why would I hurt you? You've given me more joy in my life than I've ever known." His hand stroked her gently. "I will never hurt you."

As he pondered Désirée's odd question, he turned the subject to something more cheerful. "Oh, I must tell you," he added, "Andrea and Richard are leaving for Rome in the morning to wed and go on a honeymoon."

Désirée lifted her head and looked at him with surprised eyes. "Married? Honeymoon? I didn't know they were in love."

"For quite some time, actually."

Désirée lowered her head back down on his chest. "That's wonderful news, Erik."

He wondered if she wished for the same, but couldn't bring himself to discuss marriage with her. It was such a foreign concept that he was unable to wrap his mind around the thought and no compass steered his moral thinking anyway. As long as he and Désirée were happy to share their bodies as they did, why marry?

She did not stir anymore as he held her tight. "Sleep with me, Désirée." He held her close. "I wish to sleep with you in my arms."

"Whatever you say, Erik. Whatever you want."

It was the last words spoken, and Erik drifted off into a contented sleep.

Chapter 31

The two weeks passed quickly, and the happy couple returned more radiant than ever. Erik was excited to have them both back in their midst. The opera house had been much too quiet without them. In their absence, he had enjoyed himself immensely by mingling among the surprised cast and crew. He introduced himself announcing he would be more involved in the daily operations.

New life infused into his veins thanks to Désirée, who encouraged him to share his genius with everyone. Of course, the whispers ensued about the masked man with half a face. Erik was up front with the questions that he was deformed and preferred to keep the deformity hidden from society. It was a take-it-or-leave-it statement that left no room for speculation or comment. His relationship with Désirée had begun to heal his sensitivity to the world around him, because he no longer felt like half a man; he had found his wholeness in her.

Désirée also became more active in the life of the opera, as Erik began showering her with new clothes so she could appear at his side as a lady at the evening performances. They often frequented his private box together. Her love of music grew, and she insisted that he continue to teach her the violin until she became proficient. Erik's patience held no bounds, and he encouraged her love of the instrument and love of the arts.

For the first time in his life, his happiness hit a pinnacle of personal and professional success, until shocking news arrived that threatened to test him once more. Andrea requested a private moment with Erik and showed him the morning paper. After reading it, he grabbed a nearby chair and fell into the seat.

"I read it this morning, Erik, in the society section. I couldn't believe it myself and knew you must be told immediately."

Erik stared at the words again, as he slowly read them one by one to make sure he wasn't hallucinating.

"Society is buzzing this morning with the arrival of the Vicomte de Chagny and his wife Christine to our fine city of Valletta. The Vicomtess, a celebrated soprano from Sweden, has been taking a whirlwind holiday tour with her husband across Europe, visiting the various operatic venues in major cities. She has graced the stages from Paris, Berlin, and Venice during her tour and is now planning to visit our own Royal Opera House to celebrate its restoration. Though rumors swell whether she will be asked to sing upon its stage, the word is that they will attend Friday night's performance in the company of our esteemed Governor, Sir Henry Roberts, and his wife. One has to wonder if the mysterious masked owner will show the other side of his face to welcome these very important guests in our midst. I suppose we should all purchase a ticket for the performance of *Romeo and Juliet* by Gounod this Friday evening to find out."

The paper lowered and Erik raised his eyes to Andrea. "Christine is to be here Friday evening?"

"Yes, Erik. What will you do?"

Erik folded the paper in neat folds and handed it back to Andrea. "I'm not sure," he admitted. "Whatever you do, don't mention this to Désirée. Let me speak to her privately about it, all right?"

"What does she know of Christine?"

"Not very much, I'm afraid. Her only knowledge is of the night I brought the chandelier down to take Christine. Beyond that, she has never asked me about my feelings for her or our past relationship. I assumed if she did know anything, she just preferred not to speak of the past because it held painful memories regarding her injuries that evening."

Erik thought of the implications. "I must see her," he announced with surety. "I must."

"Do you think that's wise? What purpose would it serve?"

"Much," he replied. "I must clear my conscience of many things."

"Erik, I'm sure that Christine has moved on with her life and is happy. She looks happy in the picture of her and Raoul. I wouldn't think that seeing you would accomplish a thing."

"She knows I'm here." A gut feeling rose within him, and he was sure of it. "I can feel it in my spirit. She's come to seek me out."

"Well, I doubt that very much," Andrea protested. "For what purpose now after all this time?"

"Perhaps she has changed her mind and regrets her choice."

"Erik!"

He lifted his eyes remorsefully over his words. "I'm sorry," he muttered. "I was rashly thinking out loud."

"I should think so, Erik. I wouldn't think after all you've been through that you would consider hurting Désirée."

"No, no! You are quite right," he admitted. "I'm just confused . . . upset. It will pass."

Erik rose to his feet and walked toward the door. He stopped and reminded Andrea, "Please not a word to her!"

"Of course not."

After he departed her presence, Erik felt sick inside. Old ties to his spirit tugged at his heart. *Christine . . . Christine.* He hadn't said her name for so long and to think in just a few more days she would be in his presence once more. He had so much to say to her, but how? Erik had to find a way. He would make a way the night of the performance.

※ ※ ※

Désirée wiped the tear rolling down her cheek with the back of her hand. Everyone had been buzzing around the opera house for the entire day whispering amongst themselves enough to pique her curiosity. It took little ingenuity on her part to find out why. She sneaked behind the curtains listening to Richard speak to the cast and crew about additional rehearsals before Friday evening's performance. She heard every word while she stood at the side of the stage in the shadows.

"It seems, ladies and gentlemen, that Friday evening we have a sold-out performance. The Governor and his wife will be attending, along with the Vicomte de Chagny and his wife, Christine. Some of you may not be aware, but she has sung on stage in Stockholm, Berlin, Paris, and Venice. There are no plans for her to perform during her stay here, but the owner wants us to put our best on the line for the evening's performance. That means additional rehearsals!"

A groan came from the cast and crew. A sickening feeling washed over Désirée as she caught the side of the wall to keep the stage from shifting beneath her feet.

Christine was coming here—the woman that Erik had obsessed over for years. Why hadn't he told her? She wiped her eyes and turned around to make her way back to their quarters when a wave of nausea swept over her body. *Not now,* she thought to herself. *Please not now.*

Désirée, disappointed over having been kept in the dark, worried whether Erik would do anything rash. As all the scenarios and possible avenues for Friday evening paraded before Désirée's mind, she felt as if she were on the brink of insanity. Jealousy rose in her heart over any affection that Erik might still hold for Christine. The feeling so sickened her that she scurried to the nearest bath chamber and vomited. When she was through, she knew that the news she needed to share with Erik would need to stay hidden in her heart for now. She was pregnant.

❈ ❈ ❈

"Are you all right?" Erik asked, as he tied his ascot for the Friday evening performance. "You look pale."

"No, I'm fine, just a little tired. Your snoring keeps me awake at night."

Erik raised his brow over the comment. "My snoring? I don't snore," he retorted, dismissing the accusation as purely ridiculous.

"You do too," she insisted, coming up behind him and curling her arms around his waist.

"And you, my dear, talk in your sleep!"

"I what?"

"Talk in your sleep." He sported a teasing grin, waiting for her reaction.

"I do not," Désirée protested, a blush rushing up her cheek. She squeezed him tight. "What do I say? Tell me."

Erik turned slowly around and faced her. He touched her on the tip of her nose with his index finger in a light-hearted show of affection. "You say, 'Erik, oh, Erik, yes, yes, yes . . . '"

"Oh you!" She pushed him away as he laughed.

Erik finished putting on his dress jacket, taking a deep breath over what lay ahead. He hadn't said anything to Désirée, not yet, and had struggled all day long whether to mention the guests.

"It's a busy night tonight," he began, nonchalantly. "It's a sold-out performance."

"I'm not surprised with the Vicomte and his wife in attendance," she replied snidely.

Erik swallowed hard and turned to face her once again.

"Why haven't you said anything, Erik? The entire opera house has been one buzzing bee over their arrival."

He shrugged his shoulders and pulled his eyes from her blue gaze. "I didn't wish to worry you, Désirée, with things of the past. They are only here for one performance."

"You plan on talking to her, don't you?"

"I must." Erik's heart sank. He did not want to cause Désirée unnecessary pain.

"Why?"

"Because my conscience will not allow me peace until I do so."

Erik finished dressing, while his heart pounded in his chest over the thought of seeing Christine once again. He glanced at Désirée and witnessed sadness in her eyes.

"There is nothing to worry about, Désirée," he assured her, pulling her into his arms. "I love you."

"But you once loved her," she said with remorse, pulling away from him. "Every woman, Erik, fears a man's former love."

She turned from him angrily, which put Erik on edge. He hoped that he was not pushing the boundaries between them to a breaking point.

After they both finished dressing, he offered her his arm to lead her to the performance. "I promise you," he assured her, "everything will be fine." Désirée took his arm silently, but he sensed her worry. He hoped she would believe his intentions.

As they drew closer to their private box, his heart pounded ferociously at the thought of seeing Christine one more time. It had to be done. The night he abducted her had destroyed many lives, and he needed to apologize for his insane actions. It was something he had never done to any of his victims—apologize. If he was to continue with his life, his conscience had to be clean of everything, including the matter of Comte de Chagny.

Chapter 32

Christine entered the opera box alone with Raoul. Earlier in the day, the Governor came down ill with a dreadful case of stomach flu, and his wife stayed home to nurse him. Raoul did not seem to mind the change in plans. He preferred to attend the performance alone anyway, so they wouldn't have to figure out how to dump their guests afterward.

They settled into their seats, and Christine immediately displayed her disappointment over the arrangement of boxes. "You cannot see into Box 5 from here," she exclaimed, straining her neck in that direction. Naturally, she assumed that was where he would be.

As she eyed the remainder of the auditorium, she was stunned at the beautiful perfection. Her eyes glanced about the theater of gold and reds that were reminiscent of the Garnier.

"He's done an outstanding job, hasn't he, Raoul?"

Raoul grunted in return, and she glanced at her husband. His face stoic and unresponsive worried her a bit, and Christine hoped he would be able to handle the evening together.

"Yes, very much like Paris, isn't it? I'm not surprised," he finally answered.

Christine smiled. "Andrea wrote he did a magnificent job. It has his mark everywhere in the architecture and stonework."

"It does," Raoul agreed, reaching over and grabbing his wife's hand tightly.

"Thank you, Raoul, for taking me here. If it weren't for Andrea writing to let us know he was alive and doing well, I would have thought him dead."

"That's all right, Christine," he replied, tenderly. "I'd do anything for you."

"I know you would, Raoul, and I know too how hard this must be for you knowing you'll see him again." Christine tightened her grip upon his hand.

"I intend to ask," Raoul confirmed.

"I know, darling."

She smiled warmly at her husband and settled in as the lights dimmed and the first act of *Romeo and Juliet* began. Christine wondered if Erik would seek her out. If he did not, she would find him after the performance. Christine had much to say to her Angel.

Both were impressed with the production, and as the lights rose for intermission, she turned to look at Raoul. "Be a dear and get me a glass of champagne, only take your time in returning."

He smiled at her with a light chuckle escaping his lips. "I'll give him two seconds after I'm out the box for him to enter in behind me. Make sure you time how long it takes, and let me know later if I was right."

He flashed a grin of approval and left Christine alone. She sat quietly anticipating Erik to arrive at any moment. No sooner had the air of the curtain calmed from Raoul's departure, did it move again. Christine's heart climbed in her throat, and she tightly clutched the program in her hand.

"Hello, Christine."

His voice still sounded as smooth as velvet, with the same profound power to touch her soul. She swallowed the lump in her throat and turned her head. "Hello, Erik." She patted the seat next to her. "I've been expecting you."

As she glanced at him, she was moved at how well he looked clothed in a black tuxedo. The same charismatic atmosphere filled the box in which he sat, but Christine knew in her heart he was a different man. He was at peace, and she sensed his joy. The aura of darkness that had once shadowed him was gone. When she looked into his eyes, she couldn't help the tears that welled in her own. It was good to see him.

"How is my Angel of Music?" she asked. "Well I hope."

"Yes, very well, Christine, and you?" He sat down next to her, sending a rush of fond emotion through her heart.

"I'm very happy, Erik. Raoul is a good husband and my career is doing very well."

Christine worried he would look remorseful, but he did not, and she found his actions encouraging.

"I'm glad," he admitted, reaching over and touching her hand. "I have read how well you are doing, and I'm very proud of your accomplishments in the theater." He squeezed her hand and continued. "As it should be, I would think. Things have worked out for both of us in spite of my mistakes."

"You've done marvelous work here, Erik. You should be very proud."

"It was hell, I must admit, but it did my soul good to raise something from the ashes as penance for my foolishness in Paris."

Christine shook her head. "There is no more penance to be had, Erik," she told him. "You should know the authorities never filed any charges. You are a free man."

"What do you mean?" he asked, confused. "I don't understand."

"Let's just say that Raoul took care of the matter for me. I explained to the authorities after you fled that what happened between the three of us was nothing more than a lover's spat. I refused to press any charges. Raoul paid for the restoration to the theater. It took some doing, but the past is erased. You need not look over your shoulder forever being afraid that you will pay for that night."

Erik lowered his head in shame. "Oh, Christine," he breathed remorsefully. "I wish life were so simple." He paused before his painful confession. "But you are wrong. I have paid for my sins that night in more ways than one."

"What do you mean?" she asked, concerned.

Christine listened as Erik told her about the woman named Désirée, astonished over the events that recently transpired. Her mouth gaped open as she heard it all: her mother's plan, Désirée's injuries, and the horrible night they had drugged him. When he was through, she was shocked but gloriously happy there had been a happy ending to it all.

"And you love, her?" she asked, excited over the news.

"Very much."

"Oh, Erik, I am so glad for you."

Christine squeezed his hand and a few minutes of reflective silence passed between them. Erik appeared to struggle for words.

"I will always love you, Christine," he confessed. "Your voice, your beauty, will forever stay in my heart."

He paused before continuing, his voice quivering from emotion.

"But the beauty I have found in Désirée is far more precious to me. Because of her, I've learned to love, and her love has brought healing. We are two halves making the perfect whole."

"As it should be," she responded happily. "As it should be!"

"Can you ever forgive me for the dark times I put you though," he asked.

"Of course, Erik." She reached over and hugged her Angel of Music, glad that he had finally found what he had been searching for his entire life. As they gave each other an emotional embrace, Christine heard Raoul clear his throat. She looked behind her and saw him holding two glasses of champagne in his hands with a sour look upon his face.

"Raoul!"

"Have you two made your peace?" he asked. "If so, I have—"

"Questions," Erik abruptly interrupted. He stood to his feet and walked toward Raoul. "You have questions about the night your brother died."

Raoul's eyes narrowed. "I surmised on my own, sir, that my brother's death came about because of his own irrational behavior—an accident perhaps or was it something else?"

"It was an accident," Erik said, lowering his head, recalling the dreadful details. "Your brother attempted to cross the lake in the lower cellars. Perhaps he foolishly thought he could wade across it, but there are deep sink holes that cannot be seen in the murky waters. No doubt his step felt secure, until he fell into one. Without a boat to cross, the holes are capable of dragging a man down into a black watery death."

Erik sighed, and looked at Raoul square in the eyes. "I found your brother's body floating face down, Vicomte. I retrieved him from the waters and laid him upon the bank, fearful the authorities would pin his demise upon me. I assure you, as God is my witness, I did not set a hand upon him in any way for evil." Erik looked at Christine and then back to Raoul. "It was an unfortunate accident that came about in his zeal to help you. I am sorry for the sorrow I have caused you both."

Raoul shifted his feet dealing with the knowledge of Philippe's end. It was a great loss of life that he still mourned.

"He was a bull-headed man who fought change, but I never thought it would lead to his death." He lifted his eyes and looked at Erik. "Thank you for telling me the truth of the matter," he said, reaching out his hand toward Erik and offering him a gentleman's handshake. "Apology accepted."

Erik grasped his hand in return, relieved he had made amends. "Vicomte, you better take good care of her," he said to lighten the moment. He looked endearingly over at Christine.

"I wouldn't think of doing anything less," Raoul answered. "I wish you the best as well."

Erik bid them both goodbye and left the box. He had accomplished what he came to do. Things had been set right.

The lights dimmed and the second half of *Romeo and Juliet* began.

❋ ❋ ❋

Désirée fidgeted when Erik excused himself to see Christine. He asked her kindly to stay and wait, saying he would only be a minute. What did he need to say to her that he couldn't say in her presence? She would have felt better had he taken the time to introduce them, but instead he left her to stew in a fit of jealousy until she couldn't handle it any longer.

Quickly, she stood to her feet, exited their box, and walked over a few yards to stand outside the curtain of the

Governor's box and eavesdrop. At first, their voices sounded muffled, and then with clarity, she caught Erik's heartfelt words spoken to the woman he once loved.

"I will always love you, Christine. Your voice, your beauty, will always stay in my heart."

Désirée felt the dagger of betrayal thrust into her chest. The omen her mother had given was fulfilled in her very ears. Erik still loved Christine! It wasn't that he just loved Christine; he loved her beauty too. The words cut deep, and without thinking twice, she picked up the hem of her dress and flew down the hallway, passing by patrons and bumping into shoulders and walls. Burning tears streamed down her face.

One of the attendants stopped her and asked if she needed assistance, and Désirée merely balked that she needed fresh air. He watched her retreat down the hall and out a doorway that led to the roof.

With full force, she pushed open the door and climbed the stairs, sobbing the entire way until she reached the top out of breath and dizzy from running. Once outside, she fled to the edge of the rooftop and dropped to her knees. She tried desperately to quiet the voice of her mother, who kept repeating in her mind the ominous words, *"He will hurt you . . . he will hurt you."*

Why did he still love Christine? Had this all been a joke on his part? Had he just used her body for his enjoyment?

She stood back up, staggered over to the edge of the building, and looked down to the street below. Her hands moved across her stomach as she thought of the life growing inside her. Erik had no idea he was about to be a father. Would it matter? He had just professed his undying love to Christine Daaé. He would never marry her now. Désirée wondered if he had returned to his obsession and would begin another relentless pursuit, blind to everyone and everything around him until he obtained what he always wanted.

The street below invited her to jump. A momentary madness griped her heart. She thought of her mother, who had been right all along. As she looked at the street below, she surmised it would be a quick painful fall once she hit the pavement. Her skull would crack and the taunting emotional pain would end. The mocking voice of her mother would cease. She would fly to heaven or be dragged to hell with their baby in her arms. No longer would her heart beat or bleed for the man she loved. He was still a monster. Her mother was right.

❋ ❋ ❋

Erik returned to Box 5 and was surprised to find Désirée missing when he pulled back the curtain. He thought perhaps she had made her way to the powder room during intermission and decided to wait.

He thought about his life, which finally was filled peace and happiness. All had worked out as it should. Christine would always be fond in his memories, but he had found the woman he was destined to be with for eternity. He desired none other.

The lights dimmed as intermission ended, and Erik stirred with an uneasy feeling in his gut. He had told Désirée to stay put, but she had not heeded his request nor returned. He whirled from his seat and headed down the hallway, passing a box attendant. "Have you seen Mademoiselle Hessier?" he inquired.

"Yes, sir, she said she needed a breath of fresh air and exited at the end of the hallway toward the roof."

"The roof?" In a panic, Erik ran up the stairs and flung the door open into the night air. To his horror, he saw

Désirée standing peering over the side of the building, teetering back and forth on the upper ledge.

"Désirée," he called softly, not wishing to startle her in her precarious stance. She turned around, and his heart leaped in his throat as she stood between the line of life or death.

"My God, Désirée, please get down off the edge, you're frightening me."

Her face, wet with tears, returned a blank stare. "You lied," she replied, with calm indifference. "You lied."

Erik shook his head. "Lied about what, Désirée? I haven't lied to you."

"Oh, yes," she continued, shaking her finger at him. "You said you wouldn't hurt me, but you did. Mother said you would! She warned me and you did!"

"How?" he begged, taking a few more steps closer to her. "How have I hurt you?"

"Christine. I heard you, Erik, I heard you on the other side of the curtain say to her you would always love Christine and her beauty." Her eyes grew wide with anger. "That's it, isn't it? You think I'm ugly, and you want her beauty!"

"No, no," Erik cried in his defense. "That's not what I meant, Désirée." He held out his hand toward her in desperation. "Please come down, and let's talk this over."

"No! There's nothing to talk about. I can't live without you, Erik." She balled her first and pounded her chest over her heart. "I can't breathe or think of life without you. If you leave me, I'll die, and better I die now then live through the pain of loss again."

"Oh, Désirée, you're wrong," Erik begged, his own eyes filling with tears as he drew a few feet closer. "I told Christine that I found love in you! The beauty I found in Désirée is far more precious to me. Because of you I've learned to love, and your love has brought me healing."

Erik pleaded with her to come away from the ledge. She had to believe him. "Come down, please," he cried. The thought of losing Désirée tore his soul apart. "There is no life for me without you."

Erik froze, as he struggled for air. He feared losing the love he had finally found in life, and briefly wondered if now everything he had gained would swiftly and cruelly be taken from him. His eyes begged her to listen to his plea.

Désirée looked at him with suspicion, and he knew then what needed to be done.

"Marry me, Désirée," he beseeched her, falling to one knee. "Please come down from there. I want you to be my wife." He held his hand out toward her and waited for her to respond.

Désirée studied him curiously. The anger subsided in her eyes, and he saw once again her desire that he loved so much. Finally, she put one foot down on the roof, stepped off the ledge, and left death behind.

Erik did not hesitate or wait for her to move another inch. He jumped to his feet, grabbed her body, and pulled her tight into his embrace away from danger. He trembled and sobbed as he held her in his arms.

"Oh, Désirée. Don't ever do that again. I can't live without you."

She was silent for a moment, and then whispered. "Erik, I'm pregnant. We're going to have a baby." She flung her arms around his neck and clung to him tightly.

It took a few moments for her declaration to sink into his stunned heart.

"A baby?" he repeated, questioning the truth that he could possibly become a father.

"Yes, a baby."

He pulled back and tenderly brushed the tears from her face. Erik studied her eyes and saw within them the truth that she carried new life.

"Does this mean you'll marry me?" he asked, with a sheepish grin upon his face.

She raised her tearful gaze and smiled. "Yes . . . yes, I'll marry you Erik Dante."

The starlit night twinkled above, and Erik heard the last swells of *Romeo and Juliet* from the orchestra inside the auditorium below. The tragedy on stage had ended, but there would be no tragedy on the rooftop tonight. Erik and his Juliette were going to live.

He cupped her face in his hands and breathed his heartfelt words of adoration before he claimed her lips.

"I love you, Désirée."

The End

*"Your beginnings will seem humble, so prosperous
will your future be."*
Job 8:7

Author Notes

The Royal Opera House of Valletta was designed by Edward Middleton Barry and took four years to construct. It opened on October 9, 1866. On May 25, 1873, it suffered a massive fire. The exterior was undamaged, but the interior sustained heavy damage including a collapsed roof. The cause of the fire was heavily speculated, ranging from a disgruntled tenor to employees who were derelict in their duties.

On October 11, 1877, after four years of reconstruction, the theater reopened. However, its existence was once again brought to an abrupt end when on April 7, 1942, the theater was destroyed by bombers during World War II.

The Royal Opera House of Valletta was never rebuilt, and the site remains empty today.

www.ingramcontent.com/pod-product-compliance
Lightning Source LLC
Chambersburg PA
CBHW031952120726

47898CB00002BA/361